THE
SCARS
I BARE

Also by J.L. Perq

Twist of Fate

By The Bay Series

The Choices I've Made

To all the beautifully broken, both inside and out.
Never let anyone mistake your bravery for weakness.
We are warriors, through and through.

Note from Author

While Ocracoke is a very real and beautiful place, the town portrayed in this series is fictional. Several of the locations mentioned do exist, but many have been made up to fit the storyline.

Bottom line, Molly's Inn isn't real.

But the ferry is fun, and totally not lethal, I swear.

On a more serious note—*The Scars I Bare* touches on themes that may be sensitive for some readers. Out of an abundance of caution, I've included a list of content warnings on my website for anyone who wishes to be informed before diving in.

While I do my best to be thorough, please keep in mind that the list may not cover everything.

Website:
https://jlberg.com/content-warnings/

THE
SCARS
I BARE

Dean

PROLOGUE

What I remembered most was the fire.

The way it announced its presence in the sky with a thunderous clap and a bang. Those first few seconds, looking up, my eyes still making sense of what they saw, I wanted to believe it was fireworks, some sort of celebration, or maybe a bunch of delinquent teenagers fooling around late at night.

Because, when faced with the impossible, the mind would always try to find reason. It would always try to find a suitable cause for something as horrific as fire and brimstone in the middle of the damn ocean.

But, for us, the passengers on that ill-fated ferryboat off the coast of North Carolina that night, there was no other answer.

We were all doomed.

1

ONE
Dean

Recovery Journal: Day One

I've been in this hospital bed about a week now.

Or at least, I think it's been a week. Hard to say with how much pain meds they've been giving me.

The shrink who keeps visiting, the one they send in to help me handle my transition or whatever, says this journaling thing will help me heal.

Heal.

Like that's even possible. Like the guy has a single clue about what I've been going through.

Does he know that every single letter I scribble down in this so-called recovery journal is a struggle? It looks like damn chicken scratch.

No, it was worse actually. Chicken scratch is what my mom used to call my handwriting.

Before all of this.

"Dean, I better not see that horrible chicken scratch again, or I'll bust your hide." She'd probably give anything to go back in time to those simple moments when horrible penmanship was at the forefront of our problems.

I know I would.

I didn't just lose an arm or a hand, my five working fingers, in that accident.

It was part of me.

It was freedom and normalcy.

And it was mine.

But, now, it's all gone.

So, here I am, learning how to write again like a damn kindergartner, while nurses and doctors tell me everything is going to be fine.

"Just keep writing," the shrink says.

Well, fuck that.

Fuck this whole thing.

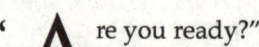

"Are you ready?"

The question startled me a bit as I stared out at the water I'd once loved so much. It had been the place I'd go to when I was angry with my overbearing mother or pissed at my annoying little brother. The waves would calm my nerves and soothe my soul…

Or at least, they used to.

But now, when I looked out at that deep blue water, churning and moving about with uncertainty—knowing it'd been there with me that night, right alongside me, offering no hope, no sense of peace in those moments before the world went black—I felt nothing.

I swallowed deeply, looking up at my oldest friend, Jake. "Yeah, I'm ready."

With a solid pat on my back, he stepped up onto the makeshift podium, and I followed. The whole town, as well as the tourists who happened to be nearby, had turned up for today's ceremony.

It was a massive crowd before us.

With one last loving glance in his fiancée's direction, Jake took to the microphone and addressed the audience before him. "Good morning. Most of you know me, but for those of you who don't, my name is Jake Jameson, and I'm the resident doctor here on Ocracoke Island. But, on the day of the ferryboat explosion, I was just a passenger, like everyone else. Just trying to get from one side to the other.

"For some of us, this one-hour trip from one shore to the other is a part of life. For others, it's a fleeting experience, a day spent with family or friends during vacation, but nothing more. However, for the sixty-two passengers who boarded the last ferry on that fateful spring night three years ago, the memories of that day will live with us. Forever."

I took a deep breath, Jake's words soaking up the air around me, seeping into my skin like a dark, penetrating fog.

Like most survivors of a life-altering event, most days, I tried not to think about it. When I looked down at my mangled arm, currently masked by the prosthesis I wore in public, I tried not to remember the way the smoke had clung to the air—so thick, I could barely breathe—or how, to this day, I could still hear the high-pitched sobs of a mother holding her young child next to me, unsure if he was dead or alive.

Like I said, I tried.

But, like most survivors, it was an uphill battle, and most of the time, I felt like I was being dragged backward.

Back into the past.

Back to the night with its fire and ash. Its chaos and—

"Dean?"

"Pardon?" I answered, blinking several times before coming back to the present. My eyes focused, and I came face-to-face with Jake crouched in front of me, the crowd silently watching us.

"You okay?" he asked, his gaze scanning me for signs of distress.

No matter how hard he tried, Jake could never stop being a doctor. Part of me couldn't wait to see him with a child of his own. He'd be a damn mess.

"Yeah," I replied, wondering how long he'd been trying to get my attention. "Yeah," I repeated. "I'm good. I can do this."

Jake didn't look completely convinced, but he rose, stepping aside to allow me room to step up to the podium. It was a short walk, maybe three or four strides at most.

But it felt like so much more.

Time seemed to slow as I concentrated on what I was about to do. When the town officials had come to me and asked if I would be willing to unveil the memorial they'd commissioned for the ferryboat victims, I should have felt honored.

Humbled.

Grateful.

Instead, I'd felt nothing but dread.

What could I say? How could I look into the eyes of the families who'd lost people that night and tell them this statue was somehow going to make it better? It wasn't going to bring them back, no matter how breathtaking it was. It wasn't going to take away the pain, no matter how long it stood here. It wasn't going to make the frustration of a three-year-old cold case the officials now deemed a fluke accident suddenly vanish, because now, there was a place they could go to mourn.

This changed nothing.

When we all left this place, the only thing that would be different was the pier. And perhaps a clearer conscience for the powers that be because they had been unable to do their job at the end of the day. My eyes darted to where Macon Green—our resident deputy, a native of the town—stood, and I wondered if this did just that.

Eased his conscience.

His eyes met mine and darted quickly away.

Probably.

I took the last step, a thousand words swimming around in my head but none of them good. I took one last breath and squeezed my eyes shut as I asked God for some sort of miracle. When they opened, I found a piece of paper waiting for me on the podium. But not just any piece of paper. A speech. I turned to Jake, and he gave me a brief nod.

He'd known.

He'd known I'd struggle, so he'd taken care of me, just as he'd taken care of me out there, in the water, on that night, saving my life when a piece of debris had severed my arm clean, causing me to nearly bleed out right there, in the middle of the ocean.

I cleared my throat and began to read the words he'd prepared. "The artist, Aiden Fisher, who was commissioned to create this memorial, was selected from an incredible list of talent. After interviewing him, many of the families involved in this endeavor said he had a certain quality that made you feel as if he were walking this journey with you rather than behind you. His understanding of grief and remembrance goes far beyond his years, and I am so honored to share his monument, memorializing the thirteen locals and tourists lost to the sea. We will never forget. Their memories will live on forever."

There was no applause, but I hadn't expected any. This was not the occasion for such. The crowd stood silent as I walked toward the covered statue, waiting for my signal to remove its covering. Several local newspaper and television crews took their places, wanting to get the perfect angle for the unveiling.

And, of course, they all wanted an interview with the amputee survivor afterward where they'd all expect me to rehash my harrowing tale of survival.

Yeah, that wasn't going to happen.

I was given a thumbs-up by a county official, my go-ahead to step forward. With my good arm, I pulled the drape off. Not too quick and not too slow. When the statue was uncovered, even my breath was taken away a little.

Two people, hand in hand, faced the waterfront, as if waiting for something.

Or someone.

The artist had left their faces and features neutral, leaving your imagination to fill in the blanks. It could be a husband and wife, a mother and daughter, or two friends.

But what lingered in my mind far after the ceremony was the subtle way their bodies leaned forward.

The anticipation.

The nerves.

The fear.

It was all there.

I hadn't expected a stupid statue to affect me as much as it did, but I found myself lurking about long after most had gone home. I stood next to the statue, staring out onto the water as the faceless figures did, wondering what they were waiting for.

A family member? A second chance?

A purpose?

It was something I'd been grappling with for nearly three years.

What did I do now? Now that life had moved on, seemingly without me, who was I?

After all this time, I still didn't know the answer.

Maybe like this bronze statue forever cemented into the ground, I never would.

"It was a lovely ceremony, wasn't it?" my mother said as I stared out at the subtle waves lapping in the bay outside her kitchen window.

"Dean?"

"Sorry. What?" I replied, turning my head in her direction.

She was fluttering around the kitchen, cooking a dinner big enough for an army even though it was just the two of us. Taylor, my younger brother, had once again gotten out of Sunday dinner, stating he had important business to attend to. A twinge of guilt gnawed at my gut.

"The dedication, it was lovely. Very well done."

I nodded my head, the haunting memory of it all still clinging to me like a second skin.

"It was nice," I agreed, swallowing deeply, trying to avoid my mother's sharp gaze.

"But?" she said, leaving the stove to plop down beside me at the small table where, every morning of my childhood, my brother and I had gathered around, fighting over cereal and action figures.

"There is no *but*," I insisted. "The county and town did a good job. It is a fine tribute to the families and loved ones."

"You know better than to lie to your mama, young man. You might have grown up and no longer live under this roof, but I can still tell when you're lying—"

"Okay," I replied, holding up my hands in surrender.

And that was when it happened. She didn't mean to. No one did, but it never failed. The involuntary eye jerk whenever attention was brought to my right side.

The startling fact that it did not match the left.

Even though my family had been living with it for three years now and had grown used to the loss of my dominant arm, nearly all the way up to my shoulder, it still didn't keep the mind from noticing it each and every time I moved. None of them meant anything by it; I knew that. But, whenever it happened, I could see a quick moment of grief sweep across their features where it was almost like they were reliving those horrific events all in the span of a few seconds.

The panic.

The fear.

The loss.

And then, like a flip of a coin, they'd come back, just as my mother was doing now, and it would be like nothing had happened. There was a time when I would have brought it up and told her I was fine and that there was nothing to fear anymore.

But, after a while, I'd learned to let it go.

Because she never would.

Just as the random stranger passing by couldn't help but look at my prosthetic hand, noticing the way the color and texture didn't quite match the other, my mother couldn't look at me and not think about what could have been.

What she'd almost lost.

"You and Jake did a fine job today. Made everyone proud."

I gave her a warm smile. "Thank you, Mama," I said, choosing to leave out the part where Jake had basically spoon-fed me my part in the whole thing.

"I imagine Jake and Molly will be getting married soon?" she asked, clearly changing the subject. She knew exactly when the happy couple was getting hitched.

"In a month or so, Mama. Remember the invitation you got? It's right there, on the fridge."

I knew she was playing some sort of game with me, acting dumb just to keep me talking. But I allowed it. She was old, and I'd caused her, a single parent, enough strife over the thirty-four years I'd been on this earth.

"And you'll be attending?" she asked.

"Of course. I'm the best man. And, before you ask another ridiculous question, no, I'm not upset over this. Hell, I think I deserve a gift, considering the amount of pushing and prodding I did to get those two together."

"Watch your mouth, Dean. You might have skipped church this morning, but it's still a Sunday."

"*Hell* isn't a bad word. It's in the Bible," I replied, grinning back at her. It was an argument I'd been using to push her buttons since I was a kid.

She made an unpleasant face, shaking her head as she rose to go back to her pork chops. "Why I didn't make you move back in here, I just don't know," she grumbled.

If she'd had her way, I would have. After my accident,

she had all but begged me to move back in, her nerves completely shot after everything I went through to make it back home. Because of the remote location of Ocracoke, my rehabilitation had meant I had to stay a couple of hours up the coast for months. Once I'd finally returned home, the thought of me being even a mile away was almost too much.

But I couldn't do it.

I'd lost so much already. Anyone who'd ever spent any time in a hospital knew how little dignity it left you with, and moving in with my mother at the age of thirty-one? It would have been the final nail in the coffin.

"A fall wedding in Ocracoke," my mom said, still carrying on about Jake and Molly. "Weren't you planning on the same?"

"Molly and I never really planned on anything wedding-related. I think we were too scared to even take the first step."

"Well, if that wasn't a giant warning sign, I don't know what is." She snorted.

"You didn't seem all that upset by the idea," I replied, remembering how she'd cried tears of joy when I announced I was going to marry Molly.

A marriage of convenience really.

Jake had left over a decade earlier to follow his dreams of becoming a world-class doctor, leaving Molly and me behind. After years of loneliness, we both began to confuse our friendship for something more. It took my accident and Jake's return to set us all straight. I'd honestly never been happier for two people in my life.

"Well, what mama wouldn't want her in the family?" she asked. "And, besides, I've been waiting my whole life for grandbabies. At this point, who am I to argue as long as I get some?"

"Well, maybe Jake and Molly will let you snuggle theirs when they get around to it."

"They'd better. Those two have been just as much family as anyone else to us. And, after everything Jake did for you…" Her voice trailed off as the emotions took hold.

"I know, Mama. You tell him thank you every time you see him." I laughed, an attempt to break the tension.

"He saved my son!"

"He saved several other people on that ferry, too, but I doubt they've sent him a gift basket every week for the last three years."

She shook her head, adding some sliced apples to the pan. "Well, they should have, and it's not every week. At least, not anymore," she said with a sly grin.

I knew not to argue. My mama was as Southern as you could get, right down to the famous cheese grits and buttered biscuits she made for breakfast. The Sutherland family could be traced all the way back to one of the founding families of Ocracoke Island. It was why, when Mama spoke, you could still hear that distinctive brogue that was so unique to this place; tourists would travel from all over the world just to hear it.

Watching my sixty-five-year-old mother bob around the kitchen, dancing to a song she'd most likely heard that morning in church, I couldn't help but feel a sadness sweep over me.

Everyone had their place here. Jake and Molly had each other. My mom had her group of friends from church. Taylor had the family business.

I used to know what that felt like. A sense of belonging.

But now, I felt like driftwood lost to the sea. Just coasting from one day to the next until I faded into oblivion.

After saying my goodbyes to my mom, I drove the short distance home, thankful for the few minutes of quiet it offered. The island was busy this time of year, the population soaring as high as the temperatures. But when the sun set, it remained fairly peaceful. The restaurants along the harbor were still alive with activity, but thankfully, it didn't spread too far.

Pulling into my small driveway, I killed the engine and headed for the front door.

Stepping into my two-bedroom cottage, I wanted nothing else but to walk into my bedroom, collapse on my bed, and fall asleep. It had been a long day, and my prosthesis was aching something fierce. Even after nearly three years, I hadn't fully grown accustomed to it yet. It made me sweat, that stupid, thick neoprene sleeve gripping what was left of my arm like a damn vise.

And the weight...

God, it was heavy.

But it eased people's minds and brought the staring down to a minimum. So, when I was out in public, I wore it, and I tried to blend in. I tried to disappear.

The people of the town had gone out of their way to make sure I got one in the first place, throwing several fundraisers for the victims of the ferryboat tragedy. I'd tried to turn down their generosity, but when the town put their minds to something, there was no backing down.

Honestly, I wasn't sure our family would have survived otherwise.

At least, not at first.

The Sutherlands were known as one of the wealthiest families on the island, owning a fishing company that could date back several generations. But the wealth was no match for the hospital bills my accident had generated. So, I had taken what I could from the town while my brother rebuilt the company in my absence, making it what it was today. And saving us from financial ruin in the process.

We'd grown from a small commercial fishing company, catering to local restaurants and markets, to a full-service tourist experience. In a few short years, my brother did what no one before him had been able to do.

He'd made our business a true success. And he had done it completely on his own.

Without me.

Not even bothering to leave the living room, I disconnected the first layer of my prosthesis, and it felt like heaven. With the weight gone, I took a moment to roll my shoulder and stretch my neck. The movement in the small mirror across the room caught my attention, and I couldn't help but stare briefly at my reflection.

Not much of me had changed in the past few years, physically-speaking. My eyes still carried the same dark green hue my mother adored, and the sandy-brown hair most of the Sutherlands were known for still hung from my head, albeit a bit longer than usual. I'd maintained most of my muscle mass, turning to long-distance jogs around the island to clear my head, something I'd learned from the shrink back at the hospital.

The one who'd forced me to write.

Tossing the pieces of my prosthesis on the couch, I took a seat at the small desk in the corner of the living room and booted up my laptop. I briefly thought about playing a game of solitaire or watching something on Netflix, but I knew none of that would do. Ever since I'd stood next to that memorial, staring out onto the water, I had known I'd end up here.

I needed to write.

When the psychiatrist had first encouraged me to do this exercise in the hospital, explaining it would be a good way to express my feelings and thoughts in a way that felt safe, I'd thought he was a nutcase.

I still did honestly.

All I knew was, it helped, and if it kept me out of a psychiatrist's office, it was a win-win for me.

Opening the drawer of my desk, I leafed through several black-and-white composition notebooks I'd already filled, looking for the one I was currently scribbling in, but before I got to it, another caught my eye. Pulling it out, my fingers traced over the date on the front, noticing how shaky the handwriting was. I remembered how much every letter had hurt back then. Thumbing through the tattered notebook, I found an entry that caught my attention.

> I met a woman today.
> A nurse actually.
> A gorgeous angel of a nurse. God, I wish she weren't my nurse.
> She greeted me on her first shift, a wide, happy smile spread across her face.
> I smiled back and...nothing.
> I said absolutely nothing. I opened my mouth to spout out something witty and charming, a skill I'd honed back in my early twenties when one-night stands with tourists was the singular most important task of my life.
> But, instead, I was left speechless.
> Like I'd lost my voice instead of my arm on that ferryboat.

She smiled again, a smaller one, as she ran through my chart, asking questions to which I could only nod.

God, I was a fucking loser.

A loser with one arm.

That's what they'll call me.

The loner with one arm.

I thought I could go back.

Back to my life.

Back to normal.

But what is normal now?

I shook my head, remembering that moment like it was yesterday. Cora, the gorgeous nurse who'd lit up my small little world for a short while. I'd thought she might be the answer to everything.

I'd thought a lot of things back then.

And none of it had led to anything.

Three years later, I was still searching for that new normal I'd written about in my journal.

It didn't exist.

I was just a loser with one arm, trying to make it through one day at a time.

TWO

Cora

Blog Entry #1

I guess I should come up with a better title than Blog Entry #1, but forgive me...I'm new to this whole online journaling thing.

And drastically behind.

I was informed by a tech-savvy eight-year-old niece of mine the other day that blogging is "so last year" and that, if I really wanted to be noticed, I needed to be on YouTube.

In front of a camera. Or do they do it with a phone?

However it's officially done, it sounds highly intimidating, so although I am grateful for my niece's recommendation, I think I'll stick to the old method.

Or the old, new method?

Whatever. At least I can do this in my pajamas.

Anyway, hi. My name is Cora Carpenter, and I'm creating this blog because I thought it sounded like a great way to stay in touch with my family and friends back in Texas and document this part of my life.

You see, I just moved halfway across the country to take a job.

I guess that's what you do when you're a young professional, but it's still scary.

I'm a Texas girl, but don't let that fool you. I grew up in Austin where we like things weird. No, literally, the city's motto is Keep Austin Weird, and my family is no exception to that rule. And I love them for it, but sometimes, a girl just needs to step out and explore.

So, that's what I did. Rather than taking the safe path, I stepped onto the old beaten one and took a chance.

So, yeah, this is my blog and the life I'm about to embark on as a nurse in Virginia Beach.

Here goes nothing.

Blake
Be safe. Tell Lizzie I love her. Let me know when you're settled.

With one last look at the text on my phone and everything it represented, I stepped out of the car and took a deep breath as the ferry left the dock.

Does the air here in North Carolina smell sweeter than Virginia?

I smiled, peeking over at the sleeping child in my back seat, looking adorable in the pink summer dress I'd picked out for her at one of those tourist-trap places along the coast.

No, it wasn't the state line we'd crossed hours ago that caused the air to shift and my body to calm. It was the feeling of freedom.

Today was the start of something new and real.

Just the two of us from now on.

Here's to starting over.

Again.

"First time going to Ocracoke?" an old man asked, leaning against the car next to mine.

His question made me jump, but I immediately calmed when I saw the pleasant-looking old man standing before me.

"Sorry, dear, I didn't mean to frighten you," he added, his hands out in front of his body like he was attempting to tame a wild animal. "It's just that you seemed so in awe of it—the water and the boat. I think I even caught a deep breath of happiness."

I smiled—a faint one but a smile just the same. "Yes," I finally answered. "First time. You?"

He shook his head, a real smile spreading across his face. How I longed to remember what that felt like. A real, honest-to-God smile. One that stretched your face and made your muscles ache from the weight of it.

"No," he replied. "We come every year."

"We?" I asked, looking around and in between the other cars until my eyes spotted an older woman at the rail, taking in the scenery with several other passengers.

"The Mrs. and me," he explained, pointing to the same woman I'd suspected he would.

Both white-haired and in casual khaki shorts, they somehow just fit together, like puzzle pieces. Even down to the nearly matching Hawaiian tops.

"We've been visiting here since our honeymoon eons ago. Growing up, our kids took trips down to the island, and now, it's just us again."

"It must be a special place," I said, noticing the way his eyes lingered on his wife.

"Oh, it is. You'll see." He stuck out his hand,

assuming I'd travel the distance to offer mine. "Thomas Lovell," he greeted.

I looked at the outstretched hand, knowing there was nothing but the warmth of a gentle-natured old man, but I couldn't.

I just couldn't.

So, instead, I awkwardly waved from the spot I'd planted myself to. "Cora," I replied before realizing I wasn't sure how to finish. "Cora Carpenter," I said finally, realizing it was the first time I'd used my maiden name since my wedding day.

But not the last, I told myself.

"Nice to meet you, Cora Carpenter. I hope your stay in Ocracoke is as lovely as I promised. Maybe you'll come back every year, like we do."

I shook my head. "No," I answered. "This isn't a vacation, Mr. Lovell. I'm moving here. Permanently."

Jake Jameson, my new boss, had offered to meet me at the dock to welcome me to my new home. Unsure of what mental state I'd be in after leaving Virginia that morning, I politely declined, agreeing to instead meet up with him and his fiancée at the inn. It had already been an emotional week after saying goodbyes to my coworkers and packing up the small apartment I rented for Lizzie and me. I didn't need to start this new adventure by sobbing all over my boss's shoulder.

I'd met Dr. Jameson a handful of times over the past few years, as some of his patients went in and out of the hospital I worked at in Virginia Beach. Since Ocracoke Island was so isolated, being only accessible by ferry, and their medical resources were limited, many inhabitants needed care off the island.

Although we weren't the closest hospital, we were the most advanced. So, for major events such as emergencies or catastrophic events, we were often the first responders.

We…

I had to remind myself that I was no longer part of that *we*. No longer a nurse managing a staff of twenty at a highly respectable medical establishment.

I was just a nurse.

The only nurse.

The two-person medical clinic Jake ran pretty much summed up the availability of help on the island. Besides a handful of volunteer EMT responders, I would be the only nurse on the island.

Me and about eight hundred or so residents and their guests.

The thought made me a little dizzy as I drove down the long, empty highway toward the sleepy town. Sure, I was used to stressful situations and handling multiple things at once, but an entire island?

It seemed like an insurmountable task.

"Mommy?" a sleepy Lizzie called out from the back seat. "Are we there yet?" she asked, her brown eyes briefly meeting mine in the rearview mirror. She had a red nose from her finger being wrapped around it while she sucked her thumb. At least a dozen mothers had told me how bad it was for an almost six-year-old to still suck her thumb.

But I didn't care.

Most of those other mothers didn't have a walking, talking encyclopedia for a child either.

Let the kid suck her thumb. That was my motto.

"Not yet, baby, but almost. You see the water there?" I pointed to the left side of the car. "Just over those dunes?"

"Did you know some dunes can be over four thousand feet high?"

"Wow!" I said. "I had no idea."

I truly didn't. Who did?

My kid—that was who. I looked in the rearview mirror and caught her looking out the window with that raw curiosity that always seemed to go with her wherever she went.

"Are you excited?"

"Kinda," she answered before adding, "Will we be able to go to the beach every day?"

"I hope so," I answered. "Although you'll be starting school soon, so it might be a little difficult."

She let out an audible breath. "I don't want to go to school."

"Why?" That was a new one. Especially for my kid. The one who loved to learn.

"What if they don't teach me interesting things? What if it's boring? What if the kids think I'm weird?"

That was a lot of questions all at once, and I heard her let out a frustrated sigh behind me. Living with a five-year-old genius was sometimes exhausting.

Scratch that.

It was always exhausting. But one thing I'd learned early on was that, deep down, she was still a kid. With deep-down kid-like needs and wants.

"I heard they sometimes go to the beach for field trips," I casually mentioned.

I saw her eyes light up in the rearview mirror.

"Really?"

I shrugged. "I mean, that's what I heard."

"Okay. Well then, it doesn't sound too bad. I guess I'll think about it."

"You do that," I said, smiling to myself as we made our way down Highway 12.

"Mommy?" she asked again, her voice sounding serious.

"Yeah, baby?"

"Do they have ice cream here?"

I nearly snorted out a laugh, but I kept it under control as a smile tugged at my cheeks. "Yes. Most definitely. Do you think I'd move to an island with no ice cream?"

"Is it good ice cream?"

Just up ahead, the dunes gave way to a scattering of buildings as we approached the town. I knew our hosts were expecting us, but a slight detour wouldn't hurt.

"I don't know. Wanna find out?" I asked as we drove into town for the first time.

"Yeah!" she answered eagerly.

There was nothing that made Lizzie happier than ice cream. Well, that and the beach. If I could give her both today, this whole moving thing would be a heck of a lot easier.

For one of us at least.

If only ice cream could solve all the world's problems.

Lizzie was a sticky mess by the time we made it to the inn. Our venture around the island in search of ice cream had taken a little more time than I'd planned, but it was well worth it. I'd not only satisfied Lizzie's ice cream fears, but we'd also given ourselves a decent tour as well.

This place was small.

I'd been told over and over that it would be.

But being told something and actually experiencing it firsthand were two different things entirely. You could travel the actual town from one end to the other in a matter of minutes by car, and during low season, I would imagine that time could be cut in half without the presence of tourists.

But, as small as it was, it was vast in beauty. From its charming small-town feel to the picturesque wildlife and never-ending water views, I could see why the Lovells kept coming back.

Pulling up to By the Bay Inn, I was immediately struck by how homey it felt. From its charming cedar roof and the large gardens surrounding it, I knew this was a place that was well cared for and loved. My parents had always put that kind of devotion into our home, painting the trim when it became dull from the summer heat and replanting flowers along the entryway each spring. I'd forgotten what it felt like—taking such personal pride in where you laid your head.

A pretty blonde emerged from the front door, waving as she walked up to our car. Either this was our hostess, Molly, or people around here really were that friendly.

"Hi, you must be Cora," she said, holding out a hand in greeting. "I'm Molly McIntyre. Welcome to By the Bay."

I took her hand, feeling its warmth and sincerity. "Thank you," I answered. "I'm so grateful to you for doing this. I know it's your busy time of the year."

She waved her hands in a dismissive gesture. "It's no trouble at all, and it's starting to slow down anyway. The end of August is always a transitional time for us. You're the one doing me the favor honestly. Jake has been so crazy lately since Betty retired, and he's been on his own at that clinic. He'll be glad for the help, and I'll be glad to have my fiancé somewhat back to sane."

I let out a small laugh. "Well, I'll do what I can."

I was starting to feel tiny beads of sweat forming around my temples. I'd always been a fan of the heat, growing up in Texas, but even after seven years in

Virginia, humidity was still new to me, and right now, I felt like I was about to melt all over the driveway.

"Is there anything I can help you carry in?" she asked. "Jake is on his way. He got stuck at the clinic, but when he gets here, I'll have him carry in your larger things."

I bit my lip, unsure of how I felt about the help. "I can manage," I finally answered.

"Okay, well, how about I show you to your rooms?"

"Rooms?" I asked, not realizing we were occupying more than one.

"Yes," she answered as she joined me on the other side of the car. When her eyes met Lizzie's, they lit up with joy, her face beaming back at my little girl as she continued to speak. "Jake and I moved out of the inn a few weeks ago now that our house is renovated. Since I haven't decided what to do with the two empty family rooms, I thought it would be a nice place for you two. It's hidden away from other guests, so you'll have a bit more privacy, and your daughter can have her own room."

As I finished unbuckling Lizzie's car seat and she hopped down, I turned to Molly, not quite sure how I was going to thank her. "That's extremely kind of you. But are you sure? I can't pay you for the extra room."

She bent down to Lizzie's height, giving her a little bop on the nose with her finger. "It's no trouble at all. And no extra charge. But I do need someone around to take care of the place when I'm gone. Nothing major. Just keep an eye on the place and let me know if the guests need anything—that sort of thing. Do you think you could help me with that?"

Realizing she was speaking to Lizzie, I kept quiet as her little head bounced up and down.

"Yes!" she answered enthusiastically. "Is there really a beach in the backyard?"

Molly laughed, rising to her full height before holding

out a hand. Lizzie, so trusting in her youth, took it without thinking.

"Let's go find out. Come on!"

Molly and Lizzie carried on toward the front door while I was left standing there, my gaze shifting between my happy young daughter and the car full of crap that needed to be unloaded. Letting out a sigh of defeat, I decided to let it go, realizing Molly had probably done this on purpose, knowing I'd follow Lizzie rather than trust her with a woman I'd only just met to cart in everything myself.

I guessed it would all have to wait.

Stepping into the inn felt like heaven—if heaven were a deep freeze. The air-conditioning made my skin prickle, but the lack of humidity was glorious. There was a faint floral scent in the air—maybe lilies or hydrangeas. It mixed with the fresh air, giving me a renewed spirit after the sweltering heat.

"Mommy! Look! It's an exact replica, right down to the coal-burning engine," Lizzie exclaimed, running into the parlor where a small train set was displayed.

"Lizzie!" I called out, giving my best silent apology to Molly. "That's not yours, baby girl. You must ask first, remember?"

Her hands, so tiny and curious, stopped mid-reach and retracted, hiding behind her back. "I'm sorry, Mama. I forgot." The sincerity in her voice slayed me.

"It's okay. You're not in trouble. Just a simple reminder, right?"

She nodded, turning her attention toward Molly, who was watching our exchange with interest.

"May I play with your train set, Miss Molly?" Lizzie asked, her hands fidgeting behind her as she waited not so patiently.

"Of course, darling. You may play with it anytime you like."

She didn't waste a second. Lizzie dived into that train set, taking each car off the track, one by one, to inspect them. Her fingers brushed over each painted color, every word and number, as if she were memorizing it.

"She's very curious, isn't she?" Molly said as we quietly watched her play.

"Very," I answered. "She always has been. You're just lucky you didn't get a plethora of train facts. She must be tired." I laughed.

Molly seemed to approve. "It's a good quality to have as a child."

I chuckled. "I agree with you most days, but every so often, that curiosity gets her into trouble."

"You must have some good stories." She laughed.

"Try a few dozen good stories. Do you have a solid week? I could start with the one where she decided to have a tea party with her pet fish."

"Well, that doesn't sound too bad."

"Did I mention he was out of the bowl? When I asked her why her very dead goldfish was sitting on her grandmother's china, she explained her swim teacher had told her that humans could hold their breath for up to five minutes underwater, so naturally, she thought fish could do the opposite."

Another laugh as Molly led me toward the kitchen. "Well, I mean, it does sound logical when you think about it. You want to tell me a couple more over coffee? It will give us time to get to know each other while we wait for that fiancé of mine."

"Sounds perfect."

With one last glance toward the parlor, I took a deep breath and let Lizzie out of my sight.

For the first time since we'd left home.

Because, for now, this was our home, and I had to start acting like it.

⁂

It was late when Lizzie and I finally retired to our rooms for the night.

Or room.

Although she found the idea of having her own bedroom intriguing, the idea of actually sleeping in it didn't appeal to her much, so for the foreseeable future, she would be in bed with me.

I'd been awake for well over an hour, lying next to the active little nugget of mine, the one who kicked in her sleep, my mind a racing whirl of activity that I just couldn't seem to shut off. I wasn't surprised. It had been a busy day.

But a good day.

For the first time in a while, it had been a very good day.

Perhaps the first of many.

Jake had finally shown up, and just as Molly had promised, he insisted on carrying in all our stuff from the car. He didn't allow me to lift one finger, assuring me that this was a service they did for all their guests.

I rolled my eyes and laughed, seeing the beads of sweat dripping off him.

No doubt, the other guests didn't have near as much luggage as we did.

But I stepped back, allowing him to help us even though everything inside me was screaming not to.

After he safely delivered our things inside, we spent the rest of the night getting to know our hosts. Molly cooked a fabulous dinner of local crab and homemade hush puppies, and afterward, Lizzie finally got her view of the backyard oasis, complete with a mini beach. It wasn't the ocean, but the gentle lapping waves of the bay suited her just fine.

She'd gone to sleep a happy girl, and it made my heart swell to see her so content in her new surroundings. I only hoped it continued. Knowing I'd never get sleep with all these thoughts swimming around in my head, I quietly got up and headed for the small sofa chair in the corner.

Pulling out the laptop, I was online in minutes and doing the one thing I hated.

Lying to my family. But it kept them content, comforted with the security of my deceit.

So, I kept doing it.

I kept writing.

I kept assuring them I was everything I was not.

Happy, healthy, and carefree.

Home from Vacation!

Sorry I haven't blogged for a while! After our vacation, I was completely exhausted and needed another week just to recover! Isn't that crazy? A vacation to recover from your vacation? Ah, that's the moment when you realize you truly have it rough, right?

Anyway, the three of us had a wonderful time. Lizzie never tires of the beach—a water baby through and through. Although she's not much of a baby anymore since our big girl will be starting kindergarten in just another week or so! It's hard to believe! Mommy and Daddy couldn't be more proud.

Speaking of which, Blake and I are both great, and hopefully, we will have the house up and running someday, so we can have guests, but until then, we're still knee-deep in renovations. I know, I know. Who said it was a great idea to buy a fixer-upper when we could have bought a brand-new house?

But at least I get to pick everything out, right?

Until next time, friends and family.

Cora

There were tears falling from my cheeks as I typed the last few words. After several years of this, I was now numb to the ease at which the lies sprang forth from my fingers. Numb to the comments from my parents and friends asking when they'd finally get to visit, followed by yet another excuse.

Just numb.

I'd created this blog to share my life with my family, and now, it was nothing but a tool to camouflage what I'd become.

Nothing.

I was nothing but an empty shell, and no one needed to see that, especially the ones I loved the most.

THREE

Dean

Recovery Journal: Day Three

I know, I know. I said I wouldn't do this.

But what else am I going to do? Have you actually ever watched daytime TV?

It's shit.

Especially in a hospital that only provides a handful of channels.

My family went back home. Honestly, I'm glad for it. None of them know what to say.

And their eyes.

It's a constant game of Let's Avoid Dean's Stump!

My mom is the worst. Her gaze will start to drift, tears will start to rim her eyes, and her lips will quiver as a wave of guilt washes over her before she suddenly jerks away.

Ten minutes later, it all starts again.

And then there are the hushed conversations. The ones with the doctors outside my room, which I'm supposed to pretend I can't hear, when they talk about my mental health and well-being and what is and is not perfectly normal for an amputee like me.

Amputee.

The word feels vile against my tongue.

The shrink says I should talk about it.

I told him to go fuck off.

In a private conversation, he told my mother it was all part of the process for me to lash out.

Oh, good. I was worried.

The overly talkative shrink also said it would be therapeutic—his word, not mine—for me to record memories from the night of the accident in this stupid book.

He said I might not always remember them as vividly as I do now.

Seriously, who is this guy?

I might not remember?

Ask anyone who was at Ground Zero what the air smelled like, and I bet, with how hard it was to breathe as ash fell from the sky, they could still describe it years later.

In vivid detail.

I wasn't going to forget the night I nearly lost my life.

I wasn't going to forget the bloodcurdling screams as cars exploded and debris went flying.

Or how my best friend, a man I hadn't seen in years, went into life-saving mode like one of those real-life heroes you read about in the papers, shouting orders while making tourniquets out of his own damn clothing.

While I sat there, in a state of shock, staring out onto the water that had been a best friend to me longer than any person on the planet. And I felt betrayed. I'd taken my first steps along the shore of the Atlantic. I'd learned to steer a boat before I could even ride a tricycle.

I wanted to stand up and scream out into that black water and ask it, Why? Why me? We were buddies. We understood each other.

And that was when the piece of debris sliced through my arm, and my life ended.

Or at least, it should have.

That night, I dreamed of the ocean—before it was the enemy.

Before it had taken away my life and everything I had to look forward to.

I dreamed I was on a boat, chasing the sunrise, both hands on the wheel, as my heart soared with such a happiness locked inside it, I thought I might explode.

And then I awoke, trembling and covered in sweat.

In that split second, when dream and reality still blurred in the twilight of morning, I felt it. Reaching up, I touched the place where my arm had once been, hoping, just hoping, that this one time, my dream might be reality.

But dreams were for suckers and small children.

And I was neither.

Rubbing the tender skin right around where the piece of debris had sliced through my arm, I tried to will away the pain and ache of the dream.

Phantom pain. That was what the doctors had called it. It was when a person still felt pain in an extremity they no longer possessed, like the body was mourning the idea long after the brain registered the information. Or maybe it was the other way around.

It really didn't matter what they called it. It sucked all the same. Because, as much as I tried to move on and forget, my body couldn't. Every morning, it'd reach out for that missing arm, and when it couldn't find it, it'd cry out in agony.

And I'd be dragged back to the past. Haunted by the events of a singular night.

Scrubbing a hand over my unshaven face, I took a deep breath and got out of bed. Looking over at the clock, I shook my head at the time.

Shit, I need to get going.

Racing to the bathroom, I took a quick shower and got dressed. Flopping down on the bed, I slid on my shoes and headed for the kitchen.

I was in desperate need of coffee.

Checking the clock once more, I let out a huff of air as my indecision ping-ponged around in my mind. Risk being late for a cup of coffee or arrive early but severely irritable?

Coffee wins.

Wishing I'd taken Molly up on her numerous offers to purchase me one of those fancy coffee machines that used the pods, I started the process of scooping out the coffee and filling the water. I could hear her voice in my head.

"It's no big deal, Dean. I'll pick it up when I'm up the coast, getting supplies, the next time. Hell, I can even write it off as a business expense."

But it was a big deal.

At least, it was to me. I didn't need her favors. If I wanted a fancy-ass coffeemaker, I'd go get one on my own.

Eventually.

While the coffee was percolating, I made sure my travel mug was ready to go and walked around the living room, picking up the journals I'd left out. My prosthetic arm was still on the floor, in the same place it had been left the night before, and I knew I needed to put it on.

Thankfully, it didn't take long at all, and by the time I was done, so was my blessed coffee. Pouring it straight into my mug, I didn't bother with cream or sugar and instead took as many sips as I could without burning my tongue as I headed to the front.

Stepping outside into the sweltering August heat, I thought briefly about walking to the clinic, but as beads of sweat began to quickly form around my temples, I quickly headed toward my truck, choosing air-conditioning over exercise for the time being. I'd get my workout in some other time.

Preferably indoors or after the sun began to set.

Growing up here, I didn't mind the heat too much, but this August was a killer. With record-breaking heat and very little rain, the island felt like it was on fire the minute the sun rose from the horizon, and nighttime didn't offer much comfort either.

Opening the door to my pickup, I slid in and didn't

waste much time in revving the engine to life. With one hand on the wheel, I began my short journey to the other side of the island.

The frigid air I'd cranked up to maximum capacity barely began to push through the vents by the time I pulled up to the small parking lot of the Ocracoke Medical Clinic. With only a handful of cars in the lot, I had no issues with parking my large truck and quickly made my way in.

A tiny bell chimed the moment the door was pushed open, announcing my arrival. Just two people sat in the small waiting room, and both waved me over.

"Dean Sutherland, is that you?" a tiny old woman called out from behind her magazine.

Her silver hair and blue eyes were familiar, but that described about a dozen of my mother's friends. Nevertheless, I did as I had been told and came forward.

"Come sit down with me and chat. God knows, I could use the company!"

Upon further examination, I recognized her wrinkled face as one of the women my mother played cards with. She was sitting next to her husband, who was fiddling around on an old iPhone, probably playing solitaire, as I took a seat next to his wife. She smelled like talc and cold cream. It was a comforting smell, soft and sweet.

"How are you, Mrs. Joyner?" I asked, putting my best manners on display. If I hadn't, I'd never hear the end of it from my mother.

Did that mean I was scared of my old-fashioned Southern mother?

Yes. Yes, it did.

That woman could be as sweet as honey, but if you crossed her? Lord, you'd better run. Fast.

"Oh, fine," she said. "Well, as fine as an old broad like

me can be. Dr. Jake does a good job at keeping this old heart ticking."

"He's always been pretty good at keeping women's hearts fluttering."

Old man Joyner let out a sort of chuckle at those words, earning him a deadly glance from his wife before they both grinned from ear to ear. It was endearing, to say the least.

Looking up at the front desk, I couldn't help but notice how disorganized it appeared. Jake didn't have the cash to hire a full-time person to man the desk, so his nurse had always done both jobs.

"He still hasn't found a replacement for Betty?"

Mrs. Joyner's eyes lit up as they met mine. "Oh, my dear, didn't you hear? She arrived yesterday."

"Who did?" I asked, completely confused.

"The new nurse."

"There's a new nurse?" I found myself saying more out of shock than anything else. Wasn't I the best friend to the island's only doctor? If he'd hired someone, shouldn't I have known about it?

"Yes. Pretty young thing. Dingbatter, too."

Dingbatter was an old-school term used when referring to anyone who wasn't native to the island. How did you define who was native to the island and who wasn't? Well, that was an entirely separate topic. Some islanders believed you weren't truly native unless you could trace your family back generations. Others believed you had to be born here.

Like I said, it was a hot button issue.

"Jake hired a nurse? From the mainland? Do you know her name? Why didn't he tell me?"

I thought Mrs. Joyner must have taken pity on me in my bewildered state. Her face turned round and warm, like that of a parent comforting a young child. But before she had time to answer all my questions, the door to the exam room opened, and my questions were answered with a single glance.

"Cora?"

I'd like to say the woman who had nursed me back to health after my accident looked up at me and fireworks exploded as our eyes met, like they did in the sappy rom-coms Molly always made me watch. But, instead, the second recognition passed across her face, I saw something closer to horror.

Or maybe it was awkwardness because that was exactly the emotion that was coursing through my veins. That, and extreme confusion. Cora Ashcroft had been there for me in a time of my life when I needed someone most.

She was the stranger I'd clung to when my family was hours away. She was the bright light I'd turned to when all I saw was darkness. And she was the woman I'd thought could be so much more...

That awkwardness in her eyes only doubled when she glanced down at the schedule she was holding and called out my name.

"Um, Dean?" she said, her voice lacking the confidence and bounce I remembered. "I guess you're next."

I placed a finger to my chest, pointing to myself like a goddamn idiot. "Me?"

She nodded, her eyebrows lifting in amusement. There was a total of three people in the small waiting room. Of course she meant me. Less than sixty seconds since this woman had crash-landed back in my life, and I was already acting like a moron.

Again.

No wonder she looked less than pleased to see me.

Rising to my feet, I walked the short distance to the door that led to the back of the clinic. With only two exam rooms and a small lab, there wasn't much to it, but I slowed to a halt and let her lead me in. She grabbed my chart from a stack on the nurses' counter, which Jake had no doubt pulled that morning, and placed it underneath her arm. As I averted my gaze, we started down the hall for the farthest room in the back of the building. As I followed her, I took a moment to reacquaint myself with the nurse who'd nearly stolen my heart.

To an unfamiliar eye, she looked the same. Her hair, although a bit shorter, was still the same deep shade of auburn. Under the harsh fluorescent lights of the clinic, the long, flowing locks appeared to be an ordinary shade of brown, but every time we passed a window and the light hit, a few strands would glisten a gorgeous mahogany red. Try as I might not to look, her body hadn't changed a bit either. Even dressed in plain-colored scrubs, I could see the curve of her hips and the swell of her breasts as she turned the corner into the exam room.

But, looking past all that, the beautiful hair and the gorgeous body, something was missing.

And I couldn't quite put my finger on it yet.

As she set my chart down on the counter, I took a seat, forgoing the exam table for one of the chairs instead.

Cora's dark brown eyes met mine before settling back on my chart. Her posture was rigid, nothing like the laid-back nurse who used to come in and visit with me on her lunch break just because she knew I might be lonely.

"So, uh...what is the nature of your visit today?" she asked, swallowing deeply before looking up at me once more.

I heard Jake's deep voice in the hallway as he said his goodbyes to a patient. Laughter broke out between them as the silence grew between Cora and me.

"Checkup," I finally answered, distracted by the commotion in the hallway. "Just my annual checkup."

"Right, okay. Then, I guess I should have gotten your weight," she said, clearly flustered. She frantically tapped her pen against the paper chart as the ruckus outside finally dissipated. "The scale is back at the nurses' station. I can just—"

"Why are you here?" I asked rather bluntly, causing her mouth to nearly fall to the floor. "I'm a solid two twenty, by the way. No need for the scale."

No longer hunched over my chart, she stood upright, staring at me with shock written on her face. "I just moved here."

"But why?" I pressed.

"Why not? You always said you loved growing up here—when you were…I mean, I think I remember something about you saying you liked it. So, when I was looking at different places in the South, I thought I'd give it a try." She shrugged, firmly crossing her arms over her chest.

At least she remembered me.

I snorted. "Your husband agreed to that? People down here don't have much need for high-priced lawyers."

Her eyes shifted to the side, focusing on a photo on the wall—something a local photographer had taken of wild ponies at sunset. "He and I aren't…we're not together anymore."

"You're divorced?" I said, my eyes homing in on her left hand and then up to her neck. Sure enough, that gigantic ring that had always swung from a chain around her neck—probably to keep the planet-sized diamond from cutting a hole through her sterile gloves, the one I somehow managed to miss every time she came into my room all those years ago, was indeed missing.

She nodded, confirming my question. "It was final just last month. We'd been separated for over a year though."

Something akin to hope blossomed in my belly as I looked up at her, the tenderhearted woman who'd been there for me in a time of my life I'd rather forget. The bouncy ball of fire who read to patients when they were too weak to do so themselves and always brought a smile to my face.

But that girl wasn't here.

And the guy she'd known in that hospital room? The one who'd still had hope of returning home like nothing had happened?

He was long gone as well.

Instead, I was sitting in a room with a perfect stranger, wondering what to say next and just how exactly I was going to kill my best friend for forgetting this bit of information in our weekly beer nights. Jake knew what a fool I'd made of myself in that hospital, convinced that I was in love with Cora when, in reality, I was just reaching out for someone.

Anyone.

Yet...

Yet she was here. Standing in front of me.

How was that for fate?

"So," she finally said, "how have you been?"

"Good," I immediately answered, almost like a knee-jerk reaction. Realizing she was probably expecting more than a one-word response, I tried to dig deep and find something else inside my muddled brain. "Everything healed up nicely," I replied, holding my arm up as proof. "The town hooked me up with this replacement, which keeps the stares down to a minimum. Except for the kids," I added. "The kids always notice."

"They're shorter," she said, reaching her hand out in front of her, about waist high. "They tend to notice things we don't."

My eyes narrowed, recalling that moment in the

hospital when I'd finally gotten the courage to ask her out and she'd refused, explaining two very important reasons.

The husband and the—

"How is your daughter?" I asked, remembering her name but not wanting to seem overly attached to our brief acquaintance so long ago. Because I had been attached.

Maybe I still am...

"Good," she replied, mirroring my answer moments earlier. Realizing she'd done so, she smiled and continued on, "She's starting kindergarten next month."

"Here? In Ocracoke?" I asked, still unconvinced she was in fact moving here permanently. It wasn't exactly the top destination for relocations. We were small and remote, and did I mention that the only way in and out was by ferryboat?

"Yes. Is it bad?" she asked, her expression showing the concern of a mother. "The school, I mean. When Jake offered me the position, I took it without much thought. I remember you gushing about how peaceful and quiet Ocracoke was, and I needed a new start for Lizzie and me. I didn't really think about the school system at all." She paused for a moment before glancing up at me. "God, you must think I'm a terrible mother."

Leaning forward, my elbows on my knees, I looked up at her, grinning. "I don't, Cora. Really, I don't. Although," I said, leaning back, "I'm kind of iffy on your nursing skills at the moment, seeing as we've been in this exam room for nearly fifteen minutes and you haven't even taken my blood pressure. But I'm pretty confident you're a good mom."

She gawked at me, her mouth slack, as she searched for words. Honestly, I was a little surprised, too, by my ability to string so many words together in her presence.

"And the school is good, by the way. It produced Jake and me, so it can't be half bad. Well, I guess, Jake turned out pretty good at least." I grinned.

"Good," she replied, using our favorite word of the day. "That's good. Thank you for that. My conscience is eased a bit, knowing she's in at least capable hands." Looking down at my chart again, she took a deep breath before speaking. "Now, if you'll excuse me."

Confused, I watched her walk toward the door. "Wait, where are you going?" I asked.

"To get your chart. I've been holding Mrs. Joyner's for the last fifteen minutes, and I was too embarrassed to say anything."

I bit my lip, trying not to chuckle, but the moment I saw a smile tug at the corner of her pretty pink lips, I couldn't help myself. Deep laughter sprang free as she opened the door, leaving me behind in search of my actual file.

In that moment, I finally felt like I'd found the dark-haired nurse who'd turned me down in that lonely hospital room. And, if she was in fact in there somewhere, hidden behind the baggage life had thrown on her over the last three years, I might be well and rightfully screwed.

Because I could fall for her all over again.

And, this time, there would be no husband or injury to blame. My whole body was screaming to turn and run, to flee, before any other part of me was lost to pain and ruin.

But, instead, I sat, firmly planted in that rickety old seat, and waited for her to return.

"What is this I hear of you harassing my new nurse?" Jake said, charging into the exam room with no warning.

I'd been sitting in here for nearly ten minutes, wondering if I'd been forgotten or simply left for dead.

"What is this I hear of you hiring a new nurse without telling me? Especially when it happens to be someone I know? Someone I used to know...well?" The last part was said in a hushed tone with a look that said I meant business.

Taking a seat on the exam table, Jake placed my chart —the correct one, I assumed—next to him and faced me as a friend rather than a doctor. Being friends with him so long, I'd now learned the difference between the two sides of him, and this was definitely Jake the friend.

"I'm sorry, Dean," he began. "I meant to; I really did. You know I've been desperate for someone for months since Betty left. And it's not easy finding a nurse who will willingly work down here. Part-time? Maybe. But full-time?" He made a disgruntled sound in the back of his throat. "I had a nurse on the mainland, offering to ferry in every day. But she would need to drive two hours each way and requested a substantial increase in pay to cover it. You know I don't have that. The clinic barely stays afloat as it is."

I nodded, knowing how much blood, sweat, and tears he'd put into this place since taking over after his father's death.

"So, when I got a résumé for a competent nurse with a familiar name to boot, I jumped at the chance before she could change her mind. Cora was willing to start as soon as possible, and things just kind of happened after that. I've been in a whirlwind ever since, trying to make sure everything was in place for her arrival."

I held up my hand, ignoring the automatic knee-jerk reaction of his eyes as they darted toward the other lying in my lap. It was the briefest of glances, but even he couldn't help but look.

"I get it; I do. Just a little heads-up would have been nice. You know, so I could have avoided making a world-class idiot of myself again."

He grinned, picking up my chart as he hopped off the table. "Wouldn't have helped in the least. You, my friend, would have done that on your own regardless of my interference. Now, let's play doctor, shall we? I have other patients today, you know."

Shaking my head, I stood up and hoisted myself up onto the exam table. "I hate you," I said, making his grin widen.

"You say the sweetest things. Now, shut up, and let me do my job."

Friend time was over, and I surrendered to the chore of answering his questions and allowing his tests, knowing he was the best at what he did—keeping people alive.

Usually, at the end of a relationship, the people involved separated and went their own ways.

This was not the case for Molly and me. At the end of our engagement that had been going nowhere, we continued to see each other.

In a platonic sort of way.

Growing up, Molly, Jake, and I had been the best of friends. When Molly and Jake naturally gravitated toward one another and their relationship became something more, we always remained a team. The three amigos.

Until Jake left.

And then it was just Molly and me.

We made the mistake of pushing our relationship past its boundaries, but soon after we broke off our engagement, we were able to find that rhythm again, the one that had bonded us together as young children and still did as adults.

When I returned home from my rehabilitation, Molly made sure of this by inviting me over to the inn for weekly dinners. At first, I had been sure it was to keep an eye on me or a secret plot with my mother to make sure I was being fed properly at least twice a week between the two of them.

Whatever the reason, it continued to this day.

Except, now, our trio was complete.

Driving up to the inn that night after my rather unusual day, I felt nothing but relief at the normalcy of this dinner. There were times when Molly would be out traveling, and we'd skip for months on end, but we'd pick back up when she returned.

Same day of the week. Same time.

When Jake had moved back home for good a few months ago, it hadn't changed. We just added more beer, and sometimes, if Molly was feeling crazy, she'd let her fiancé help with the cooking.

Parking the car in the driveway, I sincerely hoped tonight was not one of those nights. Jake had a way of destroying even the simplest of meals with a single glance. How a man who had been trained to be one of the best heart surgeons in Chicago could mangle a couple of stalks of celery was beyond me.

As I stepped out of my truck, I couldn't help but notice the other cars around mine. I'd made it a habit to do so whenever I came to the inn. I loved seeing how far Molly's guests traveled—or, in some cases, how little.

Tonight, I saw a rental from North Carolina, which suggested either a foreigner or someone from the West

Coast, and a nice-looking sports car from up north. But nothing held my attention like the dusty little SUV from Virginia.

With a car seat in the back and a Princess Anne county sticker on the dash, it suddenly dawned on me—what I'd failed to ask Cora and Jake when I was in the clinic earlier that day.

Where was she staying?

Walking up to the front door, I didn't bother knocking or ringing the doorbell. The one time I'd tried, shortly after Molly and I broke up, she'd nearly hit me over the head with a wooden spoon, reminding me that family did not knock.

Stepping into the wide foyer, I took a peek in either direction, feeling like a damn spy, as I tried to pinpoint Cora's location.

Of course she was staying here.

Why was I even surprised? Jake and Molly were two of the most giving people I knew. A single mom relocating to a town she knew nothing about? Those two had probably insisted on it as part of her employment.

"What are you doing, standing out here like a lurker?" Molly's voice filled the empty space, pulling me out of my thoughts.

"What? Who? Me? Nothing. Just wondering where you were. That's all."

Her blue eyes studied me for a moment, obviously seeing my bluff. "I was in the kitchen. Where else would I be? Come make yourself useful before Jake tries to. I sent him on a fool's errand to grab charcoal for the grill. We have gas." She grinned mischievously.

Shaking my head at her deceit, I followed her back into the kitchen, briefly looking over my shoulder like I was searching for some sort of ghost. She must have picked up on my distracted behavior because the second we entered her sacred space, her hands reaching for a wooden spoon to stir something savory simmering on the stove, she began her interrogation.

"So, Jake said you were at the clinic today. How'd that go?"

Oh, she was a sly one.

"Good. And Jake didn't say that," I answered with a smirk, refusing to give in so easily. If Molly was going to prod me for answers to something she clearly already knew, I wasn't going to make it easy for her. "You and I both know, I mentioned it last week."

She made a face, momentarily scrunching her nose but letting it go almost immediately before going for round two. "Nothing out of the ordinary happen?" she said, giving her sauce a little taste before adding a pinch of salt.

I leaned back against the counter, not surprised in the least that she hadn't given me anything to do yet. She didn't need help; she rarely did. She just wanted me to tell her all about Cora because Jake couldn't. Or he wouldn't.

Doctor-patient confidentiality and all that.

Jake was a stickler for it but living in a place where gossip was about as common as salt water, I couldn't really blame him. Whatever happened inside the walls of that clinic, whether it be a chat with a patient about the game or the results of a test, he kept it to himself. Dealing with a small town, it was the only way he found he could keep it separate—the two sides of himself. And, as much as Molly respected it, it sometimes drove her insane.

Like right now.

"Nope," I replied, enjoying the sight of her as she fought for answers.

"Are you sure? No one new there? No one you recognized?"

I pursed my lips like I was deep in thought before answering. "Mr. and Mrs. Joyner were there. Lovely couple. They remind me a little of you and Jake—or at least, you and Jake in the distant—"

"Dean Sutherland!"

A wide grin spread across my face. "What?"

Dropping her cooking utensil on the porcelain spoon rest next to the pot, she turned to face me, both hands at her hips, like she was ready to scold a misbehaving young child.

Not too far off, I thought.

"You know well and good what I'm talking about!"

Laughing, I nodded. "Of course I do. So, why don't you just come out and ask me instead of going through all this trouble to draw it out of me?"

Her eyes tore away from me, a twinge of embarrassment coloring her fair cheeks. "Because. I don't know," she replied. "I didn't know if you'd want to tell me."

"Why?"

"Because maybe it's none of my business."

Eyebrow raised, I pushed off from my spot against the counter. "Since when has my life not been any of your business? Pretty sure it was all your business at one point."

She threw her arms up. "Exactly my point! Maybe you don't want to share stuff about another woman with your ex. Maybe that's weird. Shouldn't it be weird?"

Walking to the stove, I picked up her wooden spoon and handed it to her, knowing it'd calm her down to have something in her hand to keep her occupied. "No, it's not weird. It's never been weird between us, except for that part in the middle when we made it kind of weird."

She laughed. "It really was weird."

I nodded. "I'm going to stop using the word *weird* now. But, to piggyback on what you said, Cora isn't another woman, Molly. She's just a woman I used to know, okay? So, she's moved here. That doesn't change anything."

"Why?" she asked, locking eyes with me.

I could see the warmth in them, the genuine concern for my well-being. She wanted me to be happy but not the general kind of happiness that everyone had. She wanted the true, deep-down joy she'd found with Jake, and knowing her, she'd do about anything to make sure I found it even if she had to force it on me.

"Because, Molly," I answered, "not every story ends in a happily ever after. Some just end, and rather than dwell on it, you just move on. Cora and me, we were just that—a story."

"That's bullshit, and you know it," she fired back. "Because I remember the Dean in that hospital room who told me to go for broke when it came to Jake, regardless of the outcome. You told me to fight for him even if it was just for a single day because a sliver of happiness was better than a lifetime of misery."

"I was on a lot of drugs in that hospital," I scoffed.

"Stop it, Dean."

I let out a huff. "So, what? You think Cora is my sliver? Based on what, Molly? A single encounter? She just went through a divorce, and she's raising a child on her own. What makes you think I need that kind of baggage in my life right now?"

Her eyes widened, and rather than reply, she just stared back at me like she was seeing me for the first time. Honestly, I didn't blame her. I barely recognized myself in that moment. The words had flown out of my mouth so quickly, I hadn't had a chance to realize what I was saying until it was too late.

She took several steps in my direction. "Someday, you're going to realize your life didn't end out there on that boat, Dean," she said, her voice quivering with emotion. "Someday, you're going to look past those wounds and scars that ripped open your body and realize you have more to give, more to live, and more to love. When you do, I'll be the first person in line to say, *I told you so.*"

Turning, she walked back to the counter and set her spoon down on the stove. I watched as she pressed her lips together and swallowed hard, an obvious attempt to keep the tears at bay. She left out the back door without saying a word.

I guessed there was no more to say.

Letting out a deep breath, I headed for the refrigerator and grabbed a beer, my head falling against the cool steel of the door as I let the last few minutes sink in. Had I really meant it? Did I think Cora wasn't worth the baggage she carried?

No, I didn't.

In reality, there wasn't a person for miles who had more emotional baggage than me. I didn't have the right to evaluate others when I barely had a grasp on my own.

So, why had I said it?

I remembered back in high school when my mother had sat me down and given me the talk. Not *the talk*, but the one that followed shortly after you started high school when parents remembered their own teen years and began to panic.

She'd told me, if I were ever in a situation, be it a party or an invitation to do something I knew would get me in trouble, I merely had to blame her.

"Blame you?" I'd asked.

"That's right. Ain't no skin off my back if those hooligans think I'm a square. You find yourself in the thick of things, you just tell 'em you have curfew or can't go because you're grounded. I'll back you up. The point is, keep your nose out of trouble."

I'd thought she was a little crazy at first, thinking there was no possible way I'd need such an out in a town like Ocracoke, but I'd highly underestimated the creativity of bored teenagers. While I'd dabbled in the normal stuff, like sneaking liquor from my mom's cabinet and drinking beer on the beach, I'd definitely had to blame my mom a few times when after-game bonfires got out of hand or I simply wasn't up for it.

And that was exactly what I was doing now.

Blaming someone else to protect myself from something that could possibly get out of hand. But this time, it wasn't a young boy trying to do right by his mother.

I was a scared coward of a man, running from something that could be good. Maybe even great. Yet, even admitting it to myself, I couldn't change my mind.

I couldn't take the first step.

No, I could.

I just wouldn't.

Not now. Maybe not ever.

FOUR

Cora

Dear blog family and friends,

I met a man.

A handsome devil of a man.

I never thought I'd use the term handsome devil in my life without either being seriously inebriated or trying to deliver a clever punch line of a joke, but there's no other term to adequately describe Blake Ashcroft.

He's spoiled, a bit rude even, but when I look at him, I turn to mush. We met at a bar. I know; it's totally cliché. A few of my coworkers had dragged me there after our shift, and I don't know, we just clicked. I've never been into fancy guys. You know the type—the ones with the sharp suits and the designer watches that cost more than a mortgage payment. Well, that's Blake. His family is one of the wealthiest on the East Coast, and sitting next to him makes me feel so plain. But he says he likes that about me. My genuineness. He says it's refreshing after growing up the way he did.

Now, I know what you're thinking, Dad. I'm sure you're reading this all the way from Texas, probably while drinking a cup of coffee from your Star Trek mug, muttering under your breath about how you should never have let me move away. But I'm fine.

We're taking things slow. We've been on a few dates, and he's been nothing but gentlemanly. I have a feeling this is the one, guys. I know that's crazy to say, especially after a few dates, but I can't help it.

So, stay tuned. Maybe I'm crazy. Maybe this is all puppy love, or perhaps it's intuition, and I've finally found something real.

XOXO,

Cora

"*What makes you think I need that kind of baggage in my life right now?*"

It was a single sentence, one that hadn't been meant for my ears, but I'd heard it all the same. That was what I got for being raised by parents who drilled good manners into my marrow and an over-bearing need to help whenever possible. Although Molly had pressed that I take a few days to adapt and rest after arriving at the inn, saying that I should think of myself as a full-fledged guest during that time, I couldn't help but feel an itch burning up my spine after several hours of sitting around.

The need to do something. The need to help. So I went in search of something to do. Anything really—that would help me feel like I was earning my keep.

It used to drive Blake crazy. Being born into wealth, my husband had wanted for nothing in his life, having a full staff in his ginormous house to cater to his every whim. When I had taken his name, he'd felt—no, he'd demanded I do the same.

Unlike the staff that had surrounded him, I hadn't been nearly as obedient.

I guessed that was where it had started.

Taking a deep breath, I stood a bit straighter, refusing to let those thoughts of the past drag me down, much less a few stray words from a man I barely knew.

I knew they shouldn't hurt me. What he'd said was true. I was a lot of baggage, and he didn't know the half of it.

I wasn't even looking for a relationship. I didn't think I ever would be. Not after everything I'd gone through.

Yet it hurt all the same.

My eyes stung, and my lips quivered, but I didn't let it get to me. I wouldn't indulge the pain. So, instead, I turned toward the parlor, ready to join Lizzie on the back patio where she was currently inspecting every inch of her new home.

Her temporary one, I reminded myself.

But, before I could do so, the door to the kitchen swung open, and I heard a sharp inhale of surprise. Knowing who'd just occupied the space, I didn't have to guess who was standing behind me.

"Oh, hey," he said awkwardly as I turned back around.

Always awkward, this man. Like he'd just been recently introduced to the English language after being found in the jungle or something.

Giving him a cursory glance, I couldn't help but notice how well he'd recovered since his accident. No longer bruised and wounded, Dean Sutherland proved to be quite an attractive man.

But I'd always known that.

Even when he'd been covered in bandages and laid up in a hospital bed, anyone could plainly see the appeal in this green-eyed fisherman. He carried a ruggedness that I was unused to after years of refined living. With a few days' stubble around his jawline and a well-worn pair of jeans, he looked like his body had been built for hard labor, and God help me, I wouldn't mind watching it in action.

"Hello?" he said before I realized I hadn't answered his initial greeting because I was too busy ogling the man. *Oops.*

"Oh, hi. Sorry, deep in thought," I said.

"Right," he replied, clearly unconvinced. Turning back toward the kitchen for a brief moment, he asked, "You haven't been standing here long, have you?"

Giving the best innocent blank face I could, I shook my head. "Nope. Why?"

"Oh, no reason. You headed out back?"

"Yeah, I was going to check on Lizzie. My daughter," I said, clarifying.

"I remember her name," he said as those green irises met mine.

"Oh, okay," I replied, feeling little flutters of something I hardly recognized anymore buried deep in my belly.

"After you." He motions to the parlor where the backdoors have been opened wide to the expansive patio. It's an impressive view but I can't help but stare at the man in front of me.

Feeling all sorts of flustered, I marched on ahead of him as I chastised myself for acting like a besotted teenager when I had more important things to focus on. Like finding a house and suitable daycare because, as nice as Molly was, she wasn't going to be okay with watching Lizzie indefinitely.

If it wouldn't embarrass me further, I would have put my head in my hands with the enormity of it all.

I hadn't expected it to be this hard—starting over.

I honestly hadn't thought about it at all.

My only thought when leaving Virginia was to put some much-needed distance between us and our old life. I'd tried a separate life close to Blake, I did. An entire year of it. But I couldn't move on when the Ashcroft influence was all around me, squeezing me like a vise.

So, I left it all behind.

It hadn't been easy, but it was worth it. I'd told myself I'd figure everything out when I got here.

The rest was just details.

"I know that look," Molly said, walking up to stand next to me.

Being ever the gracious host, she handed me a glass of wine, not bothering to even ask if I was interested. I looked down at it, contemplating its future for a moment before eventually giving in.

"What look?" I asked, taking a tentative sip. I was immediately in love with the fruity taste of the wine, taking another straightaway.

Molly, looking pleased with herself over the choice, joined me, holding glass to her lips as well.

"The look that says you're about to tell everyone you're fine when, in fact, you're the opposite."

I nearly choked on the rosé, biting my lip in the process. "What?" I said, stumbling over the single word like a damn roadblock. "I'm—"

"Fine?" She grinned. "I've found, in my many years of caretaking, hosting, and dealing with my own bag of crap, that particular word rarely means what people try to pass it off as."

I took a moment to locate Lizzie in the small crowd. Molly had really outdone herself tonight, inviting the entire houseful of guests to an impromptu dinner—something she apparently did on a regular basis, which, according to Mr. Lovell, was one of the many reasons she was the best innkeeper around.

"I guess you're right," I acknowledged, smiling to myself as I watched Lizzie twirl around the lazy shoreline of the bay.

"So how are you really?" she asked.

"I don't know." I laughed. "I thought if we could just get somewhere else, away from our old life, then I'd eventually sort through everything—myself included."

Someone had given her a streamer, one that reminded me of my friend Margie, who always twirled a bright green one in the high school marching band. This one, however, was bright purple, and Lizzie seemed perfectly content with running up and down the watery edge as it blew in the breeze behind her.

"I never thought past her," I said, surprising myself by the candor in my voice. "I rarely do, you know. As soon as you become a mother, this nagging voice takes over with this constant prevailing question that never seems to be answered. *How do I make a better life for her?*"

"And you think Ocracoke can give her that? A better life?"

I looked over to her, my gracious host with the big heart. I could see in her a kinship, the potential for a friendship I hadn't had for a great many years.

"I hope so," I answered honestly. "It's why I'm here. A brand-new start for both of us."

"And what about your family? Are they excited about the change? Or do they miss you terribly?"

The mere mention of family had me halting in my tracks.

Share time was over.

"They're fine with it," I replied, setting down the glass

of wine on the table beside us. "Excuse me. I'm going to check on Lizzie."

Our eyes met for a brief moment as I fled, and I could see the shock written all over her face. How could it not be? The about-face in my demeanor had been abrupt, even to the most oblivious of persons.

But I couldn't risk it.

Friendships, growing attached to someone. I needed to protect my family from the truth. The last thing I needed was a misguided friend reaching out to my parents.

It was a good reminder as I walked past the small group of people I'd started to recognize since arriving. The Lovells, Jake and Molly, and most of all, Dean.

The broken and beautiful Dean.

He was more than a friendship. More than another face in the crowd.

He was something different altogether.

I'd felt a connection to him all those years ago, something I'd refused to acknowledge back then. Something beyond what a nurse should feel for a patient. Something even beyond friendship.

I'd walked away then.

I could do so again.

I'd been berating myself on my horrible behavior toward Molly ever since I walked away before dinner. This woman had invited me into her home and been nothing but kind to me and my daughter, and at the first offer of friendship, I'd basically stomped all over it and walked away.

I had actually walked away.

I needed to make it right, but I wasn't sure how.

A simple apology sure, but how did I explain my behavior?

Sorry, Molly, I'm a bit of a nutter. Turns out, Dean's little outburst in the kitchen was totally spot-on. I am a walking, talking, heaping truckload of baggage. So much so that I don't know what I'm doing from one moment to the next. So, please, don't try to befriend me. I'm too big of a mess for you. For anyone really.

Yeah. That sounded about right.

"You look deep in thought," a familiar voice said from behind me.

I turned to see Dean, still nursing the same beer I'd seen him with earlier. He'd made decent progress with it, but I could tell he either wasn't much of a drinker or wasn't much of a drinker *tonight*.

"What? This?" I said, pointing to my expression with as much amusement as I could muster. "No, this is just the face they give you when you become a parent."

He smiled, something I'd grown fond of during our brief time together in the hospital. I'd do just about anything to make it appear on his face.

Even now, the lazy grin gave me a flutter in my belly I hadn't experienced in years.

"No shit?" He laughed. "Do you get a membership card, too?"

I couldn't help but join him, chuckling under my breath. "Sadly, no, but there are some pretty harsh initiation rituals. I'm still working on mine."

"Pretty sure those never stop."

"That's what I've heard," I replied as he looked down at me, those mesmerizing green eyes capturing my gaze like tractor beams.

"What's it like? Single-parenting, I mean. Being raised by one, I should know, but it's not really the type of thing you ask your mom, you know?"

I hadn't forgotten his mother—or much else about Dean Sutherland. It surprised me how familiar the Southern drawl in his voice seemed to me, like reuniting with a long-lost friend rather than a fleeting patient from years ago.

"I don't know, honestly," I answered. "I haven't been doing it terribly long. But, so far, I'd describe it as scary, intimidating, and overwhelming. Those are just the words that come to mind at the moment. But, when I look at her, running around that backyard with that silly streamer in her hand, happy as she's ever been, I know right down to my core that I've done something right, so it's got to be okay, you know?"

"It will be," he said. "And hey, now, you have an entire island to help you out."

I knew he was just joking, but the words struck a nerve.

I didn't want help.

I didn't need it.

I would not be that helpless person again.

"Hey." His hand found mine.

The warmth of it seeped into my bones, reminding me of a simpler time.

When a boy could touch me and it meant nothing more than an innocent caress.

When a man could kiss me and it wouldn't be followed with the memory of fear or violence.

Pulling away, I felt the heat vanish, and I rubbed the spot where his hand had been. "I'd better get to bed," I said before realizing it was nowhere near bedtime. "I have an early morning."

His eyes were fixated on my hand, the way I rubbed where he'd touched me, like I was trying to erase it from history.

If only I could explain. If only I could find the words.

It wasn't him I was trying to erase, just the memories he'd touched.

"Right. Of course," he said, his voice quiet and lifeless.

It was then that I realized the error I'd made. When he'd touched me, he'd reached out with his right hand. I'd been so frozen, so paralyzed by his touch, I hadn't even noticed how different it felt when the prosthetic hand rested on mine.

Was that haunted look he now carried in his eyes rejection? Was the pain he was showing because of me?

I assumed he'd seen the tragedy in my own haunted stare, but I'd failed to see it gazing back at me.

"I'd better go," I said, feeling the need to flee growing stronger.

Baggage.

It was weighing us both down, heavy and burdensome. There was no doubt we had our own truckloads of it following behind us like a lead weight. And, if there was one thing I remembered about Dean Sutherland, it was that he deserved better than me.

I'd gone to bed that night, feeling like a failure in more ways than one.

I'd made a mess of things with Molly and never had the chance to make amends, and I'd basically done the same thing with Dean less than two hours later.

It was like I'd taken a manners and etiquette class from Kanye West himself. I'd come to Ocracoke to start over, yet at the first sign of a fresh start, one full of friends and laughter and fun, I'd turned it all down.

Why?

Because I was a damn certifiable mess, and as much

as I craved it—the attention, interaction, and kindness—I wasn't sure I even knew how to be genuine anymore.

After becoming Mrs. Blake Ashcroft, I'd perfected the art of lying, of creating the perfect cover story, and now, after all this time, I wasn't sure what was left of Cora Carpenter.

If anything.

But there was more to it. In my effort to create a new life, free from Blake and his family's influence, I hadn't thought about my own.

The family who still believed I was a happy, healthy, and thriving wife and mother. One who took family vacations but always forgot the camera. One who was never happy enough with her home remodels for a visit.

I needed to protect them as well.

From what exactly?

From me.

From the mess I'd become. From the horrors I'd endured. From the failures I'd been shielding from their eyes. It might not be the right choice, but it was the one I'd made.

It kept them happy.

It kept them safe.

And, for now, it was the only option I could mentally deal with. I kept telling myself, maybe someday, I'd come clean. Maybe someday, I'd tell them the truth.

Someday was not today, and I had only one thing on my to-do list.

Lizzie.

Lizzie was my priority. To keep her happy, safe, and healthy. No matter the cost. No matter my cost.

For now, I seemed to have achieved that. So, for the foreseeable future, I'd get out of bed, I'd do my job, and slowly but surely, I'd figure everything else out.

Starting with today.

The getting-out-of-bed part was easy. Having a rambunctious five-year-old who woke up at the crack of dawn after sleeping in the same bed made it damn near impossible for me to do anything but get up.

But the everything-else part?

That was where it got murky.

Lizzie and I made it through breakfast time, helping ourselves like Molly had instructed since I had to be out the door and at work earlier than most of the guests liked to rise. But beyond that, I began to fumble.

Although Molly had offered to help out with Lizzie as much as possible over the next week before school started, today was an exception.

Or at least, I made it one.

Being on a remote island definitely had its perks, but when it came to supplying an inn, the location wasn't one of them. Molly often had to make routine trips up the coast for food and other staples, and although she'd offered to take Lizzie with her, the idea of my little girl even an hour closer to her father made my blood pressure rise.

"Are you sure?" she'd asked over the phone, checking one final time to see if I'd changed my mind. "It's really no trouble. I'll even take her out to lunch. My treat."

I'd swallowed deeply, looking over at Lizzie as she finished her cereal, knowing there was no possible chance my workaholic ex-husband would be out and about on a weekday, let alone at a fast-food joint.

But, still, I couldn't agree. "No, it's fine. Really. I'll figure something out."

Taking a deep breath, I'd ended the call, and I had done the only thing I could do.

I carried on.

"Lizzie, get your shoes," I instructed as she hopped

off the worn seat of the kitchen table. "You're coming to work with me today."

Letting out that same breath, I said a prayer to anyone who was listening, although I'd never been much of a religious person.

"Please don't let this blow up in my face."

Taking a moment to rinse out our dishes in the sink, I placed them in the dishwasher and met Lizzie at the front door. She was dressed in purple shorts and a shirt that said *Smart Girls Rule*, and I couldn't help but smile.

"Do I really get to go to work with you?" she asked excitedly. "You've never let me before."

"Well, today is a special day," I said. "It's Bring Your Daughter to Work Day!"

"Really?"

"Nope." I laughed. "But we can pretend."

She giggled as I opened the door, letting her step out before me. "Can I use the stethoscope? Or poke people with needles?"

"Um…"

"I saw a YouTube video on how to start an IV. I think I could handle it."

I rolled my eyes as we walked out to the car. *Damn YouTube.* I didn't even know how she'd managed to get online. With no phone and no iPad, I swore, this girl was the queen of internet stealth.

"That's a hard no," I answered.

"But how am I supposed to gather a sample to look at under my microscope?"

Laughing, I helped her up to her car seat. "So, let me get this straight. You want to poke my patients, steal their blood, and then examine it on your neon plastic microscope that Pappy got you for Christmas last year?"

"Yeah. Why?"

I was so getting fired.

Hopping into the car, I started the car and began the tedious process of negotiating with my five-year-old. "How about this? Why don't I download a book on my phone about blood and cells and all sorts of stuff, and you can read it while Mommy does the poking, okay?"

Looking up at her reflection in the rearview mirror, I could see a distinct moment of disappointment, but it was instantly replaced with a soft sigh of content satisfaction once the realization sank in.

She was going to have access to my phone.

All day long.

"Okay."

I wasn't sure if I'd done myself a favor or just opened about a dozen more cans of worms. With a childlike Lizzie, who found anything and everything interesting, there was no telling.

It didn't take long to get to the clinic, but as I was beginning to learn, it didn't take long to get to most places in Ocracoke.

"Is this where you work, Mommy? It's so tiny!" Lizzie said after we pulled into the clinic parking lot and I helped her out of her car seat.

Leaning down to her height, I decided it was time for a little pep talk before stepping into my place of employment.

That was, if I wanted it to remain my place of employment.

"Okay, Lizzie, you know how we talk about indoor voice and outdoor voice a lot?"

She smiled, a big, wide, ear-to-ear smile, as her head bobbed up and down making her dark curls bounce along with her.

God, she was cute.

So cute in fact, that sometimes, it made it hard to police her or be the bad guy because just looking at her made my eyes go all round and soft, and then all I wanted to do was hug and squeeze her and—

What was I saying?

Oh, right…the pep talk.

"Right, indoor voice," I said, getting back on topic. "Today, we need to use our indoor voices. Do you remember which one that is?"

"Yep! That's the one Grandmother says should be used all the time, even when outdoors." As soon as she mentioned her grandmother, her voice took on this formal, snooty quality as she tried to mimic the awful woman who had raised my ex-husband.

I tried not to laugh, but I couldn't help it. Her impression of her grandmother was spot-on, and it was indeed something the stuck-up old woman would say.

"Right. Well, ignore what Grandmother said, but do me a favor today, and talk quietly when you're inside that tiny building."

Like a lightbulb had gone off in her head, she responded, "Oh! Because it's tiny; that's why I need to talk tiny."

"Um, sure. Tiny voice for the tiny building," I answered, sort of seeing the logic in it, especially if it worked. "You ready?"

"Yep!" she nearly yelled.

I chuckled, grabbing her hand, and we headed for the door.

"God help me," I whispered under my breath.

"Mommy, we're not inside," she reminded me. "You don't have to whisper yet."

"You're right, baby. Just practicing."

And praying, I thought. *Been doing an awful lot of that today.*

Hopefully, someone was listening up there today because I had a feeling I would need all the help I could get.

FIVE

Dean

Recovery Journal: Day Seven

This room. It's too quiet. Every time I hear the shuffling of feet down the hall, I look and wait, wondering if someone will enter. Maybe a nurse or a doctor...anyone to put an end to the stifling silence.

God, I can't take it.

I never really thought of hospitals before now. I mean, does anyone really?

Not even when my mom spoke of my father's death did I wonder about all those people mulling about inside. I was so young. I know Dad must have been in one, even for a brief while after the aneurysm ruptured in his brain. Mom said he didn't suffer, and I always remember feeling some sort of comfort from those words.

But I never imagined him here.

Or anyone else.

In the fourth grade, Kyle Keswick had to have his appendix taken out. He was gone for a week. Even then, I just thought of him as being on a sort of vacation—one where he got a cool scar and got to eat a lot of Jell-O.

Maybe no one really does.

Maybe that is how we stay sane—going on with our lives while the sick and dying are tucked away, out of sight.

That is me now. I am the forgotten.

The friend who has gone on vacation and will come back with the wicked cool scar.

But how deep will that scar run?

And will I be worth anything after it heals?

❀

Before the accident, I'd never questioned my purpose in life.

Since then though, finding a reason to even get up in the morning seemed like a struggle. My family had pushed me, encouraging me to find my new niche in the family business now that my brother had expanded it.

"There's so much you can do," my mom would say.

"You don't have to go out on the water," my brother would remind me.

But every morning, I'd wake up, look at my front door, and never pass the threshold.

It'd been like this for three years.

But not today.

Something had been bothering me since dinner last night.

Something had shaken me, and I couldn't quite put my finger on it.

Try as I might, steering clear of Cora was proving to be a difficult task. I knew there was an attraction there, maybe even a mutual one, but I couldn't pursue it.

No, I wouldn't.

She'd just come out of what could have possibly been a messy divorce.

And then there was that moment.

The moment I'd touched her hand.

At first, I'd thought she'd flinched, a possible distaste for my prosthesis—an obvious error on my part and something I never did. I wish I could say I wasn't embarrassed by it, but I was. There had been far too many stares and wide eyes over the years to not be. So I'd learned to hold it close to me and protect what little dignity I had left.

But with her, everything felt natural.

Normal.

So why did she react the way she did? Was she disgusted? The more I thought about it, the less likely it seemed.

Cora was a nurse. Someone who dealt with the unpleasantries of the human body on a daily basis. A tiny touch from my plastic hand would most likely be a zero on her gross meter, right there with taking a temperature or wrapping a blood pressure cuff.

So, why did she pull away?

That was the question that had kept me up until the wee hours of the night. Sure, she could just genuinely not like me. That would be a hard blow to my ego, but I honestly didn't think it was as simple as that. And the more I thought about that hand flinch, the less I liked the answers I was imagining.

So, I decided a friendly cup of coffee with my best friend was in order. Nothing like a morning cup of joe with the town doctor, who also happened to be Cora's boss, to set things straight. Maybe he'd noticed the same thing. Maybe he knew something I didn't.

He wasn't going to tell me a damn thing—this I already knew.

Molly had tried just about everything—and I did mean everything—to get that man to tell her things about some of the townspeople, and he'd never cracked.

And all I was offering up was coffee.

But, like I said, I couldn't stop thinking about it.

Jumping out of bed, I did my usual sprint to the coffee machine, but instead of making enough for one, I made an entire pot. After that was done, I headed to the shower for a quick rinse and got dressed.

Start to finish, the whole process had taken less than fifteen minutes, and my coffee was still blazing hot as I revved up the engine of my truck and headed for the clinic.

Again.

But this time, I knew what I would be walking into, and this time, I'd come prepared.

Making the short journey in record time, I chose a spot in the back of the lot and left the prime spaces for actual patients. Jostling around the two travel mugs proved to be a bit daunting, but at this point, I'd decided nothing would tear down my upbeat mood. With some quick thinking, I shoved both mugs into the crook of my right arm, leaving my working one free to close the car door and allow me entry into the clinic.

Sometimes, my own genius really astounds me, I thought to myself as the door closed behind me.

Several people looked up at me and either smiled or waved.

Man, this place was busy.

I glanced at the front desk, seeing the mess from yesterday had doubled.

No, tripled.

Looking down at my coffees, I suddenly felt like a damn fool.

What was I thinking, showing up on Cora's second day on the job after witnessing how stressed they'd been the day before?

I was so used to dropping in on Jake, during his lunch break or just whenever the hell I needed to, knowing he'd make time between patients for whatever I needed, that I guessed I'd just assumed…

I'd assumed.

My mother's voice came in my head, screeching loud and clear, like it was on some sort of speakerphone. *"Do you know what happens when you assume?"*

Yeah, Mom, I do.

Realizing I should probably save this conversation for some other time, I decided to just leave the coffee and a note for Jake, and maybe we'd meet up for beers later on in the day.

Because, damn, this place was two patients short of a zoo.

Stepping up to the deserted front counter, I set both cups down and leaned over, grabbing the first pen I could see. But before I could, my movements were interrupted by a tiny voice.

"Are you stealing that?"

"Um, what?" I asked the disembodied voice of a cherub.

The presumed cherub, who turned out not to be a cherub but a little girl—Cora's little girl, to be exact—

emerged from under the desk and pointed to the pen in my hand. "Are you stealing that pen? I saw you grab it from the little hole right there." She pointed to the small hole next to the computer monitor where several wires had been neatly shoved down to the floor.

"Um, no," I answered, unsure of if I was being interrogated by a five-year-old or if she was just curious of my intentions. "I just planned on borrowing it."

She shrugged, seemingly unaffected either way. "Oh, okay." Her little head, covered in dark-brown curls began to disappear below the desk again.

"Hey!" I said before she disappeared. "What are you doing under there?"

She popped back up again. I took that moment to properly examine her. I'd watched her from afar the night before as she ran around the backyard, playing with a streamer as she dodged the water's edge. But I hadn't gotten the chance to interact with her or to stare into those familiar brown eyes while wondering if she'd inherited her mother's dazzling smile.

"Being tiny," she answered. "Mommy said I wasn't using my tiny voice well enough, so I told her I'd go practice. I thought, maybe if I tried to be tinier, it would make my voice tinier, too. Is it working?"

God, she is cute.

"Hmm...well, I don't know. What does your normal voice sound like?"

Her mouth scrunched to the side like she was thinking real hard. Tiny freckles dotted her cheeks. "My grandmother says it kind of sounds like a bird squawking. I didn't know what squawking meant, so I had to look it up in the dictionary."

My heart melted a little. Okay, a lot. *What kind of grandmother was this?*

"Well, I've heard birds squawk. Lots of birds, like a

whole mess of them. Big, mean birds out by the docks. And let me tell you, you don't sound anything like them."

"Really? What kind of birds?"

I leaned my arms on the counter. "Pelicans, egrets. The same kinds you had in Virginia Beach, I'm sure. But the really annoying ones are the seagulls."

She got that face again, the one where she seemed deep in thought. Her lips got all squishy, and tiny frown lines appeared on her brows. "Did you know humming-birds can fly backward and sideways?"

I was nearly thrown backward from shock. *Who was this clever kid?*

"I did not know that. Did you know an eggshell is porous so that the baby bird can breathe while inside?"

Her eyes lit up almost immediately. "No! Do you know what the fastest bird on the planet is?"

"The peregrine falcon."

She smiled a bright, happy smile, which only confirmed my suspicions.

She did indeed have her mother's smile.

I caught a glimpse of a missing front tooth, making my heart melt a little more.

"How'd you know that?" She giggled, covering her mouth with her small hands.

"How'd you know?" I pressed.

"I looked it up online." She shrugged like it was the most obvious answer in the world. Like all five- or six-year-olds in the world looked up random bird facts in their spare time.

"Is my mommy gonna fix your arm?"

"What?" I asked, briefly caught off guard.

Looking down at her slight frame, her head resting atop her arms on the desk, I saw her gaze was now eye level with my prosthesis. But, unlike many kids her age, there was no wide-eyed look of fear.

Just that flat-out curiosity again.

"That's why you're here, right? To get your arm fixed?"

My eyes briefly settled on the flesh-colored hand that rested atop the desk. "Uh, no," I answered. "I'm afraid that's as fixed as it's going to get. But it looks kind of cool, huh?"

She leaned forward a little, examining it with her inquisitive stare. A hesitant finger rose up in the air, hanging there for a moment as indecision wavered in her mind. It didn't take long before she made the choice to go ahead though, placing the tip of her index finger along the top of my fake hand.

"Does it hurt?" she asked, her young mind still trying to make sense of it all.

"Nope," I answered, knocking on a higher section of it with my fist. "Plastic," I explained. "All the way up to here."

Those dark-brown irises followed my finger all the way up to the top of my bicep near my shoulder.

"How does it—"

"Mr. Pond?" Cora's familiar voice called behind me.

Turning around, I was met with a surprised expression as she waited for the middle-aged grocer to gather his things. He'd all but moved in, bringing in several magazines, books, and other things. Realizing it might take a while, Cora stepped out of the doorway and walked in my direction.

"Um, hi?" she said, forming her greeting more like a question rather than a friendly salute. Although she said it nice enough, the meaning came across clear enough. *What the hell are you doing here?*

Yeah, I guess I deserved that.

"Hi," I replied awkwardly.

Ah, good. The painfully uncoordinated Dean was back. Excellent. He was always a hit with the ladies.

Actually, I didn't know that for a fact because this side of me—the all thumbs, couldn't talk his way out of paper bag—only seemed to come out whenever she was around. It was like, the second Cora turned up, I'd revert to that dorky thirteen-year-old version of myself who thought talking about video games and Star Wars was the way to a girl's heart.

Clearly, I'd outgrown him.

Or I'd thought I had…until I met Cora Ashcroft.

"Hey, what is your last name now?" I blurted out.

She looked up at me with a wry sense of curiosity, still trying to figure out why I was there in the first place.

Me, too, Cora. Me, too.

"It's just that, before, you were—I mean, it was different," I said, tripping all over my words as I tried to explain my meaning.

"Oh," she said. "Um, Carpenter. It's Carpenter, I guess."

Smiling, I nodded in approval. "Okay, good. Well, I just came by to drop off a cup of coffee for Jake, but then I got highly distracted by your very charming daughter. By the way, did you know that hummingbirds can fly backward?"

A smile flashed across her face. "And sideways I've heard."

Yep, I thought to myself. *Just like her mom.*

We hung in that moment, our mutual smiles reaching for each other like magnets.

"Um, Miss Cora?" old man Pond called out. "I'm ready."

"Oh, right," she said, her cheeks reddening in embarrassment. "I'd better get back to work."

"Oh, right. Me, too. I mean, going. I should get going."

I am a fucking idiot.

"Don't go!" Lizzie protested, a little too loud for her mother's liking.

"Shh!" she immediately scolded, holding her finger up to her lips.

God, those lips. What I wouldn't do to—

I cleared my throat. "Why doesn't she spend the day with me?"

Wait, what?

"What?" Cora echoed my internal thoughts.

Too late now. Can't take it back.

Might as well go with it.

"Um, sure. I'm not doing anything, and clearly, you're swamped. I could show her the birds we were talking about down at the docks and give her a tour of the town."

"We already did a tour of the town," she replied, her eyes dodging between me and Mr. Pond, who was currently standing next to her, holding his huge pile of books and magazines.

The whole thing was awkward.

There was no other way to describe it.

But then again, that was the definition of my interactions with Cora thus far.

Awkward.

Just all sorts of awkward.

"Please, Mommy?" Lizzie begged before amending her plea to something much quieter. "Please?" she nearly whispered.

Cora's gaze alternated between me, her daughter, and Mr. Pond, who was now watching the entire interaction like a true townie—with enthused observation.

"No boats," she said sternly.

"Wouldn't even dream of it," I agreed.

"And you'll feed her?"

"Best food in town," I promised.

"And bring her back before we close?"

I nodded. "With bells on."

"Bells!" Lizzie cheered, her voice breaking into laughter.

"Fine," she agreed, but took one step closer toward me.

I could feel her breath on my neck and smell the floral fragrance of her shampoo, and if I bent forward even an inch, I'd know exactly what her skin tasted like.

"Eyes forward, Sutherland," she barked, jolting me out of the lust-filled haze I'd momentarily stumbled into.

I looked down at her, seeing the seriousness in her eyes. I took a tiny step back, hoping it would help me focus.

"That right there is the most important thing to me in this whole damn world." Her finger went up to my chest as she tried to find more words to drive in the significance of what I was doing.

"I'll treat her like the treasure that she is, Cora. I promise."

Our eyes met, and once again, I tried to ignore the tightening in my chest and the yearning deep in my belly.

Because, as much as Molly wanted to believe, this was not a love story.

No fireworks, no happy endings.

Just one nice person doing a favor for another.

Period.

❦

"So, what'll it be?" I asked after nearly collapsing into the chair at the local restaurant I'd picked out for lunch.

Lizzie was a ball of never-ending energy, asking questions with every glance, about everything from street signs and local life to types of animals, and even giving her own fun facts along the way.

And, in the few hours we'd spent together, I'd grown pretty fond of the spunky little girl. Even if I did want to fall over from sheer exhaustion at the moment.

"Chicken fingers!" she announced after looking over the menu with a bit of scrutiny.

It didn't surprise me one bit that she could read the thing. Considering she was looking up random facts on birds on the internet, a simple kid's menu was a no-brainer.

It did make me wonder how she was going to fare in kindergarten though.

Or rather, how the school was going to fare with her.

"Chicken fingers?" I scoffed. "Out of everything this place has to offer, you're going to choose chicken fingers?"

She shrugged. "I don't like fish."

"You were born in a beach town. How can you not like fish?" I joked, recalling I, myself, hated the taste of anything sea-related until the age of twelve, and I was the son of a fisherman.

She shrugged again, this time even bigger, her shoulders nearly reaching the bottoms of her ears. "I don't know. I just don't."

"Hmm," I said, making an exaggerated face like I was trying to think of a solution. "Well, what if I said you could eat with your fingers? Would that change your mind?"

She slightly perked up. "Maybe. All the other fish I had was slimy."

"Slimy?" I echoed, wondering just where she had been getting her fish.

Remembering who her father was—or at least, what little Cora had spoken of him—I realized she'd probably been fed only high-priced, fancy stuff, which was good, if you were a high-priced, fancy adult.

But a kid? A kid needed something that was more at their level.

Something more—

"Hey, Dean. You two ready to order?" Billy asked as soon as he reached our table, setting two glasses of ice water down in front of us.

"Hey, Billy! Have you met our newest resident, Miss Lizzie?" I paused a moment, unsure if she was still an Ashcroft or a Carpenter. Deciding to let that go, I just smiled as Billy, a guy I knew from high school, greeted Lizzie like a queen.

"It's so nice to meet you, Lizzie," he said, shaking her tiny hand. "Can I get you anything else to drink besides water?"

She looked sheepishly in my direction, asking for permission. With eyes like those, I'd probably give her the damn world, but for now, I'd settle on giving her a soda.

"Sure," I said before she asked for a root beer. I did the same and proceeded to order our lunches, forgoing Lizzie's request for chicken fingers. I knew Billy could fry up a basket real quick if she hated the fish.

But I was pretty convinced I'd have a fish lover by the end of the meal.

"I'm glad my mommy can't fix your arm," Lizzie said, bringing my focus back to her. Now that her menu was gone, her head was resting on her hands, eye level with mine.

"Oh? Why is that?"

"Because you are kind of like a robot."

I grinned. "Pretty sure a robot can do more than just wave."

She watched as I demonstrated the point, holding up my prosthesis and giving her a lame wave with the frozen hand.

She laughed a high-pitched giggle that made me smile.

"How come it doesn't move?" she asked, that inquisitive expression taking over her face as she gave my arm a once-over. She leaned in closer for a better look, my short sleeves providing an ample view.

"Well," I said, pointing to the top of the device, "this one isn't meant to. It's just supposed to look like an arm."

"But why?" she pressed. "If it looks like an arm, shouldn't it move like one, too?"

I swallowed deeply, unsure of how to answer.

"If I were bigger, I'd make one that shot lasers out of the fingertips and could make you fly."

I laughed. "That doesn't sound like any arm I've ever met."

She shrugged just as our drinks were being delivered. "I'd make sure it could do all the other stuff, too, but definitely lasers."

In the little time I'd gotten to know Lizzie, I had no doubt she could do it, too.

Give her a few years, a little time on the internet, and she could probably build an entire robot, laser limbs and all.

"Mommy!" Lizzie's voice exploded my eardrums a second before she hopped out of her chair and darted in the direction behind me.

Alarmed, I jumped up and turned but instantly calmed, seeing Cora wrapped around her daughter.

Still dressed in her scrubs, that reddish-brown hair

pulled up in a messy bun on the top of her head, she was immediately dragged to our table and instructed to sit.

"Shouldn't you be at work?" I asked, a wry smile spreading across my face.

"I have a lunch break," she scoffed before adding, "but, no, it's a Wednesday, and I was just informed that means I only work a half-day."

I nodded. "Ah, yes. Jake usually travels up to Nags Head or Virginia Beach to the hospitals today to check on patients or meet with doctors."

"That's what he told me. Anyway, I'm free, so I can take over from here."

Her blank stare from across the table spoke volumes. Clearly, I wasn't needed anymore, and I was being dismissed.

"Right," I said, taken off guard and suddenly feeling a little pissed. Obviously, the idea of being neighborly hadn't been explained to our new resident. "I have stuff to do anyway."

"No, Mommy!" Lizzie whined. "We haven't eaten yet, and Dean hasn't shown me how to eat fish with my fingers."

Cora's eyes stared daggers into mine.

"I said I'd treat her like a treasure." I shrugged. "Not royalty. This is how we roll in the 'Coke. You can't tell me you've never dug into a basket of fresh seafood with your bare hands."

She shook her head, the annoyance still written all over her face. "Not even once."

Leaning forward, not even making a single attempt to leave, I asked, "Where are you from again? Texas?"

She nodded.

"And you've been here, living the beach life, for how long?"

"A little over seven years."

"And how many of those were spent with the lawyer?" I asked.

"All but a few months, but I fail to see how any of that —" she answered stiffly.

"You never got a proper introduction," I said. "You moved here, met the rich guy, and were shown a completely ridiculous side of shore life. You've missed out on Jeep rides, late-night bonfires, and pigging out on seafood so fresh, you can't help but eat it with your hands." I grinned, ignoring all those Southern manners my mother had drilled into me.

I mean, she'd started it by barging in here. That reminded me…

"Hey, how did you know where we were?" I asked.

"What?" Cora asked, knocked somewhat off-balance by the abrupt question.

"Well, you weren't planning on meeting us for lunch, and I don't recall getting any calls from you, so how'd you find us?"

One glance over in Lizzie's direction told me she was enrapt with the whole conversation, drinking her soda as her short little legs swung from the plastic chair on the patio, soaking up every word.

"Um, well, I just sort of drove around."

"You drove around? Why didn't you call?"

Her face went blank, a kind of innocent face you'd make when you'd been caught in a lie.

"I didn't think about it."

I grinned, folding my arms in front of me. "You got off work early, were eager to pick up your daughter, and the first thought in your head wasn't, *Maybe I should use that phone number Dean wrote down for me before he left with my kid?*"

"I—"

"You wanted to sneak up on me," I said, cutting her

off, sending Lizzie a lazy wink, which caused her to giggle. "You wanted to see just how well I was living up to my word, didn't you?"

Her arms flew up in the air. "Okay, yes!" she admitted. "I did. But do you blame me? I show up to a town I've never been to, and I'm living in someone else's house, working for another person I barely know, and then you show up and offer to babysit my child when I basically have no other choice."

"You're not a very trusting person, are you?"

"Are you?" she fired back.

"Yes," I answered firmly.

"Well, good for you. Some of us don't have that luxury."

And there it was. That haunting look I'd seen in her eyes the night before. It was here again, and the instant I saw it, I wanted to pull her into my arms and erase it, no matter the cost.

But I knew if I did, she'd bolt. Like a deer caught in the headlights, she'd run and never come back.

So, instead of pressing even further, I backed down.

"I'd better go," I said, meeting those sad eyes once more. "I need to get some things done."

"But what about lunch? And my finger fish?" Lizzie cried out.

I smiled in her direction, leaning forward, like I had a special secret just for her.

"Here's the trick, kid. Are you ready?"

She giggled, scooting up onto her knees so that she could lean forward over the table.

"Use your fingers," I whispered loudly so that her mom could hear.

Lizzie laughed wildly, her hand covering her mouth but doing little to muffle the sound.

"And make sure your mom does the same," I instructed before rising from my seat.

"But what about your food?" Lizzie asked.

I threw enough cash down on the table to cover the two meals plus an ample tip.

"Well, now, your mom will have no excuse but to eat fish with you!" I said, giving her one last wink.

Cora began protesting the money I'd just dropped. I ignored every word as I walked away. I knew my mama would be appalled by my behavior, but someone needed to show Cora Carpenter that in this town, we took care of one another.

Even if she didn't like it.

It didn't take Jake long to track me down after he returned home from his business up the coast, and we met up for a late beer at one of our favorite places in town, Taps. Since his return to Ocracoke earlier that year, I'd grown accustomed to seeing the various new sides to my childhood friend. After all, we had both changed a great deal since high school.

But, sitting across from him tonight, I could see the stress from the clinic was weighing heavily on him.

That, or it was something else.

"Dude, you look like hell," I said after several micro-brew samples arrived on the table for us to try.

In an effort to attract tourists, Gavin, the bartender and longtime friend, had recently renovated the long-standing restaurant and given it an updated taphouse feel, hoping locals would appreciate the selection of brews as well.

We did.

Jake and I came in every chance we had, slowly

making our way through the impressive menu as we dined on the equally ambitious bar food.

"Kind of feel like it, too, but thanks for bringing it up."

"Please tell me this is just clinic stress and not some precursor to you making a beeline out of here again."

He set his beer down as his face went rigid. "No. Hell no. I'm not leaving. Not ever again. This? This is just me pushing through. Betty leaving was a solid blow, one I honestly wasn't prepared for. Leave it to the highly trained, prepared-for-anything cardiothoracic surgeon to crumble at the first sign of distress when his only nurse retires."

"Is there anything I can do? I don't know shit about medical stuff, but I'm sure I could come in and—"

He held up a hand. "It's fine. Really. Cora is learning the ropes. It's only been two days. One and a half actually."

"How is she doing?" I asked. "I mean, is she acclimating well?"

He nodded, helping himself to the nachos we'd ordered. "She's going to be great. Honestly, I couldn't have asked for anyone better."

And there it was. My window. To ask about Cora. To tell him about the way she'd shied away from my touch. The haunted look in her eyes.

It was right there, hanging in the silence, but I let it go.

Why?

Because this wasn't Jake's problem.

And it wasn't mine either.

I needed to step back and mind my own business.

She clearly didn't need my help.

"I'm just desperate for it to simmer down," he continued. "Molly and I have been back together for only a handful of months, and with the wedding coming up—"

"You want time," I finished, understanding his dilemma.

"I know that's lame and selfish. But that's just where I am."

"It's not lame or selfish. You've given yourself completely to this town. Wanting a little time with your fiancée isn't asking much. Are you sure you don't need anything? And don't give me that shit about having it all under control."

He chuckled, taking a sip from one of the amber-colored glasses, before answering, "As much as I want to say no, I can't. I really do need help."

"Knew it. And who better to help than your loser best friend who has nothing to do?"

He gave me a hard stare. "That's on you, buddy. There's nothing holding you back."

I ignored him and instead pushed ahead. "So, what do you need me to do? Take temperatures? Make appointments? If you say anything that has to do with the phrase *turn and cough*, I'm out."

A familiar grin that used to get me in a lot of trouble formed across his face. "Filing."

"Filing?" I repeated, feeling less than enthused. "All my experience with bookkeeping, not to mention the fact that I own and operate my own company, and you want to use me for filing?"

"Operated."

"What?"

"Past tense. You do own a company, well, co-own, but as for the operating, that's all your brother these days. Don't take credit for that."

My eyes rolled as that familiar twinge of guilt gnawed

at my gut. How long would it continue to do so until I finally broke down and did something about it?

"Whatever," I finally answered, ignoring the churning feeling in my stomach like I always did. "Anyway, filing?"

"Yep. There're days' worth. When Betty left, I put a few in a stack and told myself I'd get to it later, but later never came. There are stacks on top of stacks. It's just damn embarrassing. And Cora is so immersed in learning—"

"I get it. You need someone to do the grunt work. Have you ever considered hiring a secretary?"

"Sure," he sneered. "Give me an extra thirty to forty thousand a year, and I'll gladly do that."

"Right. Okay, filing. I can do that," I said, holding up a half-empty glass of IPA. "Just do me one favor?" I asked.

He gave me a meaningful glance. "Anything."

"Make sure that fiancée of yours sends you into work with plenty of coffee and pastries."

He laughed, clinking his glass with mine. "Done."

It wasn't until I finished my beer that I realized what I'd just done.

I'd unwittingly reinserted myself into Cora's life.

So much for minding my own business.

By the time I arrived home, I had a full belly, a bit of a buzz, and a new purpose.

At least for the time being.

Filing.

I guessed it could be worse.

Leaning back in my desk chair, I removed my prosthesis and pulled off my shirt, feeling the crisp, cold air prickle my skin. Tilting my head back, I ran my hand through my hair. That nagging feeling I'd awoken with still hadn't abated. The image of Cora jerking her hand away from mine kept replaying in my head in a loop.

It made me recall a particularly rough day in the hospital during my recovery. It was early on when the pain had still been raw and real, and the painkillers had barely been enough to take the edge off.

I'd awoken from a nap, sweat dripping off my body, shaking from the pain coursing through my veins.

Cora was the one to respond to my call button.

And it was her touch alone that calmed me.

The soft, calming caress of her fingers against my forehead as I'd breathed through the pain. It was a connection, one I'd felt once again last night at dinner.

But this time, the one in pain had been her.

Scooting up to my computer, I booted up the screen and pulled up the internet browser, intent on finding some answers.

Starting with Cora's ex-husband.

Who was this man who'd owned her heart, and what scars had he left in his wake? What had he done to tear apart her trust, to make her pull away from human contact, to fear it even?

I had a pretty good guess, and as I pulled up the name *Ashcroft*, cross-searching it with the terms *lawyer* and *Virginia Beach*, the man I pulled up did nothing to dissuade that feeling.

Blake Ashcroft was the epitome of wealth. Or at least, what I assumed it to be. Even from the photos and articles I found online regarding his prominent cases and well-known family, I could see an arrogance in him. He carried himself in a way that said he thought he was above everyone else.

Just seeing his face caused a hatred deep in my gut,

something I was unused to feeling. I'd never been a revenge-seeking, eye-for-an-eye type person. Hell, I'd handed over my own fiancée to my best friend. But Blake Ashcroft stirred a need to protect like I'd never felt before.

Over an hour later, I was spiraling, falling down a Blake Ashcroft rabbit hole. When I'd gone so far as to pull up Google maps to view his house—or the house where he and Cora had lived—I knew I'd gone too far.

"What the hell are you doing?" I asked myself out loud.

Sitting back in the chair, I let out a deep breath and decided it was time for bed. A quick check at the clock in the corner of my laptop confirmed that.

It was late.

But before I could shut it down, I saw the pesky notification on my email.

Two new emails.

There were two types of people in this world. Those who could let their emails rack up into the tens of thousands without a care in the world. And then there were people like me. Those who saw one new email and had to immediately read or delete it. It was why I'd turned off the notifications on my phone. It'd driven me insane.

Pulling up the email program, I made quick work of deleting the first. Junk mail. I did not need a new duvet cover or whatever the hell the random department store was trying to sell me.

The second email took a bit more time.

When I clicked on it, my eyes narrowed in on the sender. I didn't recognize it at first. The email address was something abstract. Nothing straightforward like mine, which happened to just be my name.

"SmartieBeachGirl5." I chuckled. "Someone really

needs to change their email address." I laughed, feeling pretty amused until I began reading the email.

Dear Dean,
This is Lizzie.
Lizzie Ashcroft.

I found your email address on one of the small cards in the office you took me to when I needed to go to the bathroom when we were at the docks today. It had your name on it, so I figured it was yours.

Thanks for lunch. Mommy and I had a fun time eating the fish with our fingers. I think we would have had more fun eating with you though.

That's why I'm writing you.

My mommy and I moved here to get all new things.

New house, new school. She even said I'd get new toys since I couldn't take most of mine.

But I don't really care about toys.

I just want a new Mommy.

Not a different one. Just a happier one.

Mommy was not happy in our old house, but I think she can be here, in our new house and our new town and with new friends.

Will you be my mommy's friend? I want her to smile again.

Please?

Lizzie

P.S. Can you keep my email address a secret? Mommy would get mad at me if she knew, and I really like talking to you.

I stared at the email for a solid half hour, a mixture of

wonder and panic washing over me. I was in awe of this kid. I had been since the moment she popped up from under that desk at the medical clinic. She was beyond her years in so many ways. Not just in academics, but emotionally, too. She saw things most adults spent eons trying to figure out. Or ignore.

She knew her mother was sad.

I wonder what else she knew.

What else she'd seen.

Cora and I had had a rough go of it. So many false starts at this thing called friendship and even a rougher start when I'd tried to make it more.

But, for this little girl, I'd do anything.

No, for this little girl and her mother, I'd move mountains. Starting with a few files, friendship, and a fresh cup of coffee.

SIX

Cora

Hello Blogiverse,

Did I spell that right? Is that even a thing—spelling a made-up word right?

Who knows? Anyway, it's finally official!

We're married!

That's right. You can now call me Mrs. Handsome Devil!

Ha! Just kidding.

Blake actually hates it when I call him that, which, of course, makes me want to do it more.

We just got back from our honeymoon a few days ago, and I'm settling back into work nicely, although Blake would rather I not work. I don't know how many times he's tried to bribe me to quit. I'm pretty sure I could fund a third-world country for an entire year on what this crazy man has offered me just to quit my job.

But I am not a woman of leisure. Or whatever the modern term is. Trophy wife? Maybe that's not politically correct.

I need to work. I need to be useful and know I'm making an impact in another person's life. It's why I chose nursing to begin with. And I think, in time, he'll understand that. I've even invited him down to the hospital to see me in action. I think it would help immensely for him to see his wife—gosh, that's weird —doing what she does best.

And if we happened to take a stroll by the nursery and caught a glimpse of the newborns?

Well, that would just purely be accidental.

❧

"Why are there so many trucks in this town?" I barked rather loudly as I shoved the back door to the clinic open, my eyes still angry over being open so early in the morning.

It had been another late night for me.

Another sleepless night where I'd lain awake, filled with worry, guilt, and panic.

Had I made the right choice, moving here?

Could I do it all? Pay the bills, be a mom and a dad to Lizzie, and keep it all together after everything that had happened?

And then the guilt over my family had washed over me like a cherry on top of this whole messed up, emotional sundae I'd made.

Jake gave me a once-over before treading lightly. "Well, they're practical. Like SUVs and Jeeps. No point in living on a sandy beach and trying to navigate dusty, unpaved roads in a sedan."

I gave him a hard stare. "And I'll just shut up now."

He backed down, choosing to focus on the chart in his hand.

The rational side of me knew he was doing his best, deciding to answer me with a valid point.

But the irrational side that was running on fumes and a handful of Cheerios? That side wanted him to agree with me and say it was stupid just so I could vent about the jackass who had nearly run me off the road on my way here.

"If you want to take a break from shooting dangers at my head, I have coffee," he said softly, taking a sheepish step toward a large thermos. "And pastries. Still warm."

My eyes warmed slightly as he handed me a Danish. "Molly sends her love. She told me to say that." He smiled. "Probably so I wouldn't get all the credit."

His joke made me laugh, and I took the Danish, feeling calmer already.

"Thank you," I said before adding, "or I should say, *Thank you, Molly.*"

We sat in silence, eating the amazing pastries Jake's wonderful fiancée had sent over, before his concerned expression turned back to me.

"You doing okay?" he asked.

I straightened, realizing whom I'd snapped at. Not just anyone, but my boss.

The man who held my future in his hands.

One nurse on this island.

Only one.

If I got fired, I would have to start all over again.

New town. New home. New school.

"Whoa." He held up his hands in mock surrender. "Calm down. I just wanted to check in on you as a friend. I'm allowed to do that, right? I'm used to wearing two hats in this town. I'm both doctor and friend. I figured we could do the same. Sometimes, I'm your boss, and other times, I'm just a friend you work with."

Nodding, I reluctantly agreed. "Okay."

He smiled, leaning back against the counter, as I watched him shove an entire Danish into his mouth. It was the fourth or fifth maybe. How that man remained trim and athletic, I had no idea. Anyone else, and Molly would have had him looking like Saint Nick by now.

"So, you want to tell me why you hate truck drivers?" he asked.

"I was on the main road, driving here this morning, and when I got to the fork, some jerk did a total one-eighty right in the middle of the road and nearly took me out. The cloud dust he'd created made it all but impossible for me to see, but I did manage to make out the fact that he was driving a huge gray truck."

"Gray, huh?" His interest seemed piqued.

"Yeah. Luckily, it wasn't one of those monstrous things with raised wheels, but it was fairly substantial."

"Hmm. And did this fairly substantial gray truck have a trailer hitch on the—"

"Sorry I'm late!" Dean's voice announced as he burst through the back door. He was carrying two large travel mugs in the crook of his right arm, using the other to navigate. "I had to double back home for the coffee I'd left on my countertop. Pretty sure I nearly took out a tourist on my way, too."

My eyes widened as he blew out a heavy breath, placing the coffees on the countertop, only to look up and meet my piercing death stare. When he noticed the freshly brewed coffee already in my hand and the less-than-enthused expression on my face, his mood dropped a notch.

"Oh, I see you guys already have coffee."

Jake was casually enjoying the coffee his fiancée had made, with an ease about him that said he didn't have a care in the world. "Yep." He grinned. "Molly made it. Coffee and pastries, remember?"

The two old friends locked eyes and seemed to have an entire conversation without saying a word. Eyebrows raised, foreheads wrinkled.

In the end, I couldn't tell what had been said or who had won, if there was indeed a winner or a loser. But whatever had happened, I was left with one grumpy amputee fisherman while my boss sauntered down the hallway toward his office, chuckling under his breath.

I stared at the two travel mugs, wondering why he was here and why he hadn't brought three cups. *Did he just bring enough for himself and Jake?* Letting that thought go as quickly as it'd come, I finished off my cup and pastry, intent on getting on with my day, free from the distraction of Dean.

But I couldn't.

Not before…

"It wasn't a tourist," I said, my arms folded sternly across my chest. I caught him mid-bite, a homemade bear claw shoved in his mouth.

I didn't even know you could make those things from scratch. I mean, I guessed, when I actually thought about it, sure, everything could be made from scratch. But bear claws? Who took the time to make those?

Obviously, Molly did. No wonder everyone on the island wanted to marry her. Had I known all those years ago when she was visiting Dean in the hospital that she made such a killer bear claw? Well, I might have developed a bit of a girl crush too.

Hell, I still might.

"What?" Dean replied, clearly enjoying the homemade goods from his ex.

"The tourist you nearly took out this morning when you did a one-eighty in the road to retrieve your coffees? It wasn't a tourist. It was me."

He eyed the coffees on the counter, and then his gaze

traveled up to me, his mouth still chewing the last bit of dough from his bear claw. I watched his jaw work over and over, the rugged definition of it making me blush.

Who knew watching someone eat could be sexy?

"Wouldn't want to waste it then," he replied, sliding the travel mug in my direction. "I wasn't sure how you took it, so it's black. Jake has all the fixin's," he began to explain before he followed up with, "but you already know that."

I pressed my lips together, feeling awkward in his presence once more. He had brought the extra coffee for me. I didn't know why, but knowing that made me feel nervous and a whole host of other emotions.

Excited.

Anxious.

Elated.

Terrified.

"I'd better get to work," I said, unsure of what else to say.

No, that was a lie. I knew what to say.

Thank you.

But the words wouldn't come out because, as I stared at that coffee, I became increasingly aware of everything it could mean.

All those emotions I felt.

All those terrifying, wonderful emotions.

With every cup of coffee he brought, every smile and conversation we might have, these feelings I had for him, they'd only multiply.

Boundaries would be breached. Secrets would be spilled, and—

"Have a nice day, Dean," I said, leaving the coffee behind on the counter, where it belonged.

It had been a crazy day at the clinic.

But I'd come to quickly realize, every day at the clinic was a crazy day.

So far, I'd seen several locals and a few tourists, and I'd even bandaged up a local chef after a snafu with a knife.

Feeling a bit out of breath, I took a peek into the waiting room, grateful for its current empty state. Although the chairs out there were old and in need of a serious upgrade, they were calling my name, begging me to take a break after being on my feet all morning.

Thank God for the blessed lunch break.

Jake purposely blocked off an hour in the middle of the day to allow us to catch up. He'd explained to me that we'd sometimes end up working right through it depending on the day. Other times, if we were lucky and patients had arrived and left on time, we'd get a few minutes of peace to collect our thoughts, rest our feet, and even get to eat.

Right now, all I wanted to do was put my feet up and close my eyes.

And so, I did. The moment my feet left the floor felt like heaven. I nearly moaned as my body curled into a chair. Old and clumsy as it was, it could have been a freaking bed of clouds for as happy as I felt to be off my toes.

"I'm sorry about this morning." Dean's voice filled the silent room.

I cracked open an eyelid, finding him behind the counter, several files in his hands. He clearly didn't understand the lunchtime rules of rest. *Did this man ever relax?*

"Pardon?" I asked, his piercing stare already making my heart flutter.

I tried not to think about how often that happened.

"The thing on the road. I should have been more careful." He paused, setting the files down on the counter as he gathered his thoughts.

I took that moment to sit up in my chair, pulling my knees to my chest.

"I used to be able to drive without thinking, you know? Like, out on Highway 12, late at night, we'd all go off-roading on the dunes. It's funny because, back then, I never thought about it—driving with one arm on the wheel."

He looked straight ahead, deep in his memories, before he continued, "Anyway, sorry, I didn't mean to scare you. I didn't expect anyone else to be on the road. It was stupid of me."

"Why are you here?" I asked, realizing I'd been so flustered by his arrival this morning, I hadn't even bothered to ask why he was here in the first place. I'd just assumed he was bringing coffee.

But he was still here.

He held up a file. "Helping out Jake," he explained. "He said you guys were being taken over by files and needed a hand."

"Oh," I replied lamely. "I guess that's part of my job."

He saw the tip of my toes hit the floor, and he motioned me to stay. "Nope." He pointed to my foot. "You sit. This is currently my job. Not yours. So, stay." He continued with his filing. We both smiled, mine was a tentative one but a smile all the same. Dean settled into a rhythm of stacking or alphabetizing or whatever the hell he was doing while I relaxed and enjoyed the view.

I could do that, couldn't I?

There was nothing wrong with admiring Dean Sutherland. It was like window-shopping. Browsing without purchasing.

At least, that was the lie I was going to tell myself.

"Hey, guys. I'm going to go have a quick lunch with Molly, and I wanted to know if you—" Jake's voice boomed through the small clinic before he pushed his way into the waiting room. His eyes darted between me and Dean as I quickly sat up straighter and Dean gave him a look that said something.

What, I had no idea.

"I wanted to know if you needed anything. Yeah, um, want me to bring anything back? Because I could use someone to stay here. You know, keep the place open just in case of an emergency or something."

His words made sense, but I wasn't convinced he thought they did. He looked to Dean for confirmation, and I could see Dean's approving nod.

Somehow, I felt like I was suddenly being set up by these two men.

"Sure," I replied, "but maybe Dean would like to go with you."

Dean's look of surprise made me grin as he obviously tried to think of a reason he couldn't go.

"Can't." He grinned back. "Swamped." He motioned to the stacks of files spread all around him. "Not even sure I could get out if I wanted."

I gave him a blank stare as Jake watched our exchange with rapt interest.

"Oh, I'm sure you can. Here, let me take over for you. You guys go grab some lunch. You know Dean hasn't taken a break all day?"

"I didn't know that," Jake replied with a sly grin.

Dean knew I was calling his bluff and the shock of it was written all over his face. I leaped out of my seat and zipped around to the other side of the counter faster than he could come up with another excuse.

It wasn't that I didn't enjoy the view or the conversation.

It was that I did.

A little too much.

So, I did the only thing I could. I made a path for the man with the sinful stare and the soulful eyes that held too much promise, and I watched him walk away. And the moment the door shut and I was free of him, I let my head collapse into my hands as I wondered how the hell I was going to survive the rest of the day with him around. Let alone a lifetime.

❀

"So, what'll it be?" I asked Lizzie as we settled in for dinner at her new favorite spot, a local restaurant that had stunning views of the bay from its outdoor patio. Plus they had the fish fingers Dean had introduced her to. That was a big bonus.

I couldn't blame her. With its exceptional food, friendly staff, and casual atmosphere, it was quickly becoming a favorite of mine as well. Plus, it gave me an excuse to avoid the kitchen at the inn. Although Molly had given me free rein over it during the evenings she wasn't there, constantly reminding me to treat the place as a home rather than an inn, I just couldn't do it.

The constant flux of guests going in and out was a daily reminder that we were indeed not at home, no matter how homey it felt. I knew Molly meant well, and she was a saint for allowing us to stay there for basically nothing while I figured things out, but I needed to do so quickly.

Until I found a place for Lizzie and me, Ocracoke would continue to feel temporary and foreign. But something was holding me back from picking up the paper or looking online for vacancies. It wasn't that hard. More than half of Ocracoke was rentals. I just needed to find an owner who was willing to rent for an extended period of time, and now that the summer season was coming to a close, it was an ideal time.

So, what was I waiting for? Why was I stalling?

"Fish! With my fingers!" Lizzie announced.

"What?" I asked, clearly zoned out.

"You asked me what I wanted for dinner. I want fish!"

Remembering I had indeed asked her what she wanted, I nodded, deciding to go for the same. Billy, the owner, came by and greeted us like locals, a feeling that warmed my soul. I ordered our usual and leaned back in the patio chair, allowing the sun to warm me up for a few precious moments.

I was given exactly three seconds before my phone began to vibrate in my purse.

"Mommy! Your phone is ringing!"

"I know," I answered, hoping I could just ignore it.

"Mommy! It's Pappy!"

My eyes flew open. Lizzie had my phone in her hand.

"I'll answer it!" she announced excitedly.

"No!" I nearly screamed.

She looked alarmed.

I dialed it back a notch. "I mean, I'll do it," I said. "I'll answer it. You wait for our food. I need to talk to Pappy about your birthday, so I'm just gonna sneak over here," I explained, pointing to the entrance of the patio, "and talk to Pappy about all the super-secret birthday stuff I can't say in front of you. Okay?"

She nodded, her chin nearly touching her chest as she bounced in her chair.

"Okay," I said once again, mostly for my own reassurance.

I snuck off toward the bar, which also happened to be where the patio entrance and exit was. It was early evening, so the crowd was still light. It was as good a place as any, and at least I could still see Lizzie from this spot.

"Hi, Daddy," I said the moment after I answered the call and brought the phone to my ear.

"Well, there's my girl. It rang so much, I thought it might go to voicemail again!"

I did my best impression of a laugh. "No," I said. "Just had to wrestle it out of Lizzie's hands."

He laughed. A real one. Not the fake shit I was putting out there.

"How is my baby girl? She's turning six soon, you know."

I let out a breath, looking up at the sky as I tried to hold in the emotions. "I know," I said. "Hard to believe, huh?"

"It is," he said. "Especially since I haven't seen her since she was two."

He tried to play it off as no big deal, but I knew him. I knew my father, and this was a big damn deal.

"Any chance we might be able to see her? And you and Blake? Maybe for her birthday? Or possibly Thanksgiving? We could even fly out there for Christmas. We don't mind staying in a hotel if the house isn't done. And, hey, think of all the movies we could catch up on. Don't tell me you went to go see the new *Thor* movie without your old man."

I swallowed deeply, tears stinging my eyes.

"Of course I didn't," I managed to say. "But I don't know. I'll have to check with Blake. The house is still in shambles. Nothing is done. Our contractors quit. Can you believe that?" My lips were quivering as I spoke.

There was nothing but silence on the other end. He'd probably already expected this. It had been nothing but the same answer for years now.

God, I was such a joke.

"But maybe…" I said. "Blake has a business trip over Thanksgiving, so maybe we could come your way. Just Lizzie and me."

I had no idea what I was doing. Maybe it was the pain of hearing his voice. Maybe I just missed my dad too much, but I couldn't stop the words once they started.

"Oh, really? That would be lovely, sweetheart."

"I'd better go, Daddy. I love you," I said, my voice cracking as a dam broke, and my emotions spilled over. I didn't wait for him to answer. I couldn't. I hung up as the tears began to fall.

One more second on that phone, and he would have heard everything.

The pain, the loss, the suffering.

And then he would have known what a liar his daughter had become.

SEVEN

Dean

Recovery Journal: Day Nine

Today wasn't such a bad day.

Molly came by to visit.

It was good to see her and to apologize for ending things between us the way I had.

But I know it was for the best. She and Jake were meant for each other, and I know they'll figure it out.

Eventually.

I also got the chance to tell her about Cora.

Cora is the reason for all of my recent good days.

She makes this hellhole bearable.

She's more than a nurse to me; she's a salve for my pain, a cure for my loneliness, and the light when the world feels bleak.

I know it's the worst timing.

I know I sound crazy.

But could it be...could she be the answer to my prayers?

❦

I knew the moment I turned the corner onto the patio area of Billy's restaurant that I shouldn't listen in on that phone call.

Cora had all the telltale signs of someone who was in the midst of a private conversation.

Head lowered, voice hushed, red splotchy eyes.

I shouldn't listen.

But I did.

And what I heard told me everything and nothing, all at the same time.

Why is she lying to her father? Why is she crying over it? And what am I going to do about it?

Wait, what?

Before I had a moment to contemplate that last part, my feet, as if they had a mind of their own, were on the move, stepping forward, making my presence known, like I was some sort of knight in shining armor.

Cora looked up at me, her mascara running down her tear-stained cheeks, as she hastily tried to brush the moisture away with the back of her hand. Her gaze darted to Lizzie, who was busy with a bucket of crayons and several paper menus.

Before Cora could rush away, I opened my mouth, and words came out.

Words I had no right asking.

"Why were you lying to your father?"

Her eyes went wide, and it was all there. Fear, anger, pain, regret. Her lips quivered from the weight of it, and it took every ounce of strength in my broken body not to reach out and pull her into my chest.

But I wouldn't touch her. Not without her consent.

I didn't know what had happened to Cora in her life since I'd been her patient, but I recognized wounds and battle scars, and the woman who stood in front of me was bathed in them.

"Because I'm a fraud and a coward, and it's easier if he doesn't know."

My forehead furrowed in confusion as she began to turn away.

"Doesn't know what?" I asked.

She looked back, a sad, nearly blank expression splashed across her otherwise animated face. "Everything."

She meant to leave it at that and simply walk away, and I was going to let her.

After all, I had interrupted her private moment. I had stolen her secret and pushed for information that wasn't mine to know.

But then Lizzie caught sight of me standing by the bar, waiting for my to-go order, and if there was one thing I'd learned about this tiny genius in pigtails, it was that, when she put her mind to something, she always got her way.

"Dean!" she hollered, her high-pitched voice carrying over every other noise in the bay. "Dean! I ordered fish! Fish Fingers!" she said proudly, holding up her fingers to demonstrate.

I simultaneously held up my thumbs as Cora took her seat once more next to her daughter. She'd done a decent job of cleaning up the tears, but anyone with a good eye could see she was still visibly shaken. One proper gaze in her mother's direction, and Lizzie would notice, too.

As Billy dropped off my takeout in front of me, I realized I had a choice to make. Go home and pretend like this never happened, or go sit down at that table and distract one very observant little girl until her mother had a chance to calm down.

Knowing it wasn't much of a choice and I'd already made it, I grabbed my bag of food and headed over in the direction of Lizzie's shouting.

"Yay!" she exclaimed, clapping her hands together as I took a seat across from Cora.

The movement caused her to look up from her plate, that haunted stare still firmly planted on her face.

"Hey, Lizzie," I said, turning my attention back toward the task at hand. "I bet you can't make a list of all the foods you can eat with your fingers," I said, setting the challenge.

She scrunched her little nose as the wheels started spinning. "I bet I can!"

"Without looking it up on a computer?"

She sat up in her chair, her height growing with the help of her knees. "Yep!"

"Think you can do it right now?" I asked, unpacking my dinner as she stuffed a french fry into her mouth. Another glance in Cora's direction showed she hadn't even touched her meal.

"Of course I can."

"Okay then, show me," I said, digging into my own fries.

"Mommy, are you going to eat your finger fish?" she asked, her attention turning back toward Cora.

She looked up, struggling to answer.

"We had a big lunch today at the clinic, so she's probably just full. Maybe, in a bit, we can have Billy wrap up everything for leftovers?"

She gave a lingering glance in Cora's direction and nodded. I wasn't sure I'd entirely convinced the kid, but it was enough that she began sputtering off finger foods a second later. By the end of our meal, she had a list of at least fifty, which was impressive, considering I'd only come up with maybe five.

She also argued with me over the finer points of whether ice cream could be considered a finger food. I was firmly on the pro side while she was hell-bent on proving me wrong.

"But you eat it on a cone!" I said, feeling pretty proud of myself. "And a cone is a finger food!"

She folded her little arms across her chest. "And, when it's in a bowl, do you scoop it out with your fingers?"

I eyed Cora, who had slightly perked up during this exchange and was now watching with interest. She smirked a little and leaned back as her protégé slayed me alive.

"You could," I said, straight-faced. "Don't you eat your ice cream with your fingers?"

She giggled, vigorously shaking her head.

"No? Why not?"

"Because it's messy!" she answered, her voice rising in pitch.

Cora joined in on the laughter.

"Billy!" I hollered. "Bring this girl some ice cream. No spoon!"

A very confused Billy slid up next to me by the table. "Uh, Dean, I don't really carry ice cream. I might be able to throw together a s'more or something."

I laughed, patting my old classmate on the back. "It's okay, Billy. Maybe another time."

He seemed relieved, running back to the kitchen as the three of us laughed together. It felt good, and I could see appreciation in Cora's eyes, which only made me want to stay longer.

I'd promised Lizzie I'd befriend her mother.

But what I felt growing inside me, what I'd felt since the first moment she walked into my hospital room and every moment since, went way beyond friendship, and if I was half the man Lizzie believed me to be, I'd walk away.

I'd tell Lizzie to ask someone else to befriend her mother.

Someone with good intentions and a pure heart.

I was not that person. I was the man who wanted everything from Cora Carpenter—friendship, love, and all the happily-ever-after crap Molly had been drilling into me for years.

But I had a feeling that Cora had already given everything she had away to someone else, and what I was looking at was a broken shell of what used to be there.

Kind of like me.

Somehow, the little mastermind had managed to talk me into walking them home, and I'd left my truck behind at the restaurant.

Her reasoning?

Mommy needed company while she looked for shells and rocks.

Lizzie looked back at Cora and me, the sun slowly starting to fade into the horizon, as we walked down the path. She gave me the cutest stern look. I guess I was supposed to be talking.

About what, I wasn't sure.

Was I being set up by a five-year-old?

"She'll be okay, running ahead," I said, awkwardly clearing my throat. "Not many cars out at this time of day. Or any time of day, really. Mostly just golf carts."

I shoved my hands into my pockets and let out a deep breath.

Real smooth, Dean. Good job.

"What is it with the golf carts?" Cora finally asked.

I shrugged. "I don't know. They weren't around when I was growing up, but they sprang up about a decade ago when an ordinance passed. The tourists like them and the locals, too."

"But not you?"

I shrugged again. "I've never driven one."

She looked surprised. "Really? Never?"

Shaking my head, I replied, "Nope. Molly talked about getting one for the inn when we—I mean, but, uh...no, I've never driven one."

"There it is," she said slowly, like she'd found a long-lost wallet or something.

I turned my head as we continued walking. "What?"

She smiled. "The awkwardness I've been looking for."

"What?"

"You know, the awkwardness that is always around when two people break up. I've been looking for it with you and Molly, but you guys all play it off like it's no big deal. But, right there"—she pointed in my direction—"when you spoke about the golf cart, I saw it."

I let out a sigh and stopped. She stumbled a little after my abrupt halt but did the same, still keeping a watchful eye on Lizzie, who'd stopped to pick up a pebble.

"You're misinterpreting my awkwardness."

"I am? There are different types?"

I nodded. "Well, with you, there only seems to be one."

Her eyebrow rose in curiosity.

"See, Molly, Jake, and I are fine. There's never been any residual awkwardness between us since they got back together. What makes it weird is you."

She seemed taken aback.

Honestly, I didn't blame her.

"Me? But why?"

"Because it's you," I blurted out. "Everything about you turns me into a blithering idiot. I used to be a cool guy. Or at least, a guy who could form legitimate sentences in front of a woman. But you waltz in, and I can't seem to talk about anything, let alone string two words together."

She pressed her lips together, her eyebrows rising in what appeared to be amusement. "Seems to me like you just did," she replied with a shrug.

"What?"

"Strung two words together. Or rather, more than two actually."

She continued on down the path, following Lizzie, who'd now moved on to another rock, leaving me in the dust. I looked at both of them strolling along like neither had a care in the world.

Jesus, these two females were going to drive me insane.

Catching up to Cora, who'd made no attempt to wait for me, I noticed a marked change in her expression. The happy-go-lucky smile she'd left me with was gone, replaced with something more contemplative. The phone call with her father was still eating at her, and it showed in her gaze.

"My dad thinks Blake and I are still married. He doesn't know about the divorce."

I nodded. "I gathered that from the phone call."

She ignored me and kept speaking, as if I wasn't even

there, "Honestly, I don't even know how it started, the lying I mean. I guess maybe it was a tiny thing. No, that's not true. I know exactly what it was, but I don't want to say."

"That's okay. You don't—"

She cut me off, "And that's my problem. It always has been. No matter what, I always try to make excuses for the bad stuff, you know?"

I opened my mouth to respond, but once again, I realized, this wasn't for me. This conversation was for her, and I was the silent listener, receiving her confession. So, I softly and slowly walked next to her and let her speak as much and for as long as she needed, hoping the dusty road to the inn would be enough for her to bare her soul.

Or at least, the parts she was willing to show me.

"It was a little thing," she finally said. "I mean, I thought it was at the time. My parents were going to come visit for the weekend—it wasn't that long before I met you. Anyway, I could do that, you know—just fly them in whenever I wanted. We had the money, and Blake didn't care what I did as long as it didn't conflict with any of his work functions."

She was rambling now as Lizzie skipped ahead of us as I tried to come to terms with what she'd just told me. She'd been lying to her family for three solid years. Maybe more.

That nurse I'd met in the hospital, the one I thought was happy and full of life. Was that all a lie?

"It was my mother's birthday, and I'd planned every moment of the weekend. Cirque du Soleil was in town, and I'd gotten us front row tickets and reservations to the best restaurant in town, plus beach time with Lizzie and a trip to the Children's Museum. I'd checked Blake's schedule, I had, but I guess it changed, and we were suddenly hosting a dinner for twenty. I tried to convince him that my parents wouldn't be an imposition, but he refused."

"Did he hit you?" I asked. I wasn't sure why I'd jumped to that conclusion. Maybe it was the way she'd jumped away from my touch that night at the inn or the vacant, haunted expression in her eyes every time she spoke of the past, but the moment I asked, I already knew the answer.

She swallowed hard and turned away. "I called my parents and said Lizzie had come down with the flu. That was my first lie. After that, they just kept coming, like excuses for his poor behavior, until I couldn't tell what was real and what wasn't."

"So, why don't you tell them the truth now? Now that you're free from him?"

Her eyes settled on Lizzie. We'd reached the entrance of the inn. She'd gathered up all her findings on the porch, and she was now inspecting them one by one. She looked up at us, giving a big smile and wave in our direction. We both did the same back.

"I don't know," Cora responded. "I've thought about it, but I don't know how to tell them. And, honestly, isn't it better this way? For everyone?"

"You mean, for you?"

Her face heated in anger. "So what? Not all of us can be brave and perfect like you, Dean."

Her gaze settled on my arm. The one I held close to my chest in hopes that people wouldn't notice it.

"Like me? What the hell is that supposed to mean?"

"I see the way people look at you around here. You're a glorified hero. You can do no wrong. You're Dean Sutherland, the survivor. You might as well get it tattooed on your forehead."

My gaze dropped to the ground as a couple of choice curse words fell from my mouth. "Jesus Christ," I said.

"You want to know something about your glorified hero, Cora?"

Her eyes widened at my language. A Southern boy using the Lord's name in vain was serious business.

"I haven't worked a single damn day since I returned home. Not a fucking day," I said, my voice lowering so that Lizzie couldn't hear me. "I've been putzing around this island for nearly three years, feeling sorry for myself. My little brother does all the work, and I freeload. I like to call other people out on their baggage, including you, because I'm too scared to deal with my own. I wake up nearly every morning, reaching out for a part of my body that doesn't exist anymore, only to relive that stupid fucking night all over again. People around here stare at me because they feel sorry for me. Sorry for the piece of shit I've become. So, how's that for glorified hero?"

Silence settled between us as our eyes locked. She stared up at me as I stared down at her.

Finally, she took a deep breath, lifted her chin, and said, "Wow, you're pretty messed up."

A smirk tugged at the corner of my mouth. "Yeah, well, so are you, I've gathered."

She joined me in a laugh. "Want to come in for tea?"

"I thought you'd never ask."

I must have smiled the whole way home. Like a fucking lunatic.

Good thing the streets were empty, and the sun had set; otherwise, the people of Ocracoke might have thought I'd finally gone crazy.

I knew they'd all been thinking it since the day I came home from rehab.

They saw me wandering around here, letting my little

brother take on the burden of the family business while I did nothing all day, and they all thought it.

Dean Sutherland lost his damn mind out there on that ferry.

Well, if they saw me tonight, walking down the road, smiling and grinning to myself, as I thought back over the evening, it would be all over the island by morning.

I had the blanket of darkness to thank for my solitude now.

And I was thankful indeed.

Thankful for probably the first time in three years.

More times than I could count, people had told me that I should be thankful.

Thankful I was alive.

Thankful Jake had been there to rescue me.

Thankful it was just my arm and not something awful like, God forbid, my leg.

That was my favorite one.

A reporter had come to the island to interview me and had the nerve to say on camera, "Well, at least you didn't lose something really important, like a leg."

I asked him to think of me the next time he tried to get dressed in the morning or make his wife a nice dinner.

It took the moron a few seconds to figure it out. He probably had to picture himself going through the motions of undressing himself with one hand.

Finally, his eyes met mine.

Eyes filled with pity.

My mom had sent him pies for a week straight as an apology.

Not my finest hour.

But tonight, I truly believed I was lucky.

To be alive.

To be in this town. In this moment.

With this woman and her daughter.

I knew I was crossing a line, going way beyond the friendship I'd promised Lizzie. But, for the first time in three years, ever since a bubbly nurse had sprung into my hospital room, I felt alive.

Truly alive.

And, this time, I wasn't going to waste it.

The long walk home did nothing to dull my spirits, and the moment I bolted through my front door, I immediately went for my journal.

I spent hours writing about Cora and Lizzie.

I wrote about how worried I was over her past, how much I hated her ex for everything he'd put her through.

I wrote of Lizzie's email and mine in return, and I wrote about Cora.

Her smile and the way she laughed. How I could spend hours making her do so. How she'd invited me in for tea tonight, but we never actually drank any. We'd just sat around the kitchen table, holding hot mugs between our hands until they went cold, and the night grew dark.

By the time I finished, it was well past midnight, and my hand ached from the effort. Closing the notebook, I did a quick check of my email, nearly missing another message from Lizzie amid all the junk.

Hi,

It's Lizzie Ashcroft again. Thank you for having dinner with Mommy and me tonight. You made her tears go away. She cries a lot when Pappy calls. I think she misses him. I miss him, too. Or at least, I think I do. I don't remember him much. Or my Nana either. I have a picture of them in my bedroom. Well, it's in a box right now, but I can show it to you if you want.

Anyway, thanks for making my mommy smile.

Can you keep making her smile?

Also, I came up with ten more finger foods.

They're listed below.

Love,

Lizzie

Sure enough, right below her name, there was a list of ten random foods she'd come up with, including a Japanese dessert, mochi ice cream. *How the hell did she even know what that was?* Even I had to Google it. But she knew.

The list didn't distract my eyes for too long before they settled back on the one word in the email I couldn't keep from noticing.

Love.

Love, Lizzie.

I swallowed hard as my heart clenched under the weight of that single word because I knew what it meant to this little girl.

I wasn't just jumping into one life here. I was diving into an entire family.

Was I ready?

I stared straight ahead at the screen for a long time before my fingers found the keys and typed my reply.

Dear Lizzie,

I'll promise to keep making your mom smile if you promise to go to bed…

Love,

Dean

I waited less than a minute before I got the reply I had known would come flying back. A single word.

Okay!

I smiled to myself once more, and as I climbed the stairs to my room that night, I realized I wasn't falling for these two.

I'd fallen.

Hard.

EIGHT
Cora

Dear friends and family,

There have been a handful of days in my life that stand out. A few that make a list of greats.

My first day of nursing school.

The day I met Blake.

My wedding day.

But today? Today tops them all. Because, today, I became a mother.

Today, I gave birth to the most perfect little girl. She has ten tiny toes and ten little fingers, and when she looks at me with those newborn eyes, I feel like I understand my purpose for the first time.

To bring her happiness.

To give her joy.

To show her strength.

When the nurse handed her to Blake, I got to experience firsthand what it was like to watch someone fall in love because that is exactly what I saw when he looked into her eyes.

Pure, unconditional love.

And, in that moment, I knew that, no matter what happened in the future, whatever path life had for the three of us, we would love that little girl.

Forever.

Happy birthday, Elizabeth Ashcroft.

"Mommy, how do you know if a boy has a crush on you?"

The orange juice I'd just drunk got stuck in my throat, and I nearly choked. "What?" I sputtered. "Why are you asking this?"

She shrugged, chomping on her mouthful of Cheerios. "It's my first day of school."

I took a deep breath. "Well, I guess that's logical."

"So, how do I know?"

"He might follow you around," I said before adding, "and maybe compliment you. Or make you laugh. I don't know. I'm a little out of practice."

She seemed to be contemplating everything I'd said, holding a spoon in the air in front of her face. "I think Dean has a crush on you."

Second choking attack of the day. "Say what?"

"Dean Sutherland. I think—"

"I know who you're talking about. I just—" My brain was about to explode. *Of all the children in the world, how did I end up with the overly clever, extremely observant one?*

"He likes to make you laugh. A lot. And he's always around. Like now," she said.

"Huh?"

She raised her arm and pointed to the back door that led to the garden. I looked over, and lo and behold, there was the man of the hour, walking up the path, holding a small bouquet of flowers.

My stomach did that stupid flip-flop thing it had done every single time I saw him over the past week. I'd been an official resident of Ocracoke for nearly two weeks now, and in that time, my belly had felt like it was on a constant roller coaster ride.

All because of Dean and his charming good looks.

It had made work incredibly difficult, seeing as he was still there.

All the time.

Him and his gorgeous smile.

I ran to the back door and greeted him before he had the chance to knock.

His smile sent shivers down my spine.

"Hi," he said.

"Um, hi."

"I just wanted to drop these off for Lizzie. I know it's a big day."

I looked down at the flowers in his hand, and my heart instantly melted into a pool of goo on the kitchen floor. Thankfully, he didn't seem to notice as he stepped inside and presented her with the small cluster of daisies.

"Thank you!" she said happily. "Did you know daisies can be found everywhere on Earth, except Antarctica?"

He smiled, brushing back a wisp of hair from her face. "I did not know that. But I'm not surprised in the least that you did."

"Mommy got me an encyclopedia for kids. It's fairly decent. Not as good as Google, but it's entertaining," she said with another shrug.

His eyes met mine, and that smile he held hit me so hard, I had to grip the doorframe to keep myself upright.

God, he was handsome.

And seeing him with Lizzie, kneeling down and brushing the hair from her face, made him ten times more handsome in my eyes. I'd told myself I wouldn't get involved, I wouldn't give away my heart again, but damn if Dean Sutherland wasn't making it hard.

"Are you ready? Scared? Excited?" he asked her, standing upright to allow her to finish her breakfast.

"Um, can I be all three?" she asked, scooping her last bit of Cheerios into her mouth.

"Absolutely. I am most days."

"What if they don't like me? The other kids?"

My brows furrowed. She hadn't expressed this concern to me lately. I stepped forward, but Dean intervened before I could.

"You're adorable, and you can rattle off fun facts faster than most adults. What's not to like?"

Her face went slack as she looked up at him with concern. "Yeah, but I'm kind of weird, you know?"

"Weird? You mean, like this?" He waved his prosthetic arm in her direction.

She giggled as I joined them.

"You're gonna do just fine," I assured her. "Besides, you already met most of your classmates at orientation."

"I only met three kids," she said.

Dean laughed. "You did explain to her how small Ocracoke was, right?"

I pressed my lips together, trying to keep from laughing as well. "We might need to go over it one more time in the car."

"Well, I'll leave you to it then." He gave one more meaningful glance in Lizzie's direction. "Good luck, brainiac. Let me know how it goes." He followed it with a quick wink.

She did the same.

I was about to ask where she'd learned to wink, but she ran off to find her backpack, and I was left with Dean.

"I'll be in the clinic again today, so I'll see you short-ly," he said before stepping toward the door.

"I never knew filing could take so long," I joked.

He grinned, turning back around. "Well, I'm very thorough. But I've convinced Jake to invest in an electronic system, so I'm going to start entering everything soon."

"Are you kidding?" I asked, not bothering to cover up the elation in my voice.

"Yeah, I know they're expensive, but honestly, it's either that or he hires someone to manage the place. He opted for the computer system. And, with the extra room, he might actually have room to put in another exam room."

"That's amazing. Seriously. It will make our jobs so much easier. Thank you."

He looked down.

Without thinking, I'd reached out and grabbed his hand as I was talking. It was a meaningless gesture.

To anyone but me.

My gut reaction was to pull away. To take it back and pretend like it had never happened. But I didn't. I let out a breath and squeezed his hand, feeling the flesh beneath my fingers, letting him know I meant it.

Letting him know it meant something. For both of us.

The feeling of it stayed with me long after he left. I felt almost dazed from it as I went through the motions of the rest of the morning, loading the dishwasher and drinking my coffee. I was finally pulled out of it when Lizzie came bounding back into the kitchen, backpack on, ready to go.

"Can you watch over my flowers while I'm at school today?"

"Sure, sweetie, but I'll be at work. Would it be okay if I left them in your room?"

She'd finally agreed to move into her room, although

she would often sneak into my room late at night. Still, it was progress.

"Okay," she answered. "But make sure they have plenty of water."

I did just that, placing them in a small vase and neatly arranging them to her approval. She nodded as she looked them over.

"You know how I was saying this morning that I thought Dean had a crush on you?"

I gave the flowers a once-over, smiling to myself as I touched one of the silky white blooms. "Yeah?"

"I've changed my mind."

That caught my attention. "Oh?" I said, turning to her.

She, too, was admiring the flowers. "I think he has a crush on me. Sorry, Mommy."

And, with that, she took the flowers from my grasp and walked away.

After three ignored phone calls on the way to school, I knew the text was inevitable.

I hadn't spoken to Blake since I left Virginia. He knew where we were; I couldn't avoid that. I couldn't disappear. I wasn't supposed to, no matter how much I wanted to.

An amicable split—that was what we were calling it. Anything to preserve the Ashcroft name. No one wanted the truth to get out.

That the son of one of the wealthiest families on the East Coast was a wife beater.

When his mother had found out, she'd been inclined to let it all slide under the rug, where all the other family secrets were kept. But when I threatened to go to a judge for full custody of Lizzie? Well, that was when it got complicated. And, by *complicated*, I mean, I got my way for a change.

I was granted a divorce.

Nothing more, nothing less.

No alimony, and what child support Blake gave, I put directly into a savings account for Lizzie's college fund. After everything was said and done, I figured we'd be forgotten. After all, in the Ashcroft world, he could just find himself a shiny new family.

But this was Blake, and as hard as I tried to forget, he did care for his daughter even if he'd turned out to be a shitty husband.

Looking down at the text as I pulled into the small parking lot of the school, my heart clenched slightly.

Blake
Cora, could you at least send me a picture of her on her first day?

My lips pressed together as the engine turned off. Lizzie bounded out of the car, full speed ahead. Grabbing my purse, I jumped out of the car and followed behind. I wasn't sure this was standard protocol.

Am I supposed to follow her in? Or say goodbye to her at the door?

Is there a guide for this? Kindergarten for Newbies?

She obviously didn't know either because she grabbed my hand the instant I caught up to her and pulled me toward the entrance. Ocracoke was a small town; I'd known that much when I chose it.

But it really showed when I walked up the ramp and through the double blue doors to the one and only school that housed all twelve grades, plus kindergarten. I tried to think of the positives—one-on-one time, the low child to teacher ratio—but I also worried her advanced intellect might put her at an extreme disadvantage.

What if the teachers had no idea what to do with such a gifted child? What if she didn't fit in?

My nerves raced as we walked down the hall to her classroom. The next few moments were a blur as we found her desk and met her teacher again, and then I said goodbye.

I'd thought this day would be kind of monumental. Every parent talked about it—the moment you sent your child off to school. I'd imagined it in my head so many times. I'd kneel down and bestow some sort of epic wisdom, making her feel right at home with her new surroundings, and I'd walk off, newly crowned as the Queen of Mothers.

Instead, I wandered out of the classroom, kind of in a daze, wondering if I could ask for a do-over.

I checked my phone again, the message from Blake still on my screen.

I let out a breath and hit Delete as I tried to keep my mascara in place. I took this bad mood with me all the way to work, waltzing into the clinic with a storm cloud above my head for all to see.

"Whoa, you okay?" Dean asked, seeing me attack my coffee with a vengeance.

I attached the travel mug lid and worked my hair into a bun before pulling the sweater I kept in the office over my shoulders. "I'm a good mom; we've established this, right?"

"Right," he agreed right away.

"So, why is it that, every time one of those moments comes—you know, the pivotal moments, like the first step or first day of school—I'm always screwing it up?"

"How do you screw up a first step?"

I looked him dead in the face. "Why are you naturally assuming I screwed up the first day of school?"

His expression went blank, and he began to backpedal. "I, uh...I mean, I just assumed because of—"

The backpedaling was actually kind of adorable. I felt the corner of my mouth upturning into a grin. "It was a total disaster. You can chill. Also, my five-year-old thinks you have a crush on her."

His face went blank as he tried to come up with a response.

"What do you do when you have a crush on a girl? You bring her flowers. So, naturally, she deduced you have a crush on her."

"I really don't know what to say about that. But, holy crap, do they teach you that death stare you just did on me in parenting class, or is that something you learned on the job? Do you use that on Lizzie? Like, full force? Because, dear God, I think my life started to flash before my eyes."

I laughed. "That was only at half-volume, and yes, she whimpers just like you did. But seriously, I drove up to the school, ready to be awesome, and then nothing. I remember a chair and a desk and maybe a hug. But that's it. I blame Blake. If he hadn't called and texted me, I would have been on my—"

Dean stepped forward, all levity and humor gone from his face. "He called you?"

"He's still Lizzie's father. He's allowed to call and text."

"Says who?"

"The judge who gave him joint custody."

His face reddened. "You let him have partial custody?"

My heart galloped into motion as I stepped back. I

noticed the way his fist was balled up tightly at his side and how hard he was breathing. "I didn't let him do anything. But it was the only way I could get out. You don't know the man I married, the family I married into."

Our eyes met, and in that single second of connection, he backed down.

Taking a step back, he retreated. "You're right. I'm sorry. I'm so sorry, Cora. It's just...these feelings I have for you, they're real, and when I think of the things you must have gone through—both you and Lizzie—it makes me want to give you a better life. I'm sorry. You just got out of one mess, and I have no right to ask you into another—"

"Mess?" My mouth upturned into a sort of smile.

"I guess you could call it that, huh?" His expression matched my own before he turned serious again. "I know I scare you," he said.

"You don't," I protested.

"I do."

"Sometimes," I conceded. "But it's not you." I was at a loss for words as I quickly checked my watch. We had less than five minutes before the doors opened. "It's hard to explain."

"I'm not going anywhere."

"Come over for dinner tonight?" I asked, my heart beating wildly in my chest.

"You cooking? I seem to remember a nurse I had years ago, who said she couldn't cook anything beyond ramen and boxed macaroni and cheese."

I laughed. "You have an excellent memory. And, no, I will not be cooking, Molly has been trying to drop off some meals for me, and I keep refusing. Maybe it's time I cashed in on that offer?"

"Now, wait a minute, is that...are you asking

someone for a favor? Be careful, Cora; people might start calling you a local yet."

I couldn't help the grin that was plastered on my face as I walked away.

A local? Someone who gossiped with their friends, borrowed cups of sugar, and participated in town events?

The idea would have scared me a week ago.

But today? Today, I kind of liked it.

Dean telling me he had feelings for me? That thought still scared me.

But not enough to change my mind about dinner.

Lizzie was in her third retelling of her first day of school when the back door to the kitchen opened. I'd just sat down with a glass of iced tea and a mound of paperwork from the school when Molly came through with several grocery bags and an old woman.

"Um, hi."

"Hi! Oh, hey, Lizzie! How was your first day?"

I made a hand gesture, trying to let her know to avoid the question entirely unless she wanted to be here for the next five hours, but it was too late. Thankfully, Lizzie must have decided to keep the long version for only me.

"Good," she responded. "Some of the kids think I'm weird, but after I said that Dean was my boyfriend, everyone liked me."

"Lizzie!" I squeaked.

"I said he might have a crush on you, too," she said before I caught her giving an obvious shake of her head in Molly's direction.

That, of course, sent both women into a fit of laughter.

"Speaking of Dean, I heard you were having him over

for dinner, so I thought I'd come over and cook something rather than sending you over frozen stuff."

My cheeks flushed red. "You don't have to do that."

"Of course she does," the older woman said. "She's
been trying to marry off that man since the day she took
off his engagement ring."

I really had no words, so I instead just stepped
forward and helped them with the bags they'd carried in.

"Oh, where are my manners?" Molly said, setting
what was left of the bags on the counter. "This is Terri.
Terri, this is Cora and her daughter, Lizzie. They just
moved here—"

"I know. You told me in the car on the way here!"

Molly smiled sheepishly. "Right. Anyway, Terri is an
old family friend. Jake grew up living next door to her,
and now that we live in his family home, we have that
privilege, too."

Terri chuckled under her breath. "Privilege? It'd be a
privilege if you two would get curtains so I didn't have to
see your naked behinds all the time. You wouldn't
believe how much those two—"

"Okay!" Molly exclaimed, her eyes wide with shock.
"Wasn't there something you wanted to check out while
you were here, Terri?"

She smiled like the Cheshire Cat. "Nope. Just being
nosy."

"Well, why don't you make yourself useful and chop
all these wonderful vegetables from the garden?" She
turned her attention back to me. "Terri supplies a lot of
the fruits and veggies for the inn. She has been for several
years since I took over."

"I can't take all the credit anymore."

"Yes, you can," she said. "Just because you're using
our land to grow more doesn't mean it's not your
handiwork."

The woman made a grumbling sound but seemed pleased by the praise. She helped herself to some of the carrots from one of the bags and began making quick work, chopping like a pro. It was an impressive sight. Molly did much of the same with some onions and a few stalks of celery, giving me some time to look over several sheets of paperwork I needed to review.

"What are you working on?" Molly asked.

"Mommy has homework." Lizzie snickered.

"Oh, yeah?"

"Yep, my teacher sent home a big packet and told us to make sure to give it to Mommy or Daddy for homework. Since Daddy doesn't live with us anymore, I gave it to Mommy."

It was the first time she'd mentioned Blake in days, and every time she had, it had been just like this. A nonchalant, matter-of-fact type of thing. I'd asked her about it one night, and she'd kind of shrugged it off and changed the subject.

I didn't know what that meant, and I wasn't sure if I should be alarmed.

Like the first day of school, there wasn't a manual for divorce. I let out an audible huff, focusing on my paperwork, as Molly and Terri chopped away in the kitchen while Lizzie organized her backpack for the tenth time. There were literally three things in there, but she was convinced it was necessary to know exactly where they were at all times.

How I'd managed to give birth to the female version of Sheldon Cooper was beyond me.

"So, uh…is that what you were planning on wearing tonight?" Molly asked.

It took me a second to realize the chopping had stopped—at least, from her corner of the kitchen. I looked up from my paper stack and saw her taking a few steps in my direction, appraising my appearance with a determined eye.

"Yes," I said, suddenly feeling on display. "Why?"

Her gaze roamed over my hair and down to the dark blue scrubs I was still wearing from work. "It's just…well —" Her hand shot out, grabbing mine, as she wasn't bothering to wait for an answer. "Come on. Terri?"

"Yeah, I got it. Little Bit and I can take over from here. Right, Lizzie?"

As I was dragged off toward my bedroom, I heard a familiar giggle, followed by the old woman talking about the proper way to make a dinner. "If you start it off with bacon, you're doing it right!"

Another giggle.

Molly let me free the moment we crossed the threshold of her old bedroom. Using one of the master keys she still carried, she made herself at home while I took a seat on the bed.

"You've barely moved in!" she commented the second her eyes met the pile of boxes in the corner.

My cheeks reddened. "I know, but I figured it would be too much of a hassle to unpack everything if I was just going to move again."

"Hmm," was the only response I got from her.

She checked my closet, rummaging through several dresses I'd taken from my home in Virginia Beach and rounded out her tour at the dresser where I kept the few cosmetics I used. I'd never been much into makeup, only using a dab of concealer and a bit of mascara.

"I'm not really a makeover kind of girl. My ex-husband tried. More times than you can count. It was like *Pretty Woman* in our house every other week," I explained before adding, "minus the hooker part, of course."

That made Molly laugh, tiny lines forming around her bright blue eyes. She was a beautiful woman, tall and lean in all the right places. Her blonde hair fell down her back effortlessly. In fact, that was the word I'd use to describe her whole appearance. Effortless. As if she just radiated beauty without batting a single eyelash.

I felt woefully underwhelming next to her.

"I don't want to make you over, Cora," she explained. "I'm sorry if it came out that way. I just kind of wanted to talk, but I will say, there is something to be said about putting on a lovely dress or top. It can do wonders for the soul—or so my younger sister tells me."

A faint smile pulled at the corner of her mouth. "Look," she sighed, "Dean is important to me, and before you start getting nervous, thinking I'm about to give you the ex-fiancée speech, don't. This is the best-friend speech, so it's infinitely worse."

I let out a laugh that was more like a cough.

"But seriously, he is special. Not just to me, but also to everyone he meets. But he's broken. So broken, I don't know how to fix him, and I can't help but feel somewhat responsible." Her eyes turned away, and she stared out the window. "I should have known, you know? You don't go through what he went through and bounce back so quickly. I was just so caught up in my own shit, in everything that was going on here, that I wanted to believe so desperately that he was okay. He swore he was okay."

"He made a very convincing argument," I agreed, remembering those weeks after his surgery in the hospital. I'd thought he'd overcome the loss of his arm incredibly well—too well in fact. But who was I to judge? I hadn't known the guy, and I was nothing more than a nurse who visited him a few times a day.

"But then he came home, and I saw it—remnants. He wasn't whole anymore. It was like everything he'd been before was scattered all over, and every day since, he's been roaming around, searching for the missing pieces." She paused for a moment. "I see that same look in your eyes. Like a wounded animal."

"What?" I reacted sharply.

"Sorry. It wasn't meant as an insult. Let me explain," she offered, turning back toward me to take a seat next to me on the bed.

I wasn't sure I wanted to hear much more, considering the woman had just compared me to a woodland creature, but I allowed it.

With my arms firmly planted across my chest and a scowl plastered across my face, I listened as she continued.

"A year or so ago, I was out on the patio, enjoying a bit of time to myself. About a glass of wine into my solitude, I noticed a funny-looking bird along the shore. Now, it usually takes several glasses of wine before I start seeing things, so naturally, I sat up from the lounge chair and took notice. It was then that I saw the bit of plastic wrapped around its wing."

My scowl fell a little as I tried to imagine the poor bird with its impaired wing. I still remembered my mom being so distraught over seeing a photo on TV one night of a bird wrapped in soda can rings that she'd run to the kitchen and begun cutting all of them up before the commercial ended.

"I knew I should have called someone, but then my night would have been ruined by paperwork and animal control. It was just one tiny bird, right?"

My gaze briefly traveled up to the ceiling as I began to rise from the bed. "Look, I'm sure this is a lovely story, but I've got to—"

"Sit," she commanded.

My eyes widened, and I did as I had been told.

"Anyway," she continued without a hitch, "I marched

down toward the beach. Well, I didn't march really, more of a tiptoe."

Oh, for the love of God, did this woman have a point?

"When I reached it, the poor thing put up a fight, wanting no help from me. He...or she—I don't know which honestly—pretty much tried to claw and peck me to death as I did my best at removing the piece of plastic that was keeping him grounded."

As much as I hated to admit it, I was beginning to see her point.

"I finally had to run back up to the house and grab a towel. The bird tried to peck me to death the entire way there and back. Hindsight, I probably should have left it at the beach and gone by myself, but like I said, I'd had a bit of wine. Anyway, I kept telling it, 'I'm only trying to help. Just let me help you,' but it just kept thrashing at me as I wrapped it in the blanket, for both of our sakes. Finally, I was able to loosen the mangled piece of trash and set him free. But, man, he was a fighter."

"And you think I'm this bird? Dean and me?"

She nodded. "Oh, I know you are. You walk around here, licking those wounds of yours, refusing help when you need it."

"Dean doesn't," I argued, seeing an obvious flaw in her logic. "In fact, he's just like you, always pointing out how little help I take."

She pressed her lips together. "And have you seen Dean take any since you moved here? The man with a company his brother runs? The man who's been wandering around, doing nothing, for three years? Do you think we haven't offered to help him a hundred times over?"

"He's helping Jake," I said.

"He's helping you," she pressed.

I swallowed hard. "And so, you think I've come here

to, what? Save him? You're right; I am wounded. So deep, sometimes, I wonder if I'll ever recover. That's why I'm so scared to start anything with Dean. I can't open myself up to another person. Dean might be searching for his broken pieces on this island, but I'm just looking for a new start. A new beginning with Lizzie. Besides, I've been here for only two weeks," I added. Like an irate child, I wrapped my arms around my middle.

"Why Ocracoke?" she suddenly asked, her change in subject nearly startling me.

"What?"

"Of all the places in all the world, why here?"

"I, uh." I fumbled for a moment before answering, "I liked the idea of being remote. Far away from everything. I knew Blake would never come to a place like this."

"And who told you about Ocracoke?"

I sucked in a breath. "Dean."

Her eyebrow arched, and then she once again made her way to the closet, picking out a floral summer dress. She neatly set it down on the bed. "Dean? The handsome patient who happened to fall in love with you right before your marriage came crashing down around you? How's that for coincidence? There's nothing wrong with a new beginning, Cora," she said. "Just don't close yourself off to the possibility of whom it might include."

She didn't say another word. She simply sauntered out of the room, leaving me in a sort of daze.

I'd never really considered Dean's part in my move to Ocracoke. Sure, he'd mentioned his hometown when we talked during his stay in the hospital, but I'd heard of it before. Everyone had. You couldn't live in Virginia or anywhere near it without knowing of the Outer Banks and the tiny little island at the end.

Had Dean been in my thoughts when I made my decision to make Ocracoke our home? Had his face lingered in my thoughts all those years after, like Molly had suggested, reminding me there was hope outside of my hellish life, if I chose to find it?

Looking at the end of the bed, I saw the floral dress Molly had left me. The one she'd promised would give me confidence and do wonders for my soul.

Hell, I could use all the help I could get.

NINE

Dean

Recovery Journal: Day Seventeen

I saw the ocean today.

I saw the ocean today, and I cried.

I cried so hard, my throat burned, and my ribs ached. I cried for everything it had taken from me—the lazy days, the working days, and every moment in between.

It had once been my home.

My solace.

My peace.

And, in one night, all that had been stripped away.

I was moved today to a rehab facility. Moved like a piece of furniture or a box of junk.

I was no longer a person. Just a job.

The rehab facility is closer to home by a

couple of hours. I'm in North Carolina, but home is still a world away.

Driving down the highway in the van the rehab team had sent up felt like I was being thrust into live-action role-play where everyone knew the game but me. I'd been holed up in that hospital room for so long, I'd almost forgotten what life was like on the outside. I'd almost forgotten there were people out here, going on with their daily lives with no real thought to the ferry or how it'd impacted them.

Because it hadn't.

It's an odd feeling, realizing how your life can be so utterly altered by a single event while the world is completely unaffected.

I sat back in the van while the rehab team talked about their weekend, laughing about the movies they had seen and the restaurants they had gone to, as I stared out the window, coming face-to-face with the monster of my nightmares.

The taker of all my hopes and dreams.

No doubt, I'll be thrown in some sort of psych ward now after my mental breakdown in the van. I'm not even sure they have those in this place.

Whatever. I don't care.

I don't care about any of this.

Oh, and in case you're wondering, Cora shot me down. She's happily married. With a young daughter.

Happily. She used the word a lot when she told me. Like she was afraid I'd forgotten the meaning of it.

Not quite, Cora, but I have a feeling I'm about to.

❦

B y the time I arrived at the inn for dinner, I was a goddamn mess. Sweat was running down my back from the heat, even after changing my shirt twice. I'd changed my mind three times on whether to bring flowers for Cora, doubling back to the house at the last minute to grab them after I firmly decided to leave them at home.

When I finally arrived, I was a solid twenty minutes late and probably looked like a psychopath from all the sweat and the mangled flowers in my hand.

But all of this was forgotten the moment the door opened, and Cora greeted me.

"Jesus," I cursed, giving her a once-over before she even had the chance to say hi. "You look insane."

"Insane is good?" she asked, pink staining her cheeks.

I'd never seen her in anything beyond scrubs and shorts. Granted, this woman could wear a paper bag and be the hottest woman in the room. Tonight though, she'd dressed up, wearing a short, strappy number with tiny pink flowers dotting the fabric.

"Insane is really good," I clarified.

Her cheeks reddened even more. The shade of them was now quite possibly my new favorite color.

"You two gonna stand there, ogling each other all night, or are you gonna invite the boy in?"

My eyes widened as I recognized the voice inside. "Is that Terri?"

She nodded. "Molly insisted on making dinner from scratch tonight, and Terri stuck around to make sure I wouldn't ruin it."

I laughed. "How very Terri of her."

She motioned for me to come in, and as I crossed the threshold, she leaned in toward me, the smell of her hair instantly hitting me. "How do I get rid of her?" she whispered.

Smiling, I whispered back, "I have no idea. She's never been overly fond of me. I tend to just duck out when she's around."

"I might be old, Dean Sutherland, but I can still hear you jabbering on in there."

"Come on," she said as both of us tried not to laugh. "Before she scolds us."

She took my hand just then, pulling me behind her. It was such an innocent gesture but felt monumental for so many reasons. It was only the second time she'd willingly touched me, and unlike so many others who shied away from it, she'd grabbed my right hand—boldly, unapologetically, and without hesitation.

I missed feeling the warmth of her skin under mine as she held onto my prosthetic hand, but the gesture sent reverberations through my whole body, and it took the entire walk to the kitchen for me to process it.

"Nice flowers," Terri said, glancing in my direction as she grabbed her purse from the counter. "They for me?"

I looked down at the pathetic excuse for flowers I'd brought with me, the ones I held in my left hand.

Was that why she'd grabbed my right hand? Maybe it hadn't been on purpose? Maybe she hadn't realized it?

"Um, no," I said, fumbling for words. But then I

looked into Cora's eyes, and for a single moment, everything disappeared.

"What do you do when you have a crush on a girl? You bring her flowers."

"They're for Cora," I said softly.

Terri gave me a quick wink before heading for the door. "You kids have fun. Everything is ready, and there are rolls in the oven."

"Thank you, Terri. This is more than I could have asked for."

"Ah, well, I don't get to cook for a family much. Henry, my husband, owns a restaurant in town, so we mostly eat there. And, before that, when I was single, I was cooking for one. So, this is nice."

"...cook for a family..."

I knew she'd said it on purpose. I didn't know Terri as well as Molly and Jake did, but I knew one thing about the old broad. She didn't say anything by accident. The thought stuck in my mind after she let herself out, so much so that I didn't hear Lizzie ask about the flowers until she came bursting into the kitchen.

"Flowers again?"

"What? Oh, uh, actually, these are for your mom," I said. "Maybe you can put them next to yours?"

She made a sour face. "But then they'll be in my room, so technically, they'd be mine. I'll let her keep them."

I smiled. "Seems fair. So, how'd your first day go?"

Cora made a chuckle, taking the flowers from my hand, and then she looked around for a vase. Clearly, I'd asked the wrong question because, suddenly, I was reliving the day in vivid details only Lizzie could provide.

"Ms. Haley took my crayons."

"What now?" I asked, immediately sorry I had.

I caught Cora dishing up whatever was on the stove

onto plates. I couldn't help but notice the way her hips swayed back and forth as she hummed to herself.

"And I told her, communal crayons just didn't make sense."

"Huh?"

Clearly, I'd missed something while I was checking out Cora.

"They make us share crayons. Isn't that ridiculous?"

I looked to Cora for guidance. Her eyes widened, and she made a nodding gesture. Apparently, I was to agree.

"Yes, totally absurd."

"What if the kid next to me presses too hard or, for heaven's sake, eats the crayons? That kind of improper use should not affect me, should it?"

"I should think not?" I said, almost phrasing it as a question because, really, I had no clue what the rules were when it came to Crayola rights.

My eyes drifted back to Cora and the short dress. Her legs seemed to go on forever. *What I wouldn't do to—*

"So, you'll speak to my teacher then?"

"Um, what?"

"About having my own crayons. We haven't moved on to using colored pencils or markers, but I'm guessing it will involve the same kind of stuff. Better if you include them in your discussion."

My face went blank as I found Cora's.

She was taking her place next to me at the table. She shrugged. "She's already tried asking me, Molly, and Terri. You were the next viable option."

"Who knew kindergarten could be so complicated?"

Cora laughed. "When your name is Lizzie Ashcroft, everything is complicated."

As with anything Molly cooked, dinner was amazing, and Lizzie spent the entire evening entertaining us. Although, somehow, I thought I'd been talked into going to her kindergarten class and pushing for crayon rights.

Or at least, starting a petition.

"She's smart," I said the moment Cora and I found ourselves alone for the first time that night.

Lizzie was in bed, and we'd settled ourselves in the parlor, enjoying the peace and quiet for a change.

"I know," she replied.

"I mean, she's, like, really smart. I'm not even sure there's a word for it."

"Savant," she said. "Or so she told me."

I couldn't help but grin.

"Does it ever make you nervous? How gifted she seems to be?" I asked, turning to her on the couch.

Her hands were wrapped around a hot cup of tea, although she hadn't taken a single sip.

"Always," she said. "I wonder if I'm doing enough or too much. When she taught herself to read at three, I thought, *Wow, what an amazing child I have*, and of course, I still think that, but I often worry about the things she reads because it's hard to block a child who can literally hack her way into any computer. I mean, the kid was teaching me about internet security just last week."

She let out a frustrated breath. "I just want her to be a kid. She's already gone through enough this year without having to read about all the other shit that goes on in the world.

"But then I see her excitement over the littlest things —from learning how moon phases affect the tides to teaching herself how to play the piano. Learning is what she does. I can't keep her from it."

Placing her tea down on the table beside us, her hand slid out to meet mine in the space that separated us. Just the tips of our fingers touched but I felt it. That connection. I'd felt it all those years ago; I knew I had. And, now, I was positive of it. Now, I just had to convince her of it.

"This isn't easy for me," she said, taking my hand now fully in hers and pulling it into her lap. "Not just the touching, but also the opening up."

"You don't have to—"

"No, I do," she replied. "I said I'd explain, and I will. It's just hard."

Giving her hand a gentle squeeze, I replied, "And, like I said, I'm not going anywhere."

"You see, I used to read about women who suffered abuse and think, *I'll never end up like that. I'd never be so stupid.*" She let out a strangled laugh. "Like there was some sort of IQ level that went along with it.

"In books and movies, the men who beat women are always lowlife scumbags. The moment you see them walk on camera or the minute you read about them, you know. But when I met Blake, there was no flashing sign above his head. Nothing that stood out in the back of my mind. Not even now.

"Looking back, it was a simple love story, just like any other. I fell in love. The first time he hit me felt like some sort of dream. Surely, I was going to wake up and realize none of it had really happened because my husband was not the type."

She took a deep breath.

"There is no type when it comes to abusers. They're just shitty men with shitty tempers. Just shitty, shitty men. And that's what makes them so dangerous because, if I can fall in love with one—"

"Who's to say you can't fall in love with another," I said, finishing her sentence as a single tear fell down her cheek.

She nodded.

"I'm not one of those men," I promised as I watched more tears fall from her eyes.

"I want to believe you," she said. "I do. I just...I don't know how."

"What if we leveled the playing field?" The words sprang from my mouth before I even had a chance to think it through.

"What?" Her eyebrows shot up in a mixture of confusion and amusement.

"Okay, hear me out," I said, letting go of her hand to raise both of mine out in front of me in a show of mercy. "You fear me sometimes, right?"

Guilt washed over her. "Yes, but like I explained, it's not you specifically; it's just—"

"It's a trust issue. Your trust was broken by someone you loved. He"—I did my best to control the anger I felt whenever I mentioned her ex—"asserted his dominance over you when you'd trusted he wouldn't, and now, you don't know who you can and cannot trust."

She gave a quick nod. "Yes."

"So, we'll level the odds."

She crossed her arms in front of her as a look of puzzlement splashed across her features. "I don't understand."

"You asked me a while ago if I trusted people, and I answered yes. Without a doubt, yes. Do you remember?"

She nodded as I let out a ragged breath.

"Well, that was a lie. A lie I tell everyone. Even myself. The truth is, I lost my trust in a lot of things the night I lost my arm. The ocean. People. God."

She swallowed hard as I continued, "I do my best to carry on like none of it bothers me, but, like you, I don't trust much of anything anymore. I don't trust the ocean will keep me safe. I don't trust people will accept me with this contraption on my arm, and I'm not sure God is even up there, listening to me anymore."

"Dean," she whispered.

"So," I continued, trying to keep my voice steady, "how about I do one scary thing in exchange for one of yours?

I sat up as she watched with interest, and the moment my fingers touched the neoprene fabric, my stomach began to lurch in protest. "I've never done this in front of another person—outside of rehab, that is."

No turning back now.

As I pulled the fabric completely down and began to unlock the prosthesis, her eyes widened—not so much in horror, but in fascination. She was after all a nurse, and I thought being able to see my injury healed after all this time was sort of rewarding for the woman who'd cared for it so long ago.

When the whole thing was off, sweat was beading at my temples, and my hand was shaking as she leaned forward to take a closer look.

Her hand reached out, but she stopped short. "It's healed nicely. May I?"

I nodded, swallowing hard as her fingers gently touch the skin around my residual limb. Feeling someone else's touch there was surprisingly wonderful.

"See? Not so terrifying after all," I managed to say between breaths.

She smiled sweetly. "You're beautiful, Dean."

I let out a nervous laugh. Being here with her, so exposed, so vulnerable—hell, I'd rather be naked in front of the entire town.

"Not nearly as beautiful as you," I whispered, my heart racing in my chest.

"Now, I'm supposed to do a scary thing?"

I nodded.

"What?" she asked, looking nervous.

"It's your stage, Cora. Do as little or as much as you want, but know this: I'm not going anywhere. Not now, not ever. If all we do is talk for the next five years, it will be the best five years of my life."

She smiled. "That's a lot of talking," she said, leaning closer.

I could smell her freshly washed hair as it fell in waves off her shoulder.

Coconut and wildflowers.

Her eyes lingered on my mouth as she placed a tentative hand beside me on the couch.

"You don't have to—" I began before a single finger came to rest on my lips, halting my words.

"If my heart is beating wildly and my breath is ragged, can't that be considered scary?" she whispered.

"Yes," I answered, my eyes meeting hers.

It took every bit of strength I had not to reach up and kiss her, not to taste those lips I'd been staring at for ages, or not to run my fingers through her hair.

But this was her stage.

Her moment.

So, I sat back and let her have it.

Every wonderful, torturous moment.

She bent forward and then pulled back, no doubt talking herself through it. Her fingers brushed the skin of my forearm before curling into a ball at her waist. I wanted to tell her this whole thing was too much, that I wasn't worth it.

But I knew there had already been one too many men in her life telling her what she could and couldn't do.

I could see the decision in her eyes the moment she made it. A mixture of determination and perhaps something else—desire maybe—flashed deep in those dark brown eyes of hers.

God, what I wouldn't do to make this woman mine.

Those were the words running through my mind as our lips touched. That was the prayer I sent up to a god I hoped was listening as I pulled her closer, tasting her for the first time, drinking her in as she moaned in my mouth, parting her lips ever so softly.

This was what I had been waiting for. This was what I'd been looking for.

Her.

Dear God, please don't let me fuck it up.

❀

"You need what now?" Jake asked as he sipped on his coffee in the wee hours of the morning.

I'd hustled like crazy to be the first one to get here, trying to beat the ever-punctual Cora, so I could have a few minutes of alone time with my best friend.

So that I could badger him for help.

"Dating advice."

"And you're asking me? The guy who's currently engaged to his high school sweetheart?"

Unfortunately, Molly must have been in a hurry to get to the inn this morning because there were no special deliveries today. No pastries. No doughnuts. No hot-from-the-oven scones.

Just plain old, boring clinic coffee.

But nothing could deter my good mood today.

Nothing.

I was currently over the moon. No, if there was something greater than over the moon, I was that. I was fucking euphoric.

I'd kissed Cora Carpenter.

No, I'd made out with Cora Carpenter.

I stood by the coffee pot, grinning like a damn idiot,

and poured a cup. "Yeah, but you do remember, there was a significant gap between high school and that proposal. I figured you had to have gained some experience in there somewhere."

He made an amused sound deep in the back of his throat as he leaned against the counter. "Between med school and my residency, there was time for one thing, Dean, and I doubt you came here, seeking information on one-night stands. You've dated. Why don't you use some of your own practical knowledge? Hell, what did you and Molly used to do?"

I thought back to that time in my life and gave a half-shrug. "Sat around and watched movies mostly. Maybe played some board games."

A sly grin spread across his face. "And, to think, it didn't work out."

"Hey! I was the one who dumped her!" I said, unable to hide the amusement written all over my face. "You're welcome, by the way."

His smile only widened.

"Cora thinks this is weird."

"What's weird?"

"The dynamic of our relationship. How okay we are with everything—the past, I guess. How easy it is for us to talk about it."

He shrugged. "I guess it would only be weird if we weren't over it."

I nodded in agreement. "That, or if we shared pointers."

His eyes looked up at mine in horror.

I chuckled under my breath. "Molly still like that thing with her ear?"

He pushed off from the counter, his head shaking back and forth, as if he were trying to dislodge a picture from his head. "Not cool, Dean."

"What about that sound she makes when she—"

"I will kill you," he threatened, pointing a finger in my direction, still unable to make eye contact with me. "They taught us things in med school. I could make it look like an accident."

"That's a lie," I said. "What about—"

"Dean! I swear to Christ—"

"What the heck is going on in here?" Cora shouted in the midst of my laughter and Jake's tears.

"Dean's a messed up dude; that's what. I've got to go get ready for my first patient," Jake said, giving me a look that said he was definitely going to poison my coffee later.

Cora suspiciously eyed me as she got her coffee for the morning. "What was that all about?"

I leaned against the counter and watched her, still chuckling under my breath. Still thinking about that kiss. "You know how things between Jake, Molly, and me are never weird?"

"Yeah," she answered, mimicking my behavior on the other side of the counter.

"I think I just made it weird."

"Is everything okay?" She looked concerned, pushing off the counter to come to my aid.

"What? Oh, yeah. This is what friends do. We give each other shit."

She didn't look entirely convinced.

"He'll be fine. Promise. He's probably in there right now, devising a plan to get back at me."

"And you're not nervous?"

I thought about it. "Hell yeah. But that's half the fun. Did you have a better drop-off today?"

My sudden change in conversation topic had her reeling. "Um, what?"

"School. Sorry, I didn't transition well. Did dropping off Lizzie go better today?"

She nodded. "Yes, much. I am still working on my epic mom speech, but I definitely felt more in charge today."

"Well, you didn't come in here with those laser-beam eyes, so I figured it had to have gone at least a tiny bit better."

"It did," she replied. "Although, when I saw you two yelling at each other like school kids, I thought the laser beams might be required."

"Nah." I shook my head. "All in good fun."

"Says you. Jake looked like he'd seen a ghost."

I laughed, remembering our conversation. "Probably something a lot scarier, but yeah."

"You ready for another day of data entry?" she asked, taking a sip of her coffee before she set it on the counter.

She then began her morning routine, something I'd grown fond of watching every single morning. She first stowed away her purse in one of the empty cabinets before grabbing the green sweater she wore to keep away the chill during the day. And, finally, she gathered up all that lovely dark hair, twisting it into a knot on the top of her head.

I'd fantasized what it'd be like to watch her do this every morning. To lie in bed and carry on a conversation while she was brushing her teeth in the bathroom. Maybe we'd have a quickie in the shower...

"Yep. Totally ready," I finally responded, realizing I hadn't said anything for a full thirty seconds. "But, hey, before I begin my fascinating day, can I ask you something?"

She'd just finished securing her hair with a bobby pin, and she turned to give me her full attention. Her big brown eyes stared into mine, and I felt that dopey awkwardness again. The loss for words, the fumbling sensation that I was free-falling without a net.

"Date," I blurted out.

"Date?" Her eyebrow rose.

"Yeah. I mean, would you like to go on one?"

A sweet smile peaked the corners of her mouth, and pink dotted her cheeks. "Lizzie," she answered.

"Huh?"

"I'd need to find someone to watch Lizzie."

"Oh." I breathed a sigh of relief. "Maybe Molly?"

Her lips pressed together as she thought it over.

"But you'd better ask her," I added, looking down the hall toward Jake's office. "Yeah, you should definitely ask. I think I'm on their shit list for a week at least."

That eyebrow rose again, this time a hint of amusement painting her face. "Okay. When?"

"When? Well, before the date would be good."

Her smile widened as I realized what she meant.

"Oh, tomorrow? Dinner? If that works."

"I'll let you know."

And, with that, she began to walk away but not before her fingers brushed the tips of mine.

"Dean!" Jake hollered. "In my office."

"Shit," I cursed under my breath.

"Somebody's in trouble," I heard Cora sing in the other room.

By the time I made it down the hall, I had half a speech prepared and spared no time in delivering it the second I crossed the threshold. "This isn't how we do this, Jake! You know the rules of combat when slinging the shit. I just gave you some; now, you have to wait and find the proper and right time to throw it back at me."

When I took a second to breathe, I caught him eyeing me, his arms crossed in front of him with his feet doing much of the same.

"Are you quite finished?"

"Uh…"

"Good. Shut the door."

I did as I had been told and took a seat, feeling like a delinquent child in the principal's office.

"Now, you have two options. Taps is pretty nice, but if she's not a beer drinker, then it's kind of a pointless place. Unless you're trying to sell her on the food, then it could still be an option."

I looked at him like he'd lost his damn mind.

"What? You asked me for dating advice," he said, his voice softer than usual. "So, I'm giving it."

"Yeah, and you said you didn't have any."

He shrugged. "I have my moments. Or at least, Molly seems to think I do."

My eyes narrowed. "What gives?"

He let out a huff. "Thin walls, okay? I heard you bomb out there, and that can only mean one thing. Either you really do suck at this whole dating thing, or Molly's right. And, since Molly tends to be right about most things—and I swear to God, if you ever talk about her in that way again—"

I held up my hands in front of me. "Promise, it's out of my system. Now, what is this about Molly being right?"

"You swear, man? 'Cause, literally, it's taking all my strength to even look at you right now."

A small smirk tugged at the corner of my mouth, but I quickly erased it. "I swear. Will never happen again. I honestly only did it to pull your chain. I don't think of her like that. At all," I stressed.

His eyes narrowed on mine but then he proceeded, "She thinks you and Cora are, like, destined or whatever. You know how she gets."

I nodded. "I know; she's told me."

"And?"

I let out a breath. "And I don't know. The idea that fate has something to do with my life, that there's a plan to all of this? I struggle with it because it means that, somewhere out there, someone decided this"—I pointed to my right arm—"was supposed to happen to me. And what good can come from this? But do I think Cora and I could be something great?" A small smile spread across my face. "Yeah. Yeah, I do."

"Well, all right, let's talk beaches," he said. "Women love dinner on the beach."

By the time I got out of there, I had enough date ideas to last until our fifth wedding anniversary, maybe longer.

And I'd never appreciated my best friend more.

Too bad he'd have nightmares of me and his fiancée doing the dirty for weeks.

TEN

Cora

Dear Friends and Family,

So much to update you on. Gosh, where to begin? Elizabeth—or Lizzie, as we lovingly call her—is thriving.

She's so smart.

And I know every parent says that, but I have a feeling not every parent has a kid like Lizzie. She's either going to be president one day or our evil overlord. It's a toss-up.

My parents—hi, Mom and Dad!—will be visiting soon! Mom's birthday is coming up, and as she's one of the only normal-ish people in the house who would rather go see a musical than the latest Marvel movie, I'm taking her to a show. In style. Because why the hell not?

On a more serious note, there was a terrible accident off the coast last week. Down by Hatteras, a ferryboat exploded, causing more than a dozen fatalities and nearly double that in injuries. They're calling it one of the worst ferry accidents in decades.

One of the patients I'm caring for lost his arm. I don't know why, but I'm captivated by him.

His strength and his sorrow.

The way he seems to smile only when he speaks of home.

I wonder, what kind of place could bring such joy to someone so sad?

Anyway, if any of you are the praying type, please pray for my patient.

His name is Dean.

❀

Molly was in the kitchen when I approached her. She was standing there, looking effortlessly beautiful, as usual, in a casual pair of shorts and a black tank top, humming under her breath as she put together some last-minute breakfast items for the next morning for the small family who was currently staying overnight.

Since school had started, the inn had gone from boisterous to silent nearly overnight. Molly had explained it was normal, the bookings reducing to almost nothing in the next few weeks, but for an outsider, it was a strange phenomenon.

"Hey, Molly," I said, nearly tiptoeing into the large space.

Normally, the kitchen felt kind of cozy when it was just Lizzie and me in the early hours before the guests came down. But, when Molly was at the helm, manning the burners, it felt like I was intruding on her inner sanctum.

"Hey. What's up? Are you ready?" she asked before turning around.

I bit my lip, fumbling with the hemline of my T-shirt. "Um, well…that's what I wanted to talk to you about."

She pivoted around, a wooden spoon in her hand, and her eyes widened in shock. "You're not ready! Not even a little bit!"

"I know!" I cried. "You know how I said I wasn't the makeover type? Well, I lied. I need it, Molly. I need all the help I can get because, when I look at my closet right now, sweat starts pouring from my armpits, and that's not sexy."

"No, not at all."

"And I want to look sexy, you know?"

She nodded. "Yes, of course, hon."

"So, will you help me? Because I don't want to screw this up with Dean. I really don't."

The memory of his kiss had been my constant companion for two whole days. The sweet taste of his lips, the feel of his mouth against mine, and the gentle touch of his embrace. Every moment had been ingrained in my mind, running on replay as I went through the motions of my daily life.

Had I made the right choice?

Was I moving on too quickly?

What about Lizzie?

Shouldn't my focus be solely on her?

But, when it all came down to it, I'd remember that kiss. I'd remember the feeling of rightness, and I'd keep moving forward.

With Dean.

She set the spoon down and came toward me, wrapping an arm around my shoulders. "I'm pretty sure you could show up, dressed in just about anything, and that man would adore you just the same. But yes, I know just the person who can help us. I'll need to make a call though."

"A call?"

"My little sister, Millie. Not only is she drop-dead gorgeous, but she's also got an eye for fashion that is beyond good. That is why she probably got out of here the second she could."

"Where does she live now?" I asked as we began to make our way toward the back part of the house.

"Florida," she answered. "She works for a high-end designer and travels a lot. Paris, Rome, New York City—all over really. She rarely comes back here. But she loves to FaceTime, so she can at least see the place from time to time. She doesn't like to admit it, but I think even she gets homesick."

I looked away as we walked down the hallway and toward the family room.

Homesick.

It was a feeling I was used to.

Sometimes, if I closed my eyes hard enough, I could almost imagine myself back in my parents' living room with the gentle hum of the air-conditioning and the fragrant smell of my mother's homemade enchiladas. My niece would be in high school by now, no doubt dating a cute boy and probably driving my brother crazy. God, what I wouldn't give to see that.

My heart ached. It physically ached.

"Mommy, I found this website all about Ocracoke!" Lizzie said. "Now, I can learn everything about it!"

I shook my head, pulling myself out of my dream, and put on a stiff smile. "That's great, honey," I said while I simultaneously gave Molly a sideways glance that said anything but. "I guarantee, by next week, she knows everyone's Social Security numbers," I whispered.

Molly let out a silent chuckle as she pulled out her phone and hit a few keys. Soon, I heard ringing, and true to her word, a gorgeous blonde popped up on the screen.

"Hey! Great timing. I just got off a plane."

"Where are you?" Molly asked, taking a seat next to Lizzie.

"Milan. More importantly, where are you? Is that our old room? Is that a child? Don't tell me you and Jake had a kid while I was away. It hasn't been that long, has it?"

I couldn't help but laugh at her joke as I watched her meander her way through what appeared to be an airport. She seemed to multitask perfectly, holding her phone and navigating the busy walkways without batting an eyelash.

And what beautiful eyelashes they were. Where Molly had a wholesome, girl-next-door kind of look going for her, Millie, her younger sister, was all va-va-voom. From her flawlessly styled hair to the expertly applied makeup, I could tell she was definitely a woman who stuck out in a crowd.

No wonder she'd left Ocracoke.

"No, no kids yet. You're safe. And you still have that wedding date in your calendar, right? It's this month, Millie; don't forget. I can't walk down the aisle without my maid of honor."

She grinned. "Well, I mean, you could."

"Millie," she growled.

"I know, I know. I have the date blocked off. I can't believe it's so soon. So, what's up? Have you opened a daycare at the inn?"

She laughed. "No, this is Lizzie Ashcroft, and this"—she panned the camera over to me where I proceeded to do a lame wave in her sister's direction—"is Cora Carpenter, Lizzie's mom. They're staying at the inn until they find a more permanent place to call home. They just moved here from Virginia Beach."

"Oh God, why—I mean, great!" She coughed, making no effort to disguise the mock horror on her face.

I couldn't help but chuckle. Lizzie obviously thought it was funny, too.

"Well, welcome, I guess. What's it got to do with me? Not that I'm not thrilled you called."

"We need fashion advice."

"Come again? You lost me."

Millie had stopped moving and must have seated herself at a bar or restaurant because, suddenly, she was speaking a different language. "*Si*," she said to someone we couldn't see as she pointed. "*Vorrei uno, per favore.*" Then she nodded, and her attention was turned back to us.

"She's got a date."

"The kid or the mom?"

"Me," I said, kind of wishing I had just pulled something out of my closet at this point.

"Oh, okay. Got it. Show me what I have to work with," she said. "Also, with whom?"

"What?" Molly said,

"With whom does she have a date? There are, like, five eligible men on that island, so I'm bound to know him; I might have even dated him. Figured I'd tell her whether he was worth the time."

A waiter set a fancy drink in front of her while she waited for an answer.

"Um, Dean Sutherland," I replied.

A sly smile spread across her face. "You're setting her up with your old boyfriend? Man, that place gets weirder and weirder. Okay, let's dress you up."

I guessed I'd gotten her seal of approval because, within the next twenty minutes, I'd gone from tired mom to understated sex kitten, and Millie McIntyre was officially my new best friend.

"You've got to be kidding me," I said the moment I opened the door.

There, standing in front of me, was a very well-dressed Dean, wearing a pair of distressed jeans that always seemed to hang on his hips in just the right place and a short-sleeved collared shirt that accentuated the green in his eyes.

But, as handsome as he was, it was what was behind him that really grabbed my attention.

"A golf cart?"

He grinned one of those signature Dean grins that sent shivers down my spine and made me think wonderful, evil things.

"Yep."

"But I thought you didn't like golf carts?" I asked, unable to hide my amusement.

"No," he replied, "I said, I'd never driven one, not that I hated them. They're actually pretty fun. Well, once I got the hang of my gigantic foot pressing on the tiny pedal."

I laughed as I watched his eyes settle on the short, asymmetrical white dress that seemed to do fabulous things for my legs and made my skin look ridiculously tan.

"You look…" He paused, like he was searching for a word.

"Yes?"

When he stepped forward, my stomach fluttered as his hand tentatively touched my waist. I could smell his aftershave as that grin of his came closer.

"I think I've found the perfect word," he said, lowering his voice as he got closer to my ear. "But I don't think it's very polite."

I sucked in my bottom lip, his eyes watching every

second. The tension was building as my mind filled with thoughts of breathless heartbeats and first kisses.

"Dean!" Lizzie's voice cut through, breaking us apart like two horny teenagers caught together behind the bleachers.

"Hey, there's my brainiac!" Dean greeted her with enthusiasm, not seeming to miss a beat while I had to take a deep, slow breath to pull myself out of the lust-filled haze I was currently in. He walked inside and bent down to give her a hug.

Would my heart melt every time he did that?

Her small hands barely made it to the middle of his biceps, but she squeezed him hard, closing her eyes tight before letting go.

"Molly and Dr. Jake are going to babysit me! I made a list of all the things we're going to do while you and Mommy are on a date!"

"Oh, yeah? Let me see," he said, taking the slightly crumpled sheet of paper she had balled up in her hand. His face went through a mixture of emotions as he read the list to himself. From amusement to shock and back again. "What is this one?" he asked, pointing to something in the middle.

"Jumping Popsicle Sticks," she said nonchalantly.

"And that is?"

"Oh! You take a bunch of Popsicle sticks and weave them together, creating built-up energy, and when you're done, you release them, and they kind of jump. It's really cool. I saw it on—"

"YouTube," he and I said in unison.

"How did you know?" Lizzie asked, putting her hands on her hips while she giggled.

"Well, I'm sure Jakey and Molly will have loads of fun with this very long and comprehensive list."

"Jakey?" Lizzie asked, her interest piqued.

Dean laughed, putting an arm around her as I grabbed my purse. "Ah, yes. Be sure to ask him how he got that nickname. It's adorable."

I shook my head, amazed at how those two men behaved around each other.

But then again, all of Blake's so-called best friends were business partners and guys he'd gone to boarding school with, but he never seemed to be extremely close with any of them. I'd always felt sort of sorry for him for not having a close bond with anyone besides me.

When I'd ended things, I'd realized, in giving him that missing link he'd never had, I'd lost every single one of mine in the process.

Looking over at Dean messing around with Lizzie, I couldn't help but hope that this was my first leap in getting that all back.

"You ready?" he finally said after chasing her out to the back patio to where Jake and Molly were busy putting dinner on the grill. He came back breathless, a happy smile plastered on his face.

"So ready," I said, grabbing his hand as we made our way out the door. "But are you going to tell me where we're going in this chariot of champions?"

"Nice name," he said, our hands swinging between us as we made the short walk down the driveway.

Once we arrived at the passenger side of the stark white rented golf cart, he made a grand gesture of opening the door for me.

A small laugh escaped my lips as I hopped inside, the hem of my skirt rising high on my thighs. Dean's eyes watched in wonder before he cleared his throat and ran around to the other side to hop in next to me.

"So, I thought, for this first official date of ours, I'd take you on a tour of the town."

I gave him a curious look. "But I've already had a

tour of the town," I said. "Several, in fact. I have been here for two weeks. In fact, Lizzie and I gave ourselves a pretty nice one, involving ice cream the first day we arrived."

"Yes," he replied, unconvinced. "But have you had a proper tour from a proper local?"

"No."

"Then you really haven't seen everything, have you?"

"I guess not."

He was grinning again.

"You just wanted an excuse to rent a golf cart, didn't you?"

He turned the key, an unimpressive event for the ears since the cart was battery-operated. It just sort of made a low-key hum.

"Kind of," he answered before that very large foot he'd mentioned hit the pedal.

And we were off.

❀

Thank goodness the clocks hadn't been set back an hour yet because we needed every bit of daylight to be able to do and see everything Dean had on his agenda for the night.

"No wonder you and Lizzie get along so well," I said as we rounded the corner toward the docks. "I didn't know such a small town could be so big."

He seemed pleased with himself. "You're just amazed Ocracoke is so interesting, aren't you?"

I crossed my arms in front of me as he parked the golf cart. "I knew Ocracoke was interesting. Why do you think I moved here?"

Jumping out, Dean pulled something out of the back —a basket—and looked up at me, grinning. "Actually, I don't know. I assumed it was to find me, but that might be a bit presumptuous."

I laughed. "A little."

"You ready to eat?"

I looked around at our surroundings and saw nothing but boats and several parked cars. "Here?" I asked.

"Yep."

I'd had a great evening so far. We'd been to the lighthouse and the British cemetery where Dean had tried to scare me with ghost stories and old town legends, and then we had gone for a lovely hike out to where Fort Ocracoke once stood.

But dinner in a parking lot?

Surely, there had to be more.

"Ah, there he is," Dean said, looking behind me to where I heard a car driving up.

I turned to see a truck with a familiar logo on the side. *Sutherland Fishing Company.*

Suddenly feeling very nervous, I checked my appearance. *Was I going to meet Dean's family? Shouldn't he have told me? Did I have bugs in my teeth?*

"Hey, Taylor!" Dean called out, taking hold of my hand as a green-eyed younger version of himself walked up to us.

"Hey. Here are the keys. Be careful with the throttle; she's been a little touchy."

I felt Dean flinch. "I'm not taking her out. It's just for the lights and, uh…"

The two brothers stared at one another. There was a spark of something in Taylor's eyes. Hope maybe. But it was dashed just as quickly as it'd appeared.

"Sure, right. My mistake. I just thought…well, enjoy." Taylor's gaze flickered over to me, and he smiled. "This Cora?"

"Yes, sorry. Cora, this is my younger brother, Taylor. Taylor, this is Cora."

Taylor held out his hand, and I took it. There was a warmth about him but also sadness, a worn-out tiredness beyond his years.

"Nice to meet you, Taylor."

"You, too, ma'am. You take care of my brother." He grinned.

"Yes, sir." I laughed before he turned to leave.

"And don't do anything I wouldn't do!" he hollered over his shoulder.

"What wouldn't you do?" Dean yelled back.

Taylor raised his fist in the air before he hopped into his truck. "That's the spirit!"

Dean was shaking his head as we turned back toward the docks. "Sorry about that. He's been swamped. It was the only time I could get the keys from him, and I really wanted to do dinner on the boat."

"He seems nice," I commented as we walked together.

"He is," he said.

"But?"

He let out a huff. "But he's miserable, and it's my fault."

"He's a good brother," I simply said.

He squeezed my hand as we stepped up to the boat. "The best."

Taking a quick look around, the first thing I noticed was that it wasn't a fishing boat like I'd expected. No lingering smell of fish guts, no nets, and nothing else that screamed *work vessel*. This boat was small. Much smaller than I'd anticipated and looked like it was built for fun more than labor.

"So, how do we get on it?" I asked. "Do I need to—"

Before I had a chance to finish that sentence, Dean was carrying me, one-armed, over the side.

"What? Oh my gosh!" I squealed.

Setting me down, he bent back upright and said, "I hope that was okay. I just figured it was the easiest and quickest way."

My lips pressed together as I looked up at him.

Suddenly, he began to look worried. "I'm sorry. Was that wrong? I should have asked first."

"That was ridiculously hot," I said, the words bursting out. "You did that one-handed. That was, like, one of my fantasies come to life."

"So, not wrong then?" He grinned.

"Oh no, you can do that all the time. Definitely," I gushed.

"Duly noted."

He played it off as cool, but I could see the sentiment in his eyes. I couldn't have paid him a better compliment if I'd tried.

"So, what's for dinner?" I asked as I watched him begin to set up.

"Can't tell you," he said.

"It's a surprise?"

"Nope. I can't tell you because I don't know."

I curiously looked at the basket of food. "Say what?"

He spread out a blanket along one of the built-in benches. "Well, I was thinking about how we could work on building our level of trust. And I've heard of these restaurants in big cities where you're in complete darkness. Scary, right? But I thought, maybe I could re-create a sliver of that with our food. I had my buddy at Taps make our food, and with a couple of blindfolds and a little trust—"

"You just want my hands in your mouth." I laughed.

"So bad." He grinned, handing me a long black piece of fabric. "Now, tie me up. No, wait, that's for later."

I shook my head and proceeded to wrap the heavy

piece of fabric around his head. When it was secure, I gave him a matching piece, and he did the same to me.

"Okay, now what?" I asked, reaching out into the darkness. I immediately felt his hands on mine.

"Now, we eat. I think," he said, chuckling.

Together, our hands found the basket, and we went through the task of pulling everything out.

"Now, he promised me everything is a finger food. No soups or salads, so we won't be sticking our fingers into anything weird."

"You really like finger foods," I joked, feeling slightly awkward with my wannabe Daredevil head wrap.

"Just being thorough," he said. "Are you ready?"

I nodded before realizing he couldn't see me. "Yes."

A moment passed before he spoke again, "Do you trust me, Cora?"

I bit my lip and took a deep breath. "Yes," I answered once again.

"Then, open your mouth."

My lips parted, and seconds passed as my heart began to flutter in my chest. This was more exhilarating than I'd imagined it would be.

The waiting.

The wondering.

I nearly jumped when his fingers brushed my cheek and then the corner of my mouth. Something cold and sweet hit my tongue. His thumb tugged at my lip as I bit down on a piece of fruit.

All the flavors hit me at once along with the heat from his touch.

Salt from prosciutto, sweetness from cantaloupe.

Desire all the way down to my toes.

"God, that's good," I nearly moaned before I whispered, "My turn."

I felt like electricity was running through my veins as

I picked up a piece of the prosciutto-wrapped fruit and navigated my way toward him. My aim wasn't nearly as good as his, my free hand finding the stubble of his chin first. I slowly moved down and across until I found his mouth, open and waiting.

With my other hand, the juices of the fruit already dripping down my wrist, I rubbed it over his lips and into his mouth. His teeth caught the tip of my finger, causing me to gasp as he yanked me forward.

"I'm not hungry anymore."

"Good," he said, ripping my blindfold off at the same time I went for his. "Me either."

I could still taste the cantaloupe on his tongue the instant our mouths came together. Unlike our explorative kiss days before, this was passion and desire.

Heat and lust.

And I couldn't get enough.

Every fevered glance and every dirty thought I'd had of this man since I moved to town—no, since I met him all those years ago, had been building to this very moment.

And, now, I wanted to revel in it.

His hand was in my hair and down around the curve of my waist. Everywhere at once. I straddled him, feeling a completely different hunger build between my thighs as our kiss deepened, and my heart raced.

Finally, he cupped my face and pulled away, just staring into me with such a deep emotion, I found myself doing something I'd thought I'd never do.

"Do you want to meet my dad?" I blurted out, causing his eyes to widen.

"What? Like, now?"

I couldn't help but laugh. "No. But soon?"

He sat up a little straighter, his hand still at my hip. "Does this mean you're going to tell him? Because showing up at his door with another guy would be really confusing, and I refuse to be your gay best friend."

I grinned before turning serious. "I've been thinking about it for a while. Today, right before Molly called her sister, she said something about being homesick, and it hit me. I'm homesick. So much so that it hurts."

"Then, go back," he said. "But you don't need to bring me. I mean, we're just starting something here and—"

I smiled. "I want to. Even if you're just moral support."

He seemed pleased with that. "Okay, but don't you think you should at least meet my mother first? You might change your mind."

I shook my head. Firmly. "Oh no. No way. You haven't met my family yet. Your mom can't be nearly as weird as my crazy family."

Amusement painted his features as he said, "Now, I've got to go!"

"Yes, well, just remember you said that when my dad starts quizzing you on Star Wars trivia."

"Huh?"

"So, you know how some families bond over football or other organized sports?"

He nodded, his hand still firmly wrapped around my waist.

"Well, mine is a little different. A little geekier. We like to bond over fandoms."

His eyes got all squinty as he contemplated the foreign word. "Fandoms?"

"Yeah, like, okay...let me try to explain. My dad, he's really into movies and television. He's always the guy in the front of the line for any Marvel movie, and he's always binge-watching something with aliens in it. And my brother? He loves comics. Spent every dime he'd ever earned growing up on them. I'm pretty sure his entire basement is probably filled with them to this day."

"And you?" he asked, seeming mildly amused by my story.

"Books," I said. "I'm pretty obsessed with books."

His brow rose. "Any kind of books? Like, what is your ultimate favorite?"

I bit my lip, making him all the more interested.

"Oh, come on. Now, I really want to know."

"*The Princess Bride*."

"Wait, I thought that was a movie."

I laughed. "It is. But, first, it was a book. A really amazing book."

"Any other really amazing books I should be aware of?"

"I'll make you a list." I grinned. "In fact, maybe I'll just order you a stack."

"Oh, boy."

"You asked."

"Hey," he said, smoothing back my hair as his eyes found mine, "how come I never knew this before? This different side of you? I mean, the girl in the hospital, she never spoke about book obsessions or nerdy parents."

"I don't know," I replied. "I guess, after I got married, I let a lot of me go. I thought I was still there, you know— the strong-willed, fiery Cora who kept her job and said no to nannies even though she'd married a rich guy. But I had changed. Blake thought a lot of what my family loved was silly, and in turn, so did I."

"You miss them a lot." It was a statement, not a question.

"Yeah, I do."

"Then, let's go visit them."

I smiled up at him before looking up at the stars,

feeling more at peace than I had in years. And, for once, my heart didn't ache.

ELEVEN
Dean

Recovery Journal: Day Forty-Five

I think the goal of rehab is to empower me.

To make me feel strong enough to go back out into the world.

They're reteaching me practical skills, like tying my shoes and dressing myself. They're even trying to help me cope with the changes in my body and how to embrace them.

But all I see is a broken man.

All I see is one arm where there used to be two.

All I feel is frustration where there used to be none.

All I see is a failure where there used to be so much more.

My brother says it will all be better once I come home.

"Let's get you home and get you settled back into a routine. Get you back into your old life."

What old life?

What old routine?

The only way I could go back would be if I had the old me to return with. The one with two hands and a lifetime of possibilities. He died out on that ferry, and all that's left is this new version of me.

Whoever that is.

So, how do I move forward in an old life with old routines when I'm not even me anymore?

❦

"So, you've got everything packed?" my mom asked for the tenth time as she was busy making her famous shrimp and grits.

It was a beautiful fall Sunday afternoon, and since I'd been doing an impressive job of getting out of weekly dinners the last few Sundays to spend time with Lizzie and Cora, Mom had tracked me down early today, showing up at my door the minute church was out and demanding mother-son time.

"Yes, Mom," I said. "I'm all packed."

"Extra socks?" she asked, helping herself to just about everything in my fridge. "I've heard it's hot in Texas this time of year, so extra socks are always—"

"I've got plenty of socks." I laughed. "Really, I've got this."

She made a pout and an exasperated huff in front of the stove before turning toward me. "I'm just trying to help. You know, you can ask me for it every once in a while."

Oh, boy, here it came.

"I mean, I'm a good mom, right?"

"Yes, Mama."

"And I deserve to know things."

"Yes, Mama," I said, rubbing her shoulders as the drama began.

We'd already had this conversation at least twice. This would make it the third.

"Finding out your son has a girlfriend from the owner of the coffee shop? That's just not right, Dean. And then to not be able to invite her over for supper?"

I suppressed the eye roll that was forming. "I know. But it just sort of happened. And I don't know that we're calling each other girlfriend and boyfriend yet."

She made a disgruntled sound in the back of her throat, turning back to the stove to tend to her onions. "Well, in my time, if you were spotted kissing in public, that meant something."

I smiled, running my hand through my hair as I remembered that day.

We'd been out for a walk with Lizzie, enjoying some cooler temperatures, and happened to stop by the coffee shop. I thought I was being discreet, but I forgot where I was.

In a small town like Ocracoke, there was no such thing as discreet when you were out in public.

By noon the next day, the whole town had known we were "an item," as my mother would say. And, although we hadn't put a label on what was happening between us, hearing my mom call Cora my girlfriend had me grinning like a damn fool.

But I'd been doing that a lot lately.

It had been two weeks since our first date, and every moment since, I felt like I was flying.

"It does mean something," I said finally. "It means a lot, Mama."

I could see a small smirk forming as she turned to grab something from the fridge. "Well, good. 'Cause a single mom like that deserves a good boy like you."

"She's been through a lot," I said, taking the place to the right of her. It used to be my spot, where I'd always be on Sunday afternoon. Mama's little helper—or big helper when I had gotten taller than her. But then I had come home from the hospital, and Sunday night dinners had kind of fallen apart.

My brother had gotten too busy, and I'd become too self-involved in my misery to help her.

"What if I can't be the man she needs me to be?" I asked, picking up the knife she'd been using to chop the vegetables.

I held it over some of the leftover garlic cloves and tried to chop one. The garlic clove went flying across the room. My mother smiled, taking my hand and steadying it, helping me go through the motions.

"Then, you learn," she said. "And you become the man she needs. Life is all about growth, Dean. Growing as a person, a couple." She paused. "A family."

"I've failed our family these last few years," I said, placing the knife down as I turned to face her.

"No," she replied. "We've failed each other. And now, perhaps it's time we look at fixing that." She gave me a little wink as she reached up to fix my hair, something she'd been doing since I was a kid. "Growth," she pressed. "But first, you have a cowboy hat to buy."

I laughed. "Actually, I've been told this family is more into lightsabers."

"Lightsabers, huh? Well, it's a good thing I'm a hoarder," my mom said before grabbing my hand. "I might have just the thing."

At least I had time to shut off the stove before she hauled me toward the front door.

❀

"You look like you're about to throw up," Cora said, reaching for my hand as we waited in line at the docks the night before our flight.

I swallowed hard. "I'm fine."

The warmth of her fingers wove with mine. "You know, someone once told me that the word *fine* is really just what people say when they're actually not. Or something like that. I could be paraphrasing."

I looked over at her, taking a deep breath. "That sounds like something Molly would say. She's suddenly become very wise, like her mother, since Jake came back."

"Dean, are you going to throw up?" Lizzie asked from the back seat, sounding very concerned.

"No," I assured her. "I'm okay. Really." My eyes stared out into the dark water as I felt the trepidation coiling in my gut.

"We should have flown to the airport," Cora said, the worry loud and clear in her voice. "I should have thought this through."

"Let's talk about something else," I pleaded as we lurched ahead, the signal given to load up.

"Sure, of course," Cora said, driving forward.

I desperately tried to ignore the way my heart was trying to leap out of my chest or how sour my stomach felt. The moment the car inched onto the ferry, I felt a surge of panic and a desperate need to turn back.

The one and only other time I'd been on the thing, I'd been heavily sedated. My mom, too, had offered to fly me home, but having just come out, of several months of rehab and a hospital stay where I'd basically been taken care of like a small child, asking my mother to pay for a plane to take me home because I was too terrified to step onto a ferry was something I couldn't do.

So, I'd endured it.

Medicated, that is.

Today, I was completely sober.

And completely miserable.

"I've been making a list of all the movies I'm going to watch with Pappy," Lizzie said behind me. "Do you want to hear them?"

I nodded. "Sure," I managed to squeak out.

"Okay, so first, there is *A New Hope* and then *The Empire Strikes Back* and *Return of the Jedi*, followed by *The Phantom Menace* and—"

"Whoa, whoa, whoa, whoa, whoa," I said. "You're watching them out of order."

"What?"

I turned to Cora, who was busy following directions to the correct parking spot on the ferry. I turned away, trying to stay focused on Lizzie. "*The Phantom Menace* is the first one. You've got to watch that one first."

"But it didn't come out first," she said.

I smiled weakly, feeling pretty proud of myself for knowing something Lizzie Ashcroft didn't. It was a rarity.

"No, it didn't. It's actually the fourth, but it is the first, if you go by order."

"That doesn't make any—"

"Just trust me, kid. I was a pretty big Star Wars nerd when I was younger."

"Really?" Cora asked, her interest piqued.

"Yep," I said, still looking down at my hands to avoid the windows. To avoid the water.

"I have a feeling I would have liked Dean Sutherland the teenager."

I tried my best at a laugh. "I have a feeling you've met him on occasion. Stuttering, dopey kind of guy."

"Oh, yes, right—him. Yeah, I like him." I could hear a smile in her words.

"I actually brought some of my Star Wars comics. My mom saved them; can you believe that?"

"Yes, I can. If she's anything like mine, she's saved just about everything, short of the thumbtacks you used. Make sure you show those to my dad. That might help win him over."

"You mean, it might help lessen the shock that the man he thinks you've been happily married to for the last seven years is a—" My eyes found Lizzie's in the rearview mirror and I caught myself from saying anything more.

"Yeah, right—that." She paused for a moment. It was one of those heavy pauses, and I knew she was debating on what to say next.

"Hey, do you happen to watch *Doctor Who*? Go to Comic-Con? Or maybe you're a closet Potterhead?"

Of all the things she could have said, I didn't expect that.

I couldn't help the smirk that spread across my face. "I literally have no idea what you just said."

She laughed and patted me on the leg. "Well, we will just have to work with what we have then."

"And what would that be?" I asked.

"Your charming good looks and the fact that you adore me."

Lizzie giggled in the background as I looked deep into Cora's eyes, realizing they'd done a pretty good job of distracting me. Because any Star Wars geek knew the order in which to watch the movies.

Well played, evil genius. Well played.

"Yes, I do," I answered, forgetting all about the sea and the dark grasp it had on my heart as they both continued to divert my attention for the next full hour until we were back on solid ground.

"Wake up." Cora's panicked voice rang through the darkness, causing me to bolt upright. "We're late!"

I shook my head, taking a quick look around as I tried to make sense of my surroundings. A light flipped on as Cora ripped a very sleepy Lizzie from the bed next to me.

Double beds, a cheesy beach motif. Hotel. We were in a hotel.

It was all starting to come back to me.

I looked down at the clock on the nightstand that separated me from the girls.

"Shit!" I cursed, causing a still very sleepy Lizzie to giggle from the bathroom.

"Dean said a bad word."

Jumping out of bed, I threw on the clothes I'd pulled out of my suitcase the night before and did my best attempt at a hasty dressing.

Cora came out of the bathroom just as I finished buttoning my jeans, a toothbrush in her mouth as she threw clothes at Lizzie, who was beginning to understand the situation. Mommy was not messing around.

"It's only half an hour, right?" she mumbled while she brushed. "We can make it up on the road."

"Yep," I assured her, struggling to pull my shirt over my head, but it wouldn't budge.

She ran into the bathroom and returned a moment later to help me.

"I'm fine. Really. I am just not usually this rushed," I snapped.

She averted her gaze, turning her attention to Lizzie.

I let out a giant breath as I finished getting dressed. Walking toward her, I placed a gentle hand on her shoulder. "I'm sorry," I said. "My frustration wasn't aimed toward you."

"Are you sure?" she asked, her attention still focused on getting Lizzie dressed. "Because this is me, Dean. Late and unorganized. I mess up first days of school and have random outbursts about bad driving. I sleep in when I'm not supposed to, and I don't take directions well," she confessed. "And I need…" She let out a deep breath as she finished Lizzie's hair. She kneeled down and whispered for her to go pack up her things. Turning to me with those deep brown eyes, she said, "I need someone who is going to love me. All of me. The good, the bad, and everything in between. I've already had one man try to change me into something I wasn't, and it cost me nearly everything."

"Well, let's make a deal," I suggested, looking at the clock before adding, "a quick one because we've really got to go. How about we agree to accept each other at face value, right here, in this shitty hotel room? I'll always let you be you—the sometimes unorganized but always involved mother with the heart of gold—and you let me be the smart, sexy ex-fisherman who loves you."

Her eyes widened, glistening with emotion. "Deal," she said, her voice heavy and hoarse.

I didn't know how long we stood there, staring at one

another. Too long probably, but neither of us wanted to break the spell I'd cast with my words.

"Um, Mommy? Plane?" Lizzie said.

We both blinked. A wide smile spread across my face as we each turned to see her standing by the door with her luggage neat and tidy at her side.

"Right," Cora said, "plane."

She turned to me, her face full of happiness and joy, and I couldn't help myself.

"One more second, Lizzie," I said, pulling her mom toward me.

Our noses bumped together, and she laughed as our eyes met once more. This time, I didn't need to say it.

She knew.

Bending down, I kissed her.

And I heard fireworks.

And the cheers of one happy little girl.

TWELVE
Cora

Dear World,

It's me again, Cora.

My patient left today. You know the one I was telling you about? It's something I should have been ready for. After all, that's what I do, right?

I take care of sick people, and eventually, they move on—in one way or another.

Some hurt more than others.

Last month, I was taking care of an elderly woman with cancer. She had come in with an infection, and one shift, she was doing well, but the next, she was gone.

I never got to say goodbye.

I got to say goodbye to Dean. That's his name, remember?

He asked me out.

I probably shouldn't write that.

But he asked me out with such hope in his eyes.

My wedding ring hung from the chain around my neck like a heavy weight around my heart.

That great big bear of a man with the sad eyes and the gentle soul.

God, how I wish I could have said yes.

How I wish I could have explained to him everything that was going on in my life.

The canceled plans with my parents.

The angered husband.

The bruised cheek and the pound of makeup it had taken to cover it up.

But I couldn't.

I can't.

I can't tell anyone.

Especially not any of you, which is why this will never be posted.

Ever.

Thankfully, by some act of God, we made it to our flight on time. The fact that it was thirty minutes delayed probably had something to do with it. That, and we'd made it from Nags Head to Norfolk Airport in record time.

With our early morning flight, staying in a closer hotel would have been ideal, but the idea of staying anywhere near Virginia Beach, which bordered Norfolk, was out of the question.

I knew it was silly. It wasn't like I'd married into the mob, and Blake had men combing the city for me. But I wouldn't start the trip out by stepping into my past, especially since I was currently avoiding his texts. All ten of them.

Thankfully, Dean understood, and I thought he sort of agreed, too, considering his nostrils did this sort of flaring thing whenever I mentioned Blake's name.

So, we'd stayed in North Carolina and made the short drive into Virginia in the wee hours of the morning, avoiding most of the traffic and sliding into our seats on the aircraft at the last possible moment.

"Are these TVs?" Lizzie asked the moment we got on board.

"Yep," Dean said, puffing his chest like he was some sort of plane aficionado when I knew for a fact that he'd only flown a grand total of three times—one being the emergency trip to the hospital after the ferryboat explosion.

"Maybe we can find you something interesting to watch. I'm sure they have a documentary or maybe the history—" Dean suggested.

"I want to watch *My Little Pony!*" she announced, already flipping through the channels like a pro.

He looked over at me, his face taking on this blank kind of expression.

"Still a kid"—I shrugged—"remember?"

"Gotcha. Ponies for the win."

The rest of the plane ride was fairly uneventful and short. Dean and I spent some time reading quietly until he nudged me, something obviously bothering him.

"What the hell is a Potterhead?" he asked.

I laughed, wondering how long this particular term had been bothering him. Good thing I hadn't sprung any more on him. If there was a fandom, ranging from Marvel to *Star Trek* to *The Lord of the Rings*, someone in my family was obsessed with it.

I pulled up the first book on my phone, the one I'd read over and over. If it were a physical copy, it'd have tattered pages and a worn cover. I actually had one of those, but it was Lizzie's now.

"Oh," he said. "You mean, Harry Potter. Why didn't

you just say that? I've seen the movies," he said very matter-of-factly.

I just sat there, dumbfounded.

"I'm glad you brought this up before we landed; otherwise, there might have been bloodshed in the house of Carpenter. There is a difference between seeing the movies and being a Potterhead."

His eyebrows rose in confusion. "Okay, I'm lost again."

And he would be until I properly showed him the ways of my people.

The minute we were off the plane, I dragged him into one of those magazine stores in the airport and bought him the first book in the series, handing it over to him like the precious treasure it was.

"Read it," I pressed. "You'll thank me."

His eyebrows rose once again as he looked down at me. "This is that other side of you, isn't it? The one I'm gonna have to love, no matter what?"

I smirked as we headed toward baggage claim. "Yep. Wishing you'd stayed back home?"

He squeezed my hand as he looked down at the new reading material I'd just bought him. "Oh no," he said, giving Lizzie a wink. "I'm all in."

"You'll like it," Lizzie said.

"You've read it?"

She nodded. "Last year."

He just shook his head like he should have known.

We made it down to baggage claim, stopping only one more time for a potty break for Lizzie. By the time we made it to the carousel, our few bags were the only ones left making the rotation. Dean jogged forward and pulled them off one at a time.

"I'm not even going to feel bad that I enjoyed every minute of that. Were you always this muscly?" I said after blatantly checking him out. I'd adjusted my voice to what I liked to call my Lizzie-proof voice. It was the volume I used when talking about things less than appropriate.

So, that was about fifty percent of what I'd been saying to Dean lately.

"A little more so than before," Dean answered with a wicked grin.

I leaned in closer, doing my best attempt at flirting. "And no one snatched you up?"

"Well, I mean, they tried, but I was waiting for the perfect woman."

I blushed, something I'd been doing a lot.

Grabbing my hand as we turned toward the door, he suddenly stopped. "So, are your parents meeting us here or outside? What's the deal? Are we taking a taxi, and they're just waiting for us at their house?"

Oh boy, here goes nothing.

My lips pressed together as my face turned red for an entirely different reason. I looked up, as if searching for divine intervention. "I didn't tell them we were coming," I said quickly, the words rushing out of my mouth so fast, I didn't think he'd processed them for several seconds afterward.

"What?"

I grimaced with the nervous, sick feeling I got whenever something started to go south in our relationship.

Would he get mad?

What happened when he did?

Oh god, what was I doing?

"Hey," he said, touching my shoulder, "you okay?"

I swallowed hard as our eyes met. "Yeah, I'm sorry. I just—how do you explain, you know? I didn't know how to tell them"—I waved my hands around, encompassing him and me—"this. And I was scared, if I did—"

"You'd chicken out," he said, finishing my sentence.

I just nodded, feeling like the coward I was.

"It's okay," he said, taking my hand as he offered the elbow of his prosthesis to Lizzie.

She laughed, gladly wrapping her tiny arm around it.

"Everyone loves a surprise, right?"

Tears stung my eyes as he escorted us out of Austin–Bergstrom Airport.

"And, besides, no one gets mad at the guy with the fake arm," he said, giving me a wink. "It's going to be great. Promise."

I swallowed the lump in my throat as the familiar Austin heat hit me. I breathed it in, the dry, warm air and the subtle smell of oil in the breeze.

I was home at last.

I knew every street corner and turn like the back of my hand. But none of that mattered. I doubted I could have driven that day if my life depended on it. Thank God for Dean and GPS.

I sat back in the passenger seat, watching my childhood pass by me in that car window. The gas station where I'd scraped my knee, running away from Brenda Parker, the fourth-grade bully. The ice cream parlor where I'd had my eighth birthday party. The Italian restaurant where my prom date, Larson, had taken me before the big dance.

A lot had changed. Houses had popped up where there had been nothing but wide, open spaces. Businesses had closed, and new ones had opened up in their places. But a lot had stayed the same, too, and I could see that little girl I remembered, her pigtails intact as she raced down the streets, trying to outrun stupid Brenda and her gang of misfits.

God, I'd hated that girl.

"You okay?" Dean asked, probably noticing I hadn't spoken since we left the airport.

"Yeah." I smiled weakly. "Just a lot of memories. And I'm nervous."

My breathing became weak as we drove away a short distance from town. Although I claimed Austin as my hometown when asked by mostly anyone, it wasn't entirely accurate. In truth, my family hailed from a small bedroom community about thirty minutes outside of Austin called Elgin. While my parents, both professors at the University of Texas, loved the eclectic oddness of Austin, at heart, they were small-town people. They had always wanted that for my brother and me, growing up. A place we could feel safe and secure.

"Do your parents live in the country?"

"Well, kind of," I said. "They like to think they do. But I mean, it's all kinds of country once you get out of Austin. They live on a small acreage, just a few but enough for them to grow vegetables and even have a few animals. They like to pretend they're farmers. Well, farmers with a handful of chickens and a goat named C-3PO."

He grinned as we made one of the last turns. "So, how do you want to do this?" Dean asked.

I looked up, seeing the familiar, long driveway my parents had lovingly lined with live oak trees when I was a child. They'd grown since the last time I was here.

Everything had.

"Do you want to go in alone and then have us follow after? Or maybe just you and Lizzie for a bit?" Dean was rambling as we pulled up to the house.

A single tear fell down my cheek.

I looked up at it.

The old farmhouse had gotten a coat of fresh white

paint, the wraparound porch gleaming in the afternoon sun. Mom's decorating obsession hadn't gone anywhere, her autumn wreath firmly in place on the front door as well as several hay bales on either side with an assortment of pumpkins.

"My father would always make fun of her for those decorations." I found myself smiling. "The minute September first rolled around, she would cover the whole house in pumpkins and leaves."

"Looks like she's still doing it," Dean said.

My gaze followed his. There, at the far end of the porch, was my mother, fussing over a basket of mums. She must have felt my eyes on her because, in that moment, she looked up and froze.

I didn't have a plan. I didn't know what to do or what to say. All I knew was I needed to see her. I needed my mom. To hold her and tell her a million times over how sorry I was.

Without thinking, I leaped from the car, running for the woman who'd loved me without reason, cared for me without end, and been my greatest inspiration growing up. Tears were staining my cheeks, pouring down my face, as we closed the gap.

"Cora!" she cried as her arms wrapped tightly around me at first. Then, like she still didn't believe I was there, standing in front of her, she patted me down—my hair, the curve of my shoulders, and finally my face. "You're here," she said, her voice thick with emotions. "You're finally here."

"Yeah, Mom." I smiled. "Sorry it took so long."

While she was still cupping my cheeks, like she used to do when I was little, I saw her gaze flicker to someone over my shoulder.

Or *someones* rather.

"Lizzie," she whispered. "She's so big."

There was a mixture of wonder and sadness in her voice. I couldn't help but feel responsible for the sadness.

I should have come sooner.

I should have been braver.

"There's a lot I need to tell you," I said, looking up at the old farmhouse where I'd grown up. "Is Dad around?"

She smiled, taking my hand, as I motioned for Lizzie and Dean. "Yes, he's preparing his lectures for the week, but I'm pretty sure he'd be willing to take a break." She gave me a warm smile and a wink. "Why don't we go find him?"

My heart picked up again as Lizzie ran up to us, taking my other free hand, while Dean walked behind us. I knew my mother was curious about the man who was definitely not my husband, but she didn't ask any questions.

Instead, she looked down at her granddaughter, who was being unusually shy today, and asked, "Do you like chickens?"

We stepped up onto the porch and toward the front door, and I could already see the wheels turning in Lizzie's head.

"Yes," she answered.

Dean and I looked at each other and smiled, waiting for it.

"Did you know that chickens are omnivores? That means, they eat plants and animals. Kind of like humans. Although there's a kid at school, Dalton, who says he's a vegetarian, so I guess not all humans."

My mom's eyebrow rose, a sort of mixed expression of surprise and adoration washing over her face. She looked up at me, and I simply shrugged.

"I did know that. Our chickens sometimes eat the mice and lizards that roam around the barn."

Lizzie looked up at me as her eyes lit up. "You have chickens?"

"Yep," my mom answered as we walked inside. "And a goat!"

"Wow, can we go see—"

"Cora."

There, in the hallway where I'd learned to walk, was my father. He looked nearly the same as I remembered him. Same goofy outward appearance, wearing a *Guardians of the Galaxy* T-shirt and jeans that had probably been bought when I was in high school. He had a pencil tucked behind his ear and a smile on his face.

"Hi, Daddy," I whispered.

His eyes looked down toward Lizzie, and I could almost see his heart swell several sizes. He briefly looked to Dean before moving back to me.

"Did you see the Christmas special?" he asked, grinning.

My mom made a sound in the back of her throat and threw her hands up in the air as she headed for the kitchen, mumbling something under her breath about, "...been apart for years, and that's what he asks."

"Yes." I grinned back.

"And?"

"Brilliant," I replied.

Just like I had known he would, he laughed, opening his arms wide. I ran right into them.

As I was engulfed in my father's hug, I heard Dean say to Lizzie, "What Christmas special?"

"*Doctor Who*," Lizzie informed him. "Mommy watched it after I went to bed because she thinks I'm not old enough."

"Not old enough?" my dad bellowed as I turned toward my band of misfits, his arm still wrapped firmly around my shoulders. "You're never too young for the Doctor."

I gave him a sideways glance that told him I seriously disagreed. "And, when she has nightmares over Cybermen and Weeping Angels, who will she be waking up at night, Dad?" I asked.

He shrugged. "Oh well, it's good for the character. Teaches bravery." He gave Lizzie a wink, causing her to giggle. "Now, come on. Let's go see what Nana has for us in the kitchen." He pulled me close and whispered in my ear, "And maybe you can explain who your friend is?"

I nodded as Dean was dragged into the kitchen ahead of us.

Well, here goes nothing.

After my several attempts and false starts while sitting around the kitchen table, Dean saved me.

"You know, I don't know if I've ever seen a goat up close," he said after we all finished cups of iced tea in near perfect silence. "Do you mind if Lizzie and I go roam the property for a bit?"

The collective sigh of relief was palpable.

"No, of course not," my parents both said in unison.

As I gave him a smile that said so many things but mostly *thank you*, Lizzie hopped off her chair, happy to be going outside, and headed for the back door. I watched as my parents curiously eyed Dean. I didn't blame them. I'd been so wrapped up in emotions after my arrival, I hadn't even introduced him.

So, not only did they not know what he was doing, they also didn't even know what to call him. They would soon. They would know everything soon.

I took a deep breath, my fingers clenching the empty

glass in front of me, still cold from my tea. I opened my mouth, finally prepared to own up to all my sins and—

"We know you're divorced," my dad said, halting my words.

I looked up at him, a mixture of shock and surprise coursing through me. "What?"

He let out a frustrated sigh. "We've known something was up for a while. We're not that stupid, Cora. How many times can one house be remodeled?"

I turned away, the guilt rising in my throat.

"But we kept hoping you'd come to us," my mother stressed before adding, "It's a hard job, being a parent, but it's an even harder job, being a parent of an adult. You're expected to care just as much but do very little. And when your child moves away? It's even harder. We knew you were struggling in your marriage. I could read between the lines of those fake blog posts, hear the pain in your voice when you called, but every time I asked you if everything was okay, you assured me it was."

"I know," I said, feeling my lip quiver with emotion. "I'm so sorry."

"No," she said. "We're sorry. We should have done more, but again, we don't know how to do this. When you were younger, we could just send you to your room until you fessed up."

A halfhearted laugh fell from my lips. "How much simpler life was back then."

"After your last call, I went online and found the divorce records," my dad said. "We were making plans to come visit you next month."

"Really?"

They both smiled, a warmth spreading over me that I hadn't felt in years.

"I missed you both so much."

"We missed you, too, kiddo. And we're sorry we let

you down. From now on, we're going to be in your business all the time, like those helicopter parents I see the first week of classes, who follow their kids into my lectures," my dad joked.

I laughed, happy tears falling down my cheeks.

"Yes," my mom agreed. "Starting with the handsome stranger with the soulful eyes."

Leave it to my mom, the creative writing professor, to add the touch of flair to Dean's description.

"Well, he must be important if she's brought him all the way home," Dad said.

"That, and she's blushing."

"Would you guys stop it?" I laughed. "His name is Dean, and yes, he's important. Very. Things with Blake..." I hesitated, unsure of how much I wanted to say. "Let's just say, they weren't good. I lost a lot of trust when it came to relationships. So much so, I wasn't sure I'd ever be able to try again. But Dean makes it easy, so easy that I don't even have to try. I never question the trust between us. It's just always been there since the beginning."

A moment of silence passed between my parents as they looked at each other before turning back to me.

"Okay, but serious question."

I bit my lip as my father stared me down.

"Does he like *Battlestar Galactica*?"

My mom threw her hands up once again as I burst into laughter.

"What?" he said. "If I'm going to get a shot at another son-in-law, can't I at least ask? None of you will watch the *fracking* show with me."

I let out a giant breath as my eyes squeezed shut.

God, how I'd missed this place.

THIRTEEN

Dean

Recovery Journal: Day...who the fuck cares?

I'm home.

I've been home for a while now.

Maybe a couple of weeks, or maybe it's been months now. The days kind of drag together.

Right about now would be a good time to develop a serious drinking habit, but like most things these days, I can't even seem to get my shit together enough to accomplish that.

I just don't care.

About anything.

Mama and Taylor have given up on asking when I'm returning to work. I guess, after asking for so long, they've figured they have their answer.

And the really shitty thing?

I know I'm being a dick. I have enough logic left in my head that I can step back, look at what I'm doing, and say to myself, "Jesus Christ, grow the fuck up, and get over your damn self. So you lost an arm. Big fucking deal. Man up, and get on with your life."

Yet I wake up the next morning, drag my ass out of bed, make an entire pot of coffee, and sit around, doing nothing all day.

I'm stuck.

And I don't know how to get unstuck.

Molly says it's PTSD or depression. I wasn't aware she'd gotten her psych degree while I was in the hospital.

All I know is, I want to be left alone.

Yeah, I know.

Zero chance of that happening.

❦

"My mom thinks you're hot," Cora announced as we leaned against the fence, watching Lizzie run around with her grandparents, happy as can be.

After homemade enchiladas and margaritas, we'd agreed that a little fresh air could do us all some good.

I smiled, shaking my head, as I turned to look at Cora. "What is it with you Carpenter girls? I'll be sure not to give her flowers."

She laughed, placing her head on my shoulder. "Thank you for coming with me. I know it must have been awkward for you at first, especially when my dad started grilling you at dinner."

I smiled, watching Lizzie chase after a chicken as her grandparents trailed behind. "Usually, fathers grill the guys on things like job security and what intentions they had with their daughter. Your father though? It was like sitting down to play Trivial Pursuit. Only worse."

She laughed. "He was only trying to get to know you. He just talks fast when he's excited."

"That was excited?"

She nodded. "Didn't you see his hands waving?"

"I don't know," I answered. "I think I momentarily passed out in the middle. So, he likes me?"

She nodded once more, this time with a warm smile. "Yeah, I think so. But I knew he would. You're intelligent and full of witty humor, and most of all, you adore me."

I brushed back a piece of her hair, smiling. "Yeah, I do."

Our moment of connection was broken when we heard Lizzie shout, "Pappy, can I have your phone? I want to know what these two chickens are doing over here."

My eyes traveled over to where she was standing and saw a very large rooster about to mount a chicken as a curious Lizzie looked on.

"Oh god!" Cora cursed, running toward her father as he stood there, looking perplexed, holding his phone in his hand, probably wondering what the hell he was supposed to do.

After redirecting Lizzie's attention, we all headed inside.

"Abe," Cora's father said. "I don't think we were ever properly introduced aside from being known as 'Pappy'." He stuck his hand out to meet mine. His right hand.

Although it hadn't been mentioned at dinner or

anytime after, I was sure the Carpenters had noticed my disability. Why he would greet me with a handshake like this, I had no idea.

Unless it was some sort of test.

Before I had a chance to react, Cora came between us. "Sorry," she apologized. "I'm going to go unpack, so I can get this kid to sleep." She raised her eyebrows at me as she passed. "And then I'm going to take Dean to The Hole."

"The what?"

No one answered me.

Abe just chuckled under his breath until his gaze settled on my arm once more. "How'd it happen?" he asked.

Swallowing hard, I answered, "I was on a ferryboat. The engine exploded or so we think. Piece of debris severed my arm nearly clean off."

I could see the empathy and pain in his eyes. "I know I come off as a kind of quirky guy. A chemistry professor who loves sci-fi—how much more cliché could I get? But I do know a thing or two when it comes to character. Iron Man, Captain America, Harry Potter. We identify with these fictional characters—or at least, I do—because we recognize traits in them that we see in ourselves. And, if there's one thing I've learned along the way, it's that the best heroes are made in the face of tragedy. If you are half the man my daughter claims you are, then I'm grateful to have you watching over the two of them."

I met his gaze and lifted my chin. "If you know anything about your daughter, you know she doesn't need anyone to watch over her. She's perfectly capable of doing it herself."

I waited for the shouting to begin. No doubt, he'd kick me out after that.

Way to go, Dean. I hope there's a suitable hotel nearby.

But, instead of shouting, there was laughter. Just a roaring laugh and a hefty pat on my back.

"Good man," he said. "I was hoping you'd say that. Now, you can go to The Hole with my daughter."

I looked down the hall to where Cora was leaning against the doorframe to the guest bedroom, a satisfied smirk spreading across her face.

This was the weirdest family I'd ever met.

"Should I be worried that you're taking me out into the middle of nowhere, at night, to a place called The Hole?" I asked before adding, "Or be concerned that you didn't even bring a flashlight?"

She laughed as we passed by the small barn and walked into the open field just past the house.

"No," she replied, not seeming concerned in the least. "I know the way like the back of my hand. And, besides, a flashlight would mess up our night vision."

I looked around, my eyes beginning to adjust slightly to the pitch-black surroundings. "Okay. But you still haven't explained what The Hole is."

"And I'm not going to," she said. "You'll just have to wait until we get there."

I focused on following her steps but not before I said, "You're different in Texas."

"Different good?" she asked as the house started to fade behind us.

"Just different." I shrugged. "Less burdened, I think. More laid-back."

"Is that good? Or bad?" she asked again.

I could already sense the worry in her voice. Tugging on her hand, I got her to stop for a brief moment. In the darkness, I could barely make out the gentle curves of her face as I cupped my hand around it.

"It's just an observation, Cora. It's not good or bad because it's all you, remember? The unorganized but always involved mother with the geekiest heart of gold."

She laughed at my humorous addition as I bent down and kissed her mouth. She tasted of salt and tequila, warm Texas nights and possibilities. I wanted to spend forever exploring every inch of her body with my tongue.

"So, are you going to show me where this hole is, or am I going to be forced into making a bad joke?"

"Actually," she said, tugging me toward a grove of trees, "it's just over here."

Of all the things I'd imagined in my mind, which was actually very little, I hadn't expected this. Nestled inside the grove of oaks was a large pond. The moon reflected off the water, giving plenty of light as we walked up to the edge.

"It's a swimming hole," I said, finally understanding the name.

She nodded. "Or watering hole, if you're a local."

I took a moment to look around, spotting what appeared to be a hammock tied between two tree trunks and a small paddleboat at the water's edge. There was even a rope hanging near us for diving, I assumed.

"This must be a blast during the day," I said, imagining how apeshit Lizzie was going to be when we brought her here in the morning.

A hand slid around my waist, and my focus was drawn back to her. Only her.

Cora's eyes dazzled under the moonlit sky as she looked up at me. "It can be a lot of fun at night, too," she said. "Or so I've imagined."

She stepped back, giving me a full view of every luscious curve of her perfect body. The moment her fingers touched the hemline of her shirt, I knew I had to say something.

Taking her hand in mine, I brought it to my lips. "This doesn't have to be today, Cora. I said I'd wait, and I meant it. I know you've had an emotional day and—"

Her lips halted my words, kissing away any doubts I'd had with a single breathless moment. "I know what I want, Dean," she said. "And I want you. Right here. Wet and wild, under the stars, in the water—"

It was me who didn't hesitate that time, kissing her with such passion, I thought we might burn the whole pasture down around us.

When her fingers went for her shirt, this time, I didn't stop her. This time, my hand followed hers, trailing behind, tracing over her bare skin like I was an explorer on uncharted land. But my hand wasn't enough. Soon, my lips were everywhere at once. The hollow of her collarbone, the subtle curve of her neck, and the delicate valley between her breasts.

"More," she murmured, tugging at my shirt. "I want to see more of you."

I did as she wanted, pulling my shirt up over my head, and watched her eyes roam over my body with desire.

Just seeing her reaction to my half-naked body was enough to make me hard.

Harder than I'd felt in my entire life.

We took our time undressing each other, both knowing this moment, this first, would only come once. I savored the way her skin, still tan from summer, almost seemed to shimmer in the faint light. I brushed my fingers over the tiny scar from Lizzie's C-section and the scattering of freckles that adorned her breasts.

"Will you make love to me in the water, Dean?" she asked, wrapping her arms around her neck.

I cupped her cheek with my hand. "I'll make love to you whenever and wherever I can, for however long you'll allow me the honor, Cora."

"How does forever sound?" she asked.

"Perfect."

We moved toward the water before I stopped myself. She turned back, a look of concern in her eyes.

"I can't go in the water with my prosthesis," I said, unsure why I still felt nervous about taking it off.

I'd done it once.

I should be over this fear.

Obviously, she sensed my hesitation.

Cora stepped forward, one hand reaching for the thick fabric that covered my prosthesis, the other on my waist. "You once asked me if I trusted you. Do you remember?"

I nodded as my forehead rested atop hers, and I let out a deep breath.

"Now, trust me, Dean Sutherland," she urged.

Her fingers curled around the neoprene and gently tugged. I could already feel sweat forming around my temples as my eyes darted to my arm.

"Look at me," she demanded.

I did as she'd asked. "Now, close your eyes."

I swallowed the lump of panic working its way upward and forced my eyelids closed.

"Breathe," she said.

"Right," I replied, a poor attempt at a joke.

Cool air hit the upper part of my limb as she pulled the fabric the rest of the way off and disconnected the heavy prosthesis. Her warm touch was the next thing I felt along with another trail of kisses moving up to the residual limb that remained. I let out a ragged breath, savoring the feel of her lips on my broken body. Slowly, as her mouth traveled up my shoulder, across my collarbone, and toward my mouth, the nervousness I felt dissipated, replaced by raw, relentless hunger.

"Water," I growled. "Now."

Knowing she had a certain proclivity for a few of my one-handed abilities, I bent down and made quick work of tossing her over my shoulder, and then I charged toward the shoreline.

All I could think of was having this woman wrapped around me, naked, wet, and willing. Cora was my ultimate fantasy, a pipe dream I'd thought was long gone until she stormed back into my life, like a gift from above.

I'd never stop being grateful. I'd never stop trying to be the man she deserved.

Before we got too deep, the water lapping at my waist, I tugged her back down toward my chest, her sexy little body sliding down around mine.

"Still hot?" I asked in regard to the one-armed maneuver.

She tightened her hold, pressing against me. "Very."

Having her so close and my body so ready, I realized we'd forgotten one crucial ingredient to modern-day lovemaking.

"Cora," I said, feeling like the biggest idiot on the planet, "I don't have any condoms. I wasn't exactly planning on sleeping with you for the first time at your parents' house."

She let out a small chuckle. "And you don't carry one in your wallet?"

I grinned, sliding my hand around to her ass. "Only when I was seventeen and thought it might bring me good luck."

"Oh, yeah? How long did you keep that lucky condom?"

I squeezed her ass, causing her to squeal. "Cora, focus. Your body is so fucking hot and I am currently experiencing the biggest hard-on of my life, so if we don't figure this out soon, I might pass out right here, in this watering hole. And I really don't think you want to explain that to your parents."

Her lips pressed together, a sign that she was obviously trying to keep from laughing.

"I haven't been with anyone for a long time," she said. "Blake and I were separated for over a year, and before that..." She hesitated before continuing, "It's been a while. I'm on the pill."

I nodded, reaching down to touch her hair. "I haven't been with anyone since Molly."

She seemed to be somewhat surprised. "That was over three years ago."

"I'm seriously messed up, remember?" I smiled, recalling her words from not too long ago. "I was tested though. Before Molly, I mean. I wasn't exactly the relationship type back then." I let out a breath as I scrubbed my face, the cool water dripping down my cheeks. "This is awkward."

Her arms held me tighter. "No," she said, "it's honest. And, if you were any other man, you would have just taken what was offered without a single thought. But you're not. And that's why I love you, Dean."

I looked at her under the glow of moonlight, her wide eyes full of promise and truth.

She loves me.

I couldn't say it enough times.

Dear God, she loved me.

Our mouths met in a frenzy. She moaned, deep and loud, under the starry sky. There were so many things I wanted to do to her, so many places I wanted to explore.

But, right now, I wanted to be inside her.

So goddamn bad.

She must have felt the same raging need because her

moan turned to a whimper as she moved against me, almost panicked with desperation.

With my hand on her hip, I briefly lifted her as I thrust up, never breaking eye contact as our bodies became one.

And our souls entwined.

Her arms wrapped around my neck as I let out a staggering breath, the rightness of this moment hitting me like a freight train.

"So fucking good, Cora," I mumbled, curling my hand under her ass for leverage. "You feel so damn good."

Every thrust felt like magic. Every moan and cry of passion from her lips? Poetry. Making love to her under the warm Texas night sky was what dreams were made of.

"I love you, Cora," I vowed, her arms tight around my neck as she rode my body hard and fast.

"I love you, Dean," she said, breathless in my ear as I rotated her hips against mine, pulling every ounce of pleasure I could.

Her sexy little body gripped mine like a vise.

Like we had been made for each other.

I could feel her growing close as she began to move, hot and quick, making my balls tighten and my cock weep. She cried out my name to the heavens, water splashing around us in a thunderous wave.

"Dean!" she screamed, her orgasm taking over as her head fell back and she let go.

"Fuck!" I cursed, coming hard and long inside her.

I never wanted to leave.

I'd found my home.

Right here, in the middle of nowhere, under the moonlit sky, I'd found what I'd been searching for.

A purpose.

A family.

A future.

And I was never letting go.

Although Cora had assured me we'd done a good job of sneaking back into the house the night before, I couldn't help but notice the sideways glances her father kept giving me at breakfast or the way her mother seemed to blush every time I walked by.

"It's your imagination," Cora said as we lounged on a blanket at The Hole, watching Lizzie splash around with her pappy.

"Is it? Because your mom hasn't been able to look at me without giggling or turning bright red, and believe me, I know what the Carpenter blush looks like."

She laughed, playfully hitting me on the arm. "Okay, so maybe my mom asked me if I had any laundry to wash this morning, and when I said no, she might have gotten the clue that we didn't exactly take bathing suits here last night."

"I told you!"

She just shrugged. "I'm nearly thirty years old, Dean! It's not like I'm a mischievous teenager sneaking out here with my high school boyfriend."

"Did you ever sneak any of your high school boyfriends down here?" I asked, suddenly rising up on my elbow.

Her eyebrows rose in amusement as I watched her remove the floral cover-up she'd put on to hike out here. A small smile spread across her face as she noticed my eyes lingering around the curve of her breasts and the deep valley in between.

"Wouldn't you like to know?" She jumped up and ran toward the water.

"I would kind of!" I hollered, damn near knocked back by how perfect her ass looked in that black bikini of hers.

I thought back to the night before. Her naked body wrapped around mine. That tight, wet heat. The moans. The cries of passion.

Yeah, never mind. Definitely did not want to know.

"She seems happy."

I turned to see Abe taking a seat next to me. I involuntarily coughed, realizing I had just been fantasizing about his daughter coming all over my cock, and did a quick check of myself, thanking Cora for packing extra towels.

"She is," I said, wondering if this guy had some of the superpowers he was so obsessed with because he was just in that water, like, two seconds ago.

The old man had stealth; that was for sure.

He paused for a long time, just staring out at her, watching her splash around with Lizzie and his wife. I could see a small smile forming in the corner of his mouth, full of contentment and satisfaction.

"I know much of what she told us yesterday regarding her and Blake's marriage problems was full of holes," he said. "That can only mean she left things out for a reason."

My jaw twitched as I looked ahead.

"Don't worry, son; I'm not asking you to break her trust."

"Good, because I won't. I've worked hard to earn it."

He patted my knee, a fatherly gesture—or at least, that was what I assumed fathers did. "The thing about Cora you've got to learn is, she's really quite trusting when it comes down to it. That might have been shaken in the last few years, but ultimately, the one and only person Cora has a hard time trusting is herself."

I thought about his words as we sat together in silence, watching the three of them play out in the water. Cora carried Lizzie on her shoulders before falling over, causing both of them to get soaked. Lizzie came up, sputtering water and laughing hysterically.

"Do you think she does? Trust herself, that is."

His eyes narrowed as he looked at her until he finally shook his head with uncertainty. "I don't know, Dean. I simply don't know. But I think you'd better find out before it's too late."

"Before what's too late?" I asked, turning toward him at his dire warning.

"This," he said, motioning to the happy scene I'd been staring at since he sat down. "Them."

They both chose that moment to look back at me and wave.

I held my hand up and did the same.

"Don't let them slip away like I did," he said. "Don't let her slip away like I did. Fight for her, Dean. Fight for each other. Because, eventually, she's going to lose trust in herself, and you're going to need enough for the both of you."

"Fight," I murmured, looking down at my broken body. I'd felt useless for far too long, like a tumbleweed blowing in the wind with no purpose.

But they were my purpose.

Cora and Lizzie.

And, if push came to shove, I'd fight for them and everything we had to lose.

FOURTEEN
Cora

Dear Friends and Family,

Hello from Cabo!

Okay, not really. But that's what I'll be saying next week! That's right! Blake just surprised Lizzie and me with a week in paradise.

And I know; it's during Thanksgiving break, and we won't be able to visit anyone, but who can say no to a beach vacation? And you know how much Lizzie loves the beach.

We'll figure something out for Christmas. Promise.

The contractors have guaranteed the renovations I approved will be done by then. So, Christmas in Virginia sound okay, Mom and Dad? But don't buy any tickets yet. The whole thing will be on me...and I don't want you to be out of money if the contractors don't finish on time.

But they will. Promise.

Just in case though...

Now, if you'll excuse me, I have to go do some shopping.

I have a trip to pack for.
XOXO,
Cora and family

❦

"**A**m I a bad mother for allowing my kindergartner to go on a sleepover?" I asked the moment Dean opened his door.

He looked slightly surprised but pleasantly so. Especially when I held up the overnight bag I'd packed.

"If I say no, will that mean a sleepover of our own?"

Dropping the bag in the entryway, I jumped, knowing he'd catch me with that sexy one-handed thing he did.

Seriously, it was hot.

My mouth met his as he banged into the doorframe, my hair falling down around us like a curtain. With a possessive hand on my ass, he kicked my bag inside, and we started tearing into each other's clothes.

"Shit, the door," he said. "Don't want to give the neighbors fodder for gossip fire."

"So, does that mean I need to be quiet?" I asked as he slammed the door shut and flipped around to press me against it.

"Hell no." He grinned.

"Good," I nearly purred, so hot and ready that I was nearly panting.

It'd been a long week since our return from Texas.

Being a single mom definitely had its drawbacks.

Being a single mom who lived in an inn with an extremely curious and observant genius as a daughter?

Torturous.

We'd managed to sneak into one of the exam rooms during the one and only lunch break we were lucky enough to get this week, but beyond that...

This was the first time we had been alone. And damn if I didn't want to rip his clothes off and let him fuck my brains out until the sun came up the next day.

We'd managed to do a halfway decent job in the clothes department, his shirt and mine already on the floor by the door. Reaching around, I made quick work of my bra while he stared. I could feel my nipples growing hard from his watchful gaze.

"I like the skirt," he said as his eyes made their way downward.

A small smirk tugged at the corner of my mouth as he gently set me down, one leg at a time, a single finger roaming up the length of my bare thigh.

"Come on," he said, grabbing my arm and pulling me toward the stairs.

"What?" I laughed.

"I've had you in the water, on an exam table, almost in a car—"

Oh, yeah. I forgot about that one. Stupid nosy tourists.

"But there's one place we haven't tried yet," he said as we began climbing the small staircase toward his room. "A bed."

I'd never actually been in his house before. But, honestly, I wasn't much for checking out the furnishings right now.

And neither was he.

Kicking my sandals off, I slowly climbed onto the bed with a bit of flair, letting my skirt ride high on my thighs. Turning, I lay back, leaning on my elbows as I gazed up at him.

"Goddamn, you're beautiful," he said. "Seeing you like that in my bed…"

My eyes meandered over his half-naked body, the rugged definition earned from a lifetime at sea. His haunting green eyes had managed to steal my heart and my soul. I saw everything in them. Power, strength, passion.

Unwavering devotion.

"So are you." I smiled.

His hand went to his jeans. A simple flick of the wrist and a tug, and they were on the floor.

"Did that take practice?"

A mischievous grin spread across his face. "Getting undressed, one-handed, is pretty easy," he said. "Getting dressed is the hard part."

"So, are you saying we should just stay naked for the rest of the night?"

"Definitely." He stepped out of his jeans, and he crawled onto the bed, his large body hovering above mine. "There are so many things I've been wanting to do to you for so long," he said, his lips kissing a seductive path down my rib cage and to the edge of my skirt. "So many fantasies."

I sucked in my bottom lip, feeling the tips of his fingers work their way up my inner thigh until they reached the black lace I'd worn especially for this moment.

His eyes jolted up to mine, causing me to blush.

"Now, what do we have here?"

Profusely thanking the inventor of elastic, I watched as he pulled my skirt down my legs, dropping it to the floor as he stared at the sexy little surprise I'd bought.

It'd taken an act of supreme stealth. You couldn't buy anything last minute when you lived in a place like Ocracoke, and it wasn't like they had a friendly neighborhood naughty store. So, I'd relied on good ole Austin. Just before we had been airport-bound, I'd stepped out, saying I was going to grab snacks for the plane, and—yep, you guessed it—I went to the lingerie store.

And, based on the blazing stare Dean was giving me, damn if it wasn't worth it. He looked like he was about to bend down and tear them off me with his teeth.

And, even though they had cost me a small fortune, I'd let him.

I didn't have a chance to tell him about the goldmine wrapped around my hips because that smolder turned into pure determination as he bent forward and spread me wide. I nearly yelped from the shock and surprise as he did just what I'd been dreaming about, placing his mouth right on the thin black lace.

And then he sucked hard.

"Fuck!" I cried out.

Who knew my guy-next-door type would turn out to be a kink in disguise?

And who knew I'd love it so much?

My hands fell to my sides, grasping the sheets between my fingers, as he reached for the G-string, wrapped it around his wrist, and snapped it.

Holy shit.

When he moved the lace to one side, I felt the full onslaught of his mouth on my tight, wet core. My head fell back, and I gave in to the sensations of it all.

The delirious, wonderfully exhausting sensations of being worshipped by Dean Sutherland.

I writhed under his touch as he worked my body with expert precision, knowing exactly how to squeeze out every last drop of pleasure until I was hovering on the edge, begging for an orgasm.

He kept me there, aching and wanting, rubbing my clit, and then he quickly sat up in the bed.

"Please, Dean," I whimpered, needing that release more than I needed anything in that moment.

The whole town could have paraded into his bedroom

right then, and I would have simply held up a finger and asked them to politely wait until he finished me off.

I needed relief. I needed—

"Oh my God!"

My orgasm hit as he slammed into me, joining us in the most intimate way. One thrust became two, and my climax grew, over and over, with never-ending waves of pleasure as he fucked me hard.

His mouth—that sweet, merciful mouth of his—closed over my nipple, sucking and gently biting the tip as his hand gripped my hip, demanding more.

I thought I'd given everything.

Surely, I had nothing left.

I was spent.

But, as he rocked my hips back and forth, I felt it. That flutter deep in my belly. A spark that soon grew into a flame.

A flame that roared into an inferno.

"Oh God, I'm going to come again!"

A satisfied grin spread across his handsome face as his movements became rushed and almost frenzied.

I rose up, kissing that cocky grin right off his face, as the room filled with the sounds of our lovemaking. Heavy sighs, soft groans, skin against skin.

It was beyond erotic, and as I cried out my second orgasm, I knew that this was where I wanted to be.

Wrapped in this man's broken embrace forever.

Deciding to maintain our no-clothes policy that I'd joked about earlier, we decided a night in would be best.

"I could see about having something delivered," he said as we headed downstairs, wrapped in blankets.

I shook my head, taking a seat on the couch. "That would require clothes to answer the door."

He nodded thoughtfully. "Good point. Okay, let me go see what I can throw together. Lucky for you, I always keep a stockpile of ramen on hand."

"I love ramen!" I exclaimed, taking advantage of his comfortable furniture. I'd been so blind with lust, I hadn't taken any real time to look around when I arrived.

Now that I felt satiated, for at least the moment, I let my eyes do more than a quick once-over of Dean's place.

It was well kept with a very minimal approach. The furnishings appeared to be mostly secondhand but on the newer end. The gray couch I sat on was probably the most updated thing in the room with an older leather chair in the corner. Several family pictures were scattered on the walls as well as maps and photos of the area.

I'd never given much thought to Dean the fisherman other than his outwardly appearance. But seeing him surrounded by the things he loved, I couldn't help but wonder what he had once been like.

Before.

"So, about that ramen. Turns out, I'm a liar. Pretty sure I ran out a while ago," he said, cozying up to me on the couch.

I let out a laugh as I curled up next to him.

"It's fine. I'm actually not that hungry," I said.

His eyebrow rose as he looked at me. "That's a lie."

"Okay, I'm starving. But I want to sit and talk for a while. Tell me about some of this stuff," I said, motioning to his living room.

"Like what?" he asked, our heads touching as we snuggled underneath the warm blankets.

"Like..." I said, looking around, trying to pick just one.

There were so many options. From the anchor in the

corner that looked like it weighed more than a ton to the photos on the coffee table in front of me.

"What about that?" I said, pointing to an old map, one of many lining the walls of his living room.

A warm smile spread across his face. "That," he said, "is a nautical map. An old one, too. My dad used to collect them—or so I was told." He grabbed my hand, and using my index finger as a guide, he made a long trail in the air, following the landmass on the wall. "See Hatteras there?" he said, pointing to the very tip of the inlet. "And how it stops, and just over the sound is Ocracoke?"

"It's beautiful," I said, his fingers lacing with mine. "You miss it, don't you?" I asked. "The ocean? Fishing? You never really talk about it."

He grew silent as I stared up at that map, wondering how much of that water he'd touched in his lifetime. *Would he ever again?*

"Yes," he finally answered. "But I don't know how to go back. I don't know how to look out at the water and feel anything but anger. And fear. That night we were on the boat? It was the first time I'd even been close. The fact that it was anchored was the only reason I was able to go through with it."

I rested my head on his shoulder, still staring at that map, thinking of all the times I'd caught him looking out onto the sea with such longing in his eyes. He'd lost his trust out on that ocean when that ferryboat tried to take his life.

We just had to find it once more.

"What about that?" I said, deciding a change in subject might be good as I moved toward a stack of composition notebooks on the corner desk.

"Ah"—he grinned—"if you're looking for something to help you sleep—"

I leaned in closer. "Wait a minute," I said. "You had a notebook like that when you were in the hospital. You said it was for your recovery. Don't tell me you're still writing in them."

He smiled. "Almost every day."

I placed a chaste kiss on his cheek. "You really are messed up."

He laughed. "That's what everyone keeps telling me."

I got up, taking one of the warm blankets with me. I felt his eyes on me as I walked across the room toward the desk. Reaching down, I lifted the first notebook off the stack. "Can I read them, or are they off-limits?"

I felt his breath against my neck.

I hadn't even heard him move.

"Nothing is off-limits to you, Cora," he said. "But don't start with this one." He reached into a drawer and shuffled through it, pulling one from the back. "Here," he said, but instead of giving it to me, he set it down on the desk. "But read it later."

"Why?" I asked, turning to look up at him.

A quick grin pulled at his mouth. "Because I just remembered we have a serious debate to solve."

"What's that?"

He pulled off his blanket and wrapped it around me, not in the least bit shy about his nakedness. Walking boldly into the kitchen, he opened the freezer, making me all the more confused as he took out a pint of ice cream and held it out in front of him.

"Ice cream," he said, pulling the lid off with his teeth.

I let out a laugh as he walked back over and handed it to me. He dug his finger in, using it as a giant makeshift scoop, and then looked down at me with challenge in his eyes.

"Is it a finger food or not?" He held his finger out to

me, vanilla already melting down his single digit as he waited for me to decide.

What could a good girl do?

I gave him a mischievous grin, stood on my tiptoes, and showed him just how good I could suck—ice cream, that was.

❀

"Seriously," I said, taking a wide look around the room, the inn so full of people, I could barely take a full step in either direction. "Who are all these people?"

Dean chuckled, taking a sip of his beer, as tiny children dodged and weaved between us, streamers flying, balloons hitting us in the faces.

It was extreme chaos.

"Well, when you have a party around here, everyone assumes they're invited. Kid party or not." He motioned toward the patio where it was currently raining cats and dogs, the patio where I'd planned to have one kick ass bounce house with amazing grilled food and plenty of space for all these wild children to run. "It's too bad it's raining. Although we do need the rain."

I let out a frustrated sigh. "You're telling me. But at least the company in charge of sending the bounce house came through."

"Oh?" he asked.

"Yeah, they said they were going to send someone over instead. An entertainer. Free of charge."

Dean nodded. "That's nice of them. Do you know what kind?"

I shrugged, trying to casually play it off. "I think something to do with science experiments."

I watched as he nearly spit out his beer, laughing.

"Oh God, Lizzie's going to crucify him. Did you warn them?"

I tried to keep a straight face. "No. Why?"

"Have you met your daughter? The one who, just last week, taught me all about kinetic energy, complete with a science experiment."

I bit my lip. "Okay, I see your point. I might want to warn him."

"No, don't." He smirked. "It will be hilarious."

Smacking him on the shoulder, I shook my head. "You're horrible. Let's go find her and see when she wants to cut the cake."

It took a while to locate her with Dean at my side. We were stopped by pretty much every person in the town, and if I hadn't met them yet, I did now. Everyone thanked me for the party while I agonized over whether there was enough food to feed an entire town.

Thankfully, we managed to run into Molly and Jake, coming through the kitchen, armed with food for just that —an entire town.

"You guys, I could just kiss you!" I exclaimed, immediately jumping forward to help them.

"Well, not that I would mind," Jake said, giving Dean a quick wink, "but this is all Molly. I'm just the muscle, carrying it in."

"It's true," she said. "I didn't let him near any of it," she explained, pulling out several platters of sandwiches. "But I thought you might need a hand. No one probably explained to you the party situation here in town."

I looked around, feeling a little less overwhelmed by the sheer number of people in the inn. "No," I said, "I had no idea. Thank goodness the inn is empty this weekend. What a fiasco it would have been if her birthday were next weekend!"

She shrugged. "I don't know. A birthday and a wedding? That sounds like a ton of fun."

"That sounds like a ton of stress," Jake interjected, laughing.

"Oh, please, like you've done anything besides picking out your suit. But, I do have one guest arriving today. But it shouldn't be any trouble."

I felt that anxiety beginning to rise again in my throat. "Are you sure? Because I could, I don't know, try to shoo some of these people out of here. I know you've got a lot going on with the wedding coming up in a few days."

She laughed, making a face, as she grabbed one of the platters to carry into the parlor. "You'll do no such thing. Let me do my job with the guest, and you do yours."

I looked at her while the guys made themselves useful and each grabbed a platter. "And what is mine exactly?"

She just shook her head, pointing to the counter where the gorgeous cake rested. "Go be a mom," she said.

"Oh," I said. "Right."

Grabbing the lighter and the cake, I took a deep breath and followed everyone into the parlor. Like the parting of the sea, I finally found Lizzie, laughing and acting like a regular five-year-old with a couple of friends from school. They chased each other around the parlor with a green balloon. Apparently, it was an alien, and when you got caught, you died.

Pretty typical.

When their eyes turned and saw the *My Little Pony* cake Molly had created in my hands though? Green-balloon alien was forgotten.

It was cake time.

They all started talking and yelling at once. The blonde girl with the glasses wanted the part with the pony head on it. The cute, shy boy wanted to sing Lizzie "Happy Birthday" first.

I liked him.

I set the cake down on a card table that Dean and I had set up the night before as everyone gathered around us. I realized in that moment that it didn't matter that I might not know everyone in this room. They'd all taken time out of their day to come celebrate my daughter's birthday.

Because we were part of the community.

Part of the family.

I swallowed hard, and Dean's warm hand slid around mine for comfort.

"Okay, who wants to sing 'Happy Birthday'?"

Lizzie looked wide-eyed at her cake as I lit the candles, and everyone began singing. I tried to hold back the tears I felt creeping up. This was what I'd wanted when I stepped onto that ferry not too long ago.

A new start.

I don't know how I'd managed it, but I'd found a good life here in Ocracoke.

Dean's arm crept around my shoulders as he whispered in my ear, "You're not singing."

I could detect a hint of a smile in his words.

"This is everything I've wanted for her," I said.

Cheers fell around us, and she blew out her candles.

"It's only the beginning," he said.

"Mommy! Can I have that piece?" Lizzie asked, pointing her finger to the direct center of the cake.

"Of course you can," I said, laughing.

Dean and I stepped up to begin serving the masses.

It was then that my eye caught *his*.

It was then that my happy little world stopped.

Standing in the doorway, still holding his designer suitcase, his eyes fixated on mine, was Blake.

In my perfect new life, there was my worst nightmare.

❀

Shock quickly turned to anger as I marched through the sea of people, abandoning my post as official cake-cutter.

"You can't be here," I seethed under my breath.

He smiled a smile that, once, a long time ago, had done funny things to my insides. A smile that I'd loved to wake up beside.

A smile I'd trusted.

He reached inside his pocket and pulled out his phone, holding it out to me. "Ten texts, four phone calls, Cora. That's how many times I've tried to reach you regarding our daughter's birthday. Ten texts, four phone calls. All you had to do was reply to one of them. All I wanted was a chance to see her. So, you see, I can in fact be here. Because there's not a judge around who wouldn't allow me the right to see my daughter, whom, by the way, in case you've forgotten, I still have partial custody of."

I swallowed hard, my hands shaking, as I took a step backward. I looked around and saw people politely trying to act busy, avoiding our very public display.

"Cora?"

I turned to my left, and there was Dean. He stepped up to my side with a mixture of concern and something I'd never seen before.

Raw, untapped anger.

How did Dean even recognize Blake? They'd never met before. I didn't have time to contemplate that before he turned to address my ex-husband, "What are you doing here?"

Blake's eyes darted from mine to Dean and back again, obviously making the connection. "Seems I had no choice. When my wife went missing and wouldn't allow me visitations with our daughter, I had to do what any father would do—drop everything and go looking for her."

My teeth gritted together as my fingers curled at my side. "Ex-wife. You seem to have forgotten that part."

He shrugged, giving a cursory glance in Dean's direction. "Clearly, you haven't."

Something akin to sadness spread across his face. Something I hadn't seen there in a long time.

He held his chin high, his gaze fixated on Lizzie, who was still too focused on her pony cake and friends to notice her daddy standing in the entryway. "Look," he said, letting out a puff of air, "I don't want to make a scene. That's not why I came."

Dean made a noise of disbelief next to me.

"I just wanted to see her, Cora, and I'm sorry if that upsets you. I know things between us were—"

"Bad?" Dean interjected, causing the two men to exchange glances.

"But I still want to be a part of her life. And you can't shut me out."

I let out a frustrated breath, my arms wrapped so tightly around my chest I thought I might leave visible marks from the viselike grip. "I know, and I'm sorry."

"Cora, you don't owe this man shit," Dean nearly growled, his body so on edge beside me, I could feel him nearly vibrating.

"I owed him the common decency of a reply," I said. Turning my attention back to Blake, I said, "And, for that, I'm sorry. I should have texted or called. I know, no matter what happened between us, you will always be Lizzie's father. I should never have tried to shut you out. It's just been a big adjustment, and we're not completely settled. It's why we're having her party at the inn; we still haven't found a place to live."

"And school?" he asked, sincerity in his voice.

I bit my upper lip, glancing from one man to the other. "It's been a bit of a rough go," I answered honestly, causing both of them to react accordingly.

"What do you mean?" Blake asked.

"Why didn't you mention anything?" Dean echoed.

My hands began moving along with my mouth. "It's nothing," I said. "Just a note and a meeting with the teacher. The school is worried they won't be able to provide the level of academics required for a child of Lizzie's level."

Blake was the first to talk, shaking his head like he'd seen this coming all along. "I knew you shouldn't have moved down to this Podunk shithole."

"Hey!" Dean fired back. "This Podunk shithole doesn't need you to help us solve our problems, asshat. We'll figure out something for Lizzie without you."

Blake laughed a sinister laugh I'd heard far too many times. He opened his mouth to retaliate, but I beat him to it.

"Enough!" I said, probably too loud for our private conversation.

The room quieted for a moment before picking back up.

"This is neither the time nor the place. And I will not let us ruin Lizzie's special day with our bickering. I'm sorry I didn't call, Blake; I really am. And I'm sorry to both of you for not mentioning the problems with school sooner. I obviously was in denial. It's something I'll need to figure out."

"*We'll* need to figure out," Blake interjected.

"So, until then, why don't you all plaster big, happy smiles on your faces for Lizzie and act like adults, okay?"

"Cora?" Dean said my name in a way that had me turning my head.

My heart sank. There, holding a single piece of cake in her hands, was Lizzie, her face long and sad, the birthday glow long forgotten.

"Why are you guys fighting on my birthday?"

I turned back toward the two men, uncaring if it was their fault or mine, feeling the anxiety and pressure of the day weighing down on me, and I snapped.

"Great job," I said. "You've ruined it."

And then I stormed out of the room.

What was I saying about acting like an adult?

FIFTEEN
Dean

Recovery Journal: Day 1,195

I saw her.
Cora.
I saw Cora. Here. In my town.
Which is now somehow her town.
She's divorced. I don't know why I'm writing
that first. It shouldn't be the first thing I
write. I should be writing something like why
she's here, but I can't stop thinking about that
one little detail.
She's divorced.
I still remember that day she turned me
down.
I don't blame her really.
Mentally unstable, newly single amputee asks
you out before he's even discharged from the

hospital.

> *Kind of weird, right?*

> *But I'll never forget those eyes.*

> *They were sad eyes. Not because she felt bad for turning me down.*

> *No, they were sad for some other reason.*

> *Over the years, I've often wondered what it could have been. She'd always been so upbeat when she visited, almost like she was trying too hard.*

> *Was she making up for something? Covering up a failing marriage perhaps?*

> *She's divorced.*

> *My brain circles back to that once more, and it gives me a small glimmer of hope. But I've felt something like that before when it came to Cora.*

> *Can I trust it once more?*

❀

The whole scene was something out of my worst nightmare.

Cora near tears, so on edge, she bolted out of her own daughter's birthday party. And Lizzie? Lizzie just stood there, torn between running after her distraught mother or falling into the arms of her father.

I could see the indecision on her adorable little face as her eyes drifted down the hall and back toward her dad.

Finally, with one final, apologetic glance toward the man who frankly didn't deserve any of it, she made up her mind and bolted for the family rooms in the back, toward Cora.

Leaving Blake and me alone.

Well, as alone as two men could be in a house full of people. *Let the sizing-up and heavy stares begin.*

His eyes went directly to my right side, a sly smirk spreading across his face. "And you are?"

Feeling my fist curl at my side, I did everything I could to keep it from meeting his face. "Dean. A name you'll be hearing a lot of, I'm sure."

"Well, Dean." He said my name like he'd never heard it before. Like it was foul or foreign. Beneath him.

Don't give in.

He's just messing with you.

"Do you think you could show me to my room? I have some gifts in my bag I'd like to pull out for my daughter."

The emphasis on the word *daughter* was not lost on me.

I violently shook my head. "You're not staying here," I said. "You can't."

"Excuse me?" His eyebrow rose in a way that told me he was used to getting his way. "I paid for a room."

"Jesus. You're the one guest Molly has tonight?"

"Look," he said, clearly agitated, a state I was sure he was in most of his life, "I don't know who Molly is, but the deal is, I paid for a room in this place, and I intend to stay. I haven't seen my daughter in well over a month, and despite what Cora might have told you, I do love that little girl, so if you don't mind, I'd like my room, please."

Somehow, in the course of his little speech, I'd managed to get closer to him, his face within inches of mine. That fist that seemed to have a mind of its own was beginning to vibrate, a sensation I'd felt only one other time in my life when Macon Green, the school bully turned town cop, called Molly a string bean, and I punched him.

Honestly, I hadn't even known what the term meant. I just didn't like him making fun of my friend. It had made me angry. But the anger I felt toward this very grown-up man, the man who'd abused the woman I loved, it was a hundred times greater than that.

Immeasurable.

"Dean?" I heard Jake's deep voice pull me back. "Everything okay?"

My heard turned to see him and Molly standing in the entryway to the kitchen, both looking concerned.

Well, Molly looked concerned. Jake looked ready to wrestle me to the floor.

"Yeah," I answered, my steely gaze returning to Blake. "But it turns out that Blake here might need some new accommodations," I said loud enough for the entire room to hear. "He's partial to a rental. Anyone want to help him out with that?"

It was like waving honey in front of a bear.

The locals attacked.

Many of the rentals on Ocracoke were owned by the inhabitants themselves. It was a surefire way to make money, and we were all about keeping that local. But this was the beginning of dry season, and the minute those townsfolk turned around and saw a wealthy-looking dumbass like Blake standing there, basically waving around money with his expensive suitcase and designer clothes, they all rushed forward, offering up every place they had.

I sat back, smiling like the Cheshire Cat, knowing Lizzie and Cora would be safe for the night without having to worry about him in the bedroom above theirs.

Now, I just had to figure out how to keep him out of their lives for good.

🌼

I didn't sleep a wink that night.

I'd managed to get Blake out of the inn and into one of the nicest rentals on the island, no doubt causing the owner more strife than necessary for a single night. I imagined the overly privileged Blake was no picnic to have as a houseguest, but if it meant having him away from the girls, it was worth it. Still, even an island separating him from them didn't feel like enough space.

I needed him gone. And soon.

Every time I managed to drift off to sleep, I'd have the same nightmare.

Him with that stupid smirk on his face, Cora and Lizzie by his side on the ferry as it left the dock.

And me on the shore, unable to stop them.

I would wake, covered in sweat, gasping for air, my arm aching something fierce.

It was just a dream, I'd try to remind myself.

It was just a dream.

But was it?

What if she's not over him?

I'd heard of women who'd suffered abuse going back to the men who'd caused it.

What if that was Cora? What if she went back to him?

My head was swimming by the time I made it to the clinic that morning, coffee in hand, ready to put the finishing touches on the software program I'd set up. All the records had been entered by my own hand, saving us some money in the long run, and now, I just had to run some tests—another cost-saving measure.

But as I walked through the back door, my mind was on anything but medical records and software systems.

It was on the woman in front of me.

She looked about as rough as I did, her hair drawn back in her usual bun as she tugged on the same cardigan she wore most days. But I could see the fatigue settling around her eyes

It seemed I wasn't the only one who hadn't gotten any sleep.

"Hey," I said as those dark-brown irises met mine. "I brought coffee."

She gave me a sad smile and held up an already made cup. "Thanks, but I got in early."

"Right. I'll just leave this for Jake."

A heavy, uncomfortable silence settled around us. She looked down at the old linoleum while I stared at my feet.

Finally, I got the nerve to ask, "Is he gone? I mean, did you talk to him? Is he leaving?"

She shook her head. "He's staying a little longer."

I stood up a bit straighter. "A little longer? How long?"

Her eyes met mine. "I don't know, Dean. A few days maybe. I didn't really ask."

"Why?"

"Why what?"

"Why didn't you ask?" I demanded.

"Because he was shuffling around his schedule. Because he wanted to see his daughter. Because I screwed up."

My finger went through my hair as I paced. "*You* screwed up? *You* did? Cora, this man beat you! He beat you!"

I didn't realize how loud I'd become until she matched it.

"He never beat me," she said softly. "He'd lose his temper and slap me around, but he never beat me."

My hand scrubbed over my face, feeling the stubble of the previous day. "Jesus, Cora. Do you hear yourself right now?" I asked. "Do you hear yourself making excuses for him? You do remember what he did to you?"

"Yes, I remember!" she nearly screamed. "I remember every blow. Every argument. Every tear. I remember laughing off bruises to Lizzie, telling her how dumb her mommy was for running into things so often. I remember how stupid I felt for not being able to make it stop. For not being able to walk away. So, don't raise your voice at me, Dean Sutherland, because I remember. Everything."

"Then why are you letting him do this? Why let him stay? Why not make him leave?" I whispered, taking a hesitant step forward.

Thankfully, she didn't back away.

I hadn't lost her trust. Yet.

But I had a feeling I was treading a very fine line.

"Because I also remember everything else. The way he smiled when he held Lizzie for the first time. How proud he was when she said her first word. The tender way he sang to her at bedtime. I will never, ever be able to forgive him for the husband he became, but I can never fault him for the father he turned out to be. He might be overbearing and spoiled, but he loves that little girl."

I swallowed hard, hating the idea of that man having anything less than a blackened soul. "But does he deserve her? After everything he did to you…"

My hand reached out for hers, and she let me take it, looking down at our two hands joined together with almost a sadness in her eyes.

"I don't know," she answered. "But I don't think that's up to me anymore."

"Of course it is," I pressed, thinking back to the snide sneer he had given me.

She pulled away, looking out the window toward the parking lot.

"Do you know what Lizzie told me when she came to find me during her birthday party yesterday? She said she wasn't sure if she was allowed to miss her father. Do you know how absurd that is?" She let out a somber laugh under her breath. "When I asked her what she meant, she said she knew Daddy made me sad, that he hurt me, and that's why we moved away. And, now that we were away and I was happy again, she was scared to even mention him or miss him. She thought she was supposed to forget him.

"And you know whose fault that is? You know who made her believe that? Me. I did that to my little girl. I made her think she had to forget her father.

"She fell asleep, sobbing in my arms, last night, Dean. On her birthday. Because she missed her daddy. It's not right. None of this is, but I don't know what to do. I don't know how to do any of this, but I need to figure it out. So, for the next few days, Blake is going to be around, and if you have a problem with that—"

"I don't," I said, the lie falling from my lips quicker than a lightning bolt in a summer storm.

"Good," she said, a look of relief painting her expression. "Because I need support right now. I don't think anyone really knows how to navigate this sort of thing. There's definitely not a course for How to Have Dinner with Your Abusive Ex-Husband 101."

"You're going out to dinner with that asshole?" The words exploded out of me, causing her to take a step back.

"He wanted to take Lizzie out for her birthday," she

said, her eyes wide as she looked at me with an expression I'd never seen before.

Fear.

"I don't think that's a good idea," I said, lowering my voice to something less threatening.

"And you really don't have much of a say."

"Are you going to go back to him?" I blurted out, my insecurities showing.

"What?"

I swallowed hard, shaking my head as it filled with uncertainty. "I don't like him being here, Cora. I don't think it's good for you. For—"

"You?" she said, meeting my gaze. "Look, I'm doing the best I can here with a situation that is basically impossible. But if you think me trying to figure out how to work out a relationship between Blake and Lizzie is somehow me finding my way back to him, then you're wrong. I had an entire year to go back to him, and I didn't even though there were plenty of times I'd wanted to."

Her words gutted me.

"Surprised, are you? That I could want to go back to a man who'd hurt me? That I could be that weak?"

"Cora, I don't think you're weak."

She shook her head, letting out a sound of disbelief. "Your eyes say something differently."

"Cora, I—"

"I never did," she continued. "But there were times when I'd think back and remember the man I married, the husband he used to be, and wonder if maybe he could be that again, you know? It's not so absurd—for a woman to go back. We can't shake those memories. We can't stop thinking we can fix them."

"Why didn't you?" I finally asked, realizing how little

we'd actually talked in our time together. How little I knew of this woman I loved so much.

"Lizzie," she said. "I thought I'd done a good job of sheltering her from everything that was going on in our marriage. I didn't want her to be raised in a house like that. I didn't want her to grow up, knowing her father was a monster."

I exhaled, a defeated sigh escaping my lips. "So, why invite him back into her life now? He's still a monster."

"Because he's not a monster to her. And I won't let him be."

A frustrated hand ran through my hair. "I don't know if I'll ever be okay with that. I don't know if I can forgive what he did to you."

Resigned eyes met mine as she gave a firm nod. "It's not your job to forgive him. It's mine. And this isn't about forgiving or forgetting; it's about Lizzie."

And, with that, she walked away, leaving me with an impossible decision.

A lifetime with Cora and Lizzie—and Blake.

Every major life event. Every memory.

He'd be there.

Family gatherings, birthdays, graduation. Lizzie's wedding.

He'd always be there.

Tainting our lives with his presence. Reminding me of everything he had done to the woman I loved.

But what other choice did I have?

To walk away?

To leave her, knowing he'd be there instead?

No, I couldn't do that either.

So, I'd endure. I'd endure him for Cora. For Lizzie.

And for the future I saw ahead of us.

"You okay, man?" Jake asked me as he took a place next to me in front of the mirror, both of us adjusting our ties, as the noonday sun streamed through the windows of the yellow room of the inn.

"Yeah," I said with as much enthusiasm as I could muster. "Shouldn't I be asking you that question? It is your big day after all."

He smiled at me through the mirror, a great big ear-to-ear grin. "I'm great. Been looking forward to this for a damn long time. That, and Molly and I grabbed a quickie in the closet before the guests arrived."

A quick wink, and he went off in search of his jacket.

"Isn't that against the rules? Seeing each other before the wedding? As the best man, shouldn't I have prevented that or something?"

He laughed, shrugging into his gray suit coat with ease. "Pretty sure we've broken just about every rule there is. Nothing wrong with a little stress relief before the big walk down the aisle."

I shook my head, still messing with my damn tie. Why they had to make these things so damn complicated, I had no idea.

And tight.

God, it was tight.

"Pretty sure you haven't broken all the rules. Sure, you might live together, but it's not like you knocked her up or any—"

I caught his shit-eating grin bouncing back at me in the mirror.

"Well, I'll be damned."

"We found out on Friday. We hadn't even been trying. How's that for irony? The town doctor who actively tells his teenage patients about the importance of birth control gets his soon-to-be wife pregnant before they're even wed."

"Well, it's not like you need to tell anyone."

"Are you kidding? I want to shout it from the rooftops. I'm so damn happy. But Molly says we need to be cautious."

I pressed my lips firmly shut, trying to keep from laughing. My highly trained doctor of a best friend had had to be schooled by his soon-to-be wife on Pregnancy 101.

I could already tell this was going to be fun.

"So, were you even supposed to tell me?" I asked, watching him plop down on the bed to tie his shoes as I finished up my tie.

"Yes," he replied. "She gave me a list. I'm allowed to tell you, your mother—"

"Whoa, I wouldn't," I said. "You tell that woman anything, and it will make its rounds through the whole town within hours. Plus, she's dying for a grandchild, and at this point, she's not picky on where it comes from."

He laughed. "Duly noted."

"Who else?"

"Oh, um…well, Cora. Or at least, you could. We didn't think it was fair for you to keep a secret from someone you, uh…you—"

"Love?"

"Yeah, that. So, you do love her?"

"I do. More than I thought I could love anyone."

I met his approving gaze in the bedroom mirror.

"And the ex-husband? How does he fit into things?"

I let out a discouraged huff of air. "I don't know," I said. "He's been here all week, attending meetings at the school with Cora and going out to dinner with the two of them. I'm trying to be as supportive as I can, but when I see him with them, laughing and joking around, as if nothing happened—"

"You want to kill him?"

"I want to kill him," I confirmed.

"When she applied for the position, I never asked what had made her decide to move down here. But I always had a feeling she was running. From a past that obviously caught up with her at that birthday party." He exhaled a long breath as he gave a warm smile in my direction. "I happen to know a thing or two about outrunning your past. It always has a way of catching up to you." He stood up and placed a solid hand on my shoulder. "Remember that."

"I'm not running from anything," I argued.

"Running, ignoring, avoiding—it's all the same, Dean. Take it from the guy who spent twelve years trying to forget a girl." He held his arms out wide with that same devil-may-care grin plastered across his face. "Look where it got me. Now, let's go get me married. What do you say, best man?"

His joy must have been contagious because I found myself charging toward him like a damn fool, faking one of those one-armed pick-ups Cora loved so much but instead going for an over-the-shoulder bear hug.

"All right, let's go get you married. It's about damn time."

The whole town came out to witness the wedding of Jake and Molly. Of course, the whole town pretty much came out for just about anything. But this particular event had been more than fifteen years in the making, and almost everyone felt like they had played some part in getting these two to this special day.

Even I got a little choked up, seeing Molly walk down

the aisle in her mother's lace gown, knowing everything they'd gone through to make it here.

I couldn't help but glance over at Cora at that moment and every moment after.

This was what I wanted.

Looking around at all the people crammed in the inn once more after another rainy weekend, I chuckled under my breath. Well, maybe not exactly this.

But I wanted the happiness. The moment where our lives became one. When a family was born. I knew this—a wedding might be too soon for both of us—after all, we'd only just started dating, but I saw it on the brink of the horizon, like a lighthouse beacon calling me home.

"She's a good match for you," my mom said as we watched from the sidelines while Cora and Lizzie danced along with several other guests on the makeshift dance floor that had been set up in the parlor.

The original plan had been for a reception under the stars, but the early months of autumn were turning out to be soggy ones, and last-minute preparations to move everything indoors had had to be made.

Thank goodness for it, too, because as the sun set, lightning lit the sky, making me wonder just how bad it might still get. Here, in Ocracoke, we were no strangers to weather. I had many childhood memories of hunkering down to wait out a storm and even several evacuations. Jake and Molly were lucky, and the tropical storm that was supposed to barrel toward the coast had dissipated, and we were only experiencing the remnants.

Still, remnants or not, the sky was angry.

"Did you hear me, boy?" my mother said, leaning into me.

I shook my head, smiling. "I heard you, Mama. Thank you. I couldn't agree more."

"Now, this opinion is all just speculation, you see, since I still have not been formally introduced."

I blew out a breath and turned. "You've met both Lizzie and Cora half a dozen times," I protested. "You had an hour-long conversation over iced tea the other day at the party."

She folded her arms in front of her, feigning a pout. "Yes, well"—she made a noise in the back of her throat—"that's different, and you know it."

I caved. "I'll bring them over for Sunday dinner next week."

She opened her mouth to argue, she and I both knowing that today was Saturday, and there was a perfectly good Sunday dinner happening tomorrow.

"I have a feeling, we'll all need rest tomorrow," I said, nodding in the direction of my brother, who was already zeroing in on one of the bridesmaids, an out-of-town cousin from Molly's family.

"Oh, your brother hasn't been showing up for ages," she stated.

"If I'm going to introduce Cora and Lizzie to my family, I'd like to do it properly. Cora's still upset I didn't get to meet her brother when we visited a few weeks ago."

"Speaking of her family, I thought I'd get a chance to meet her parents at the birthday party last week. I'm sorry they weren't able to attend."

I nodded. "Me, too, but it's still too early in the semester for them to take off a few days. And you know how involved a trip here is. Besides, they've made arrangements to visit over Thanksgiving break—all of them. I've pretty much booked the entire inn for the occasion."

"Oh, that will be lovely. I've always wanted a house full of people to cook for."

I gave her a sideways glance. "You always have a house full of people to cook for," I argued.

She rolled her eyes. "You know what I mean. A house full of family. Grandchildren running around and daughters-in-law helping in the kitchen while the men watch football."

I let out a laugh, taking a sip of the beer I'd been nursing for far too long. "That wasn't sexist at all."

"Stop sassing me, boy. For so long, it's just been us three. And that's been fine. Great even," she said, taking hold of my hand. "But I want to see you two happy. Rooted. Growing."

"Me, too, Mom," I said, my eyes trained on Lizzie and Cora.

Both of them were beautiful tonight. So beautiful, it almost hurt to look at them. I swallowed deeply, unable to turn away.

"But?" my mom asked, sensing my hesitation.

"Cora's ex-husband scares me. His presence in their lives. I don't know if I can handle him being around them. Every time I see him, I feel like I'm losing control."

She tugged on my hand, her warm fingers still entwined with mine. I tore my gaze away from Cora and focused on my mother.

"Life is complicated, Dean. Relationships are complicated."

I breathed out, "Yours wasn't. With Dad."

"No," she agreed. "Everything about your father was easy. I met a man, and we fell in love, had a couple of kids, and settled into a very comfortable sort of life. Until one day, out of the blue, he died. Then, it got complicated. No one goes into a relationship, knowing it's going to end badly, but you can't go back and erase your past. Besides, why would you want to? Look where it got me," she said with one last smile. "I can already hear the pitter-patter of tiny feet." Her eyes darted to Cora once more as I rolled my eyes. "Be blessed in what God has given you, son. Everything else will find its place."

My mom's version of *chill* basically.

I took her advice, heading to join my ladies on the dance floor, when I saw Lizzie turn toward the front door and yell, "Daddy!"

Her excited, definitely outdoor voice was heard across the room, and as everyone pivoted around to face the direction she was looking, I caught sight of Blake, clearly embarrassed, doing his best to sneak out of the inn.

Cora and I, along with Lizzie charging forward, arms wide, closed the distance to figure out what was going on. I looked back, hoping Molly and Jake hadn't noticed. Thankfully, they hadn't.

Actually, as my eyes scanned the room, I had no idea where they were. Considering the sexy come-hither eyes Molly had been giving him during dinner, I probably didn't want to know.

"Look at my pretty dress, Daddy. It has sequins on it. Mommy called them sparkles, but they're really not. It was made in China. Did you know that, in China, they—"

"What are you doing here?" Cora asked, placing a gentle hand on Lizzie's shoulder.

For the first time since meeting the guy, he looked genuinely embarrassed and maybe a little drunk. "Lizzie left her rain jacket at the restaurant last night. I thought she might need it," he said, holding it up for evidence. "I was just going to go drop it off by her door before heading off to the airport."

"You're leaving?" Cora said. "In this weather?"

He looked surprised. "Yes. Why?"

I lifted my arm, palm up toward the front door, the

universal sign for *duh*. "In case you haven't noticed, we're in the midst of a pretty bad storm."

"Yeah, I did," he shot back, a definite whiff of alcohol coming off his breath. "And I've flown in worse."

"Maybe in a major airport, sure. But here? No way. Besides," I said, pointing toward one of the tables in the corner, "isn't that your pilot?"

I was taking a wild guess, but the guy I was motioning toward happened to be one of the best pilots in town. And Blake seemed like the-best-of-the-best kind of guy.

"Son of a bitch," he swore.

"Guess he figured you'd make the same assumption as the rest of us. No one travels in this weather. It's just the way it is."

"So, what am I supposed to do? I left the key for my rental on the counter before I locked up."

I turned to Cora and then Lizzie before letting out a frustrated breath.

Growth. It was all about growth, right?

"Go grab a drink, I guess. You're not going anywhere until morning."

Blake gave one last longing look toward the door before Lizzie grabbed his hand, tugging him toward the dance floor.

"Yay!" Lizzie exclaimed when he finally gave in. "Come dance with me, Daddy. I promise not to step on your feet. Well, maybe not promise, but I'll try. You, too, Dean!"

I forced a laugh, hating the idea of Lizzie out on the dance floor with Blake. "You go on ahead. I'll be out there in a bit."

She didn't waste a second, pulling a less-than-thrilled-looking Blake out onto the dance floor, while Cora wrapped her arms around my waist.

"That was more than generous. More than he deserved."

"I told you I'd try. Besides, I couldn't let the guy leave, trashed."

"Thank you," she said. "But, if it helps, I'll go spit in his drink."

I laughed, a real one this time, as my hands found hers and decided to do what I'd been waiting to do all night.

I took her by the hand, and we danced until we forgot all about complications. Until all there was left was us and infinite possibilities.

The night grew late, and many of the guests had left. I sat back at one of the tables, watching my two best friends slow-dancing, laughing and smiling like they were the two happiest people on the planet.

No doubt they might just be.

Cora was once again on the dance floor with Lizzie, who refused to go to bed, holding out as long as she could. Cora, knowing she'd fail miserably with a house full of people, gave in and decided a few extra dances with her daughter never hurt anyone.

Sitting there, watching them, I couldn't agree more.

"Got everything wrapped up in a nice little package, now don't you? And record timing, too. What? A month? Or has this been going on longer than that? Are you the reason she moved down to this crappy town?"

I turned to see Blake basically falling into the seat next to me. He smelled like a bourbon distillery. I guessed my invitation for a drink hadn't gone unnoticed.

"What?" I said.

"The thing you have going on with my wife." He paused. "Excuse me, my *ex*-wife."

I shook my head, feeling a mixture of anger and embarrassment for the guy. "Not really any of your business, is it?"

"Nope," he said, staring down at his empty glass. "Not anymore. Not since she left me. She was always so difficult, you see."

"Difficult?" The word made my blood boil.

"Yeah. At first, I loved it. Growing up, no one ever defied me. Everyone did what I'd asked. Nannies, tutors. Hell, I even got my professors to change a few poor grades in college with sheer determination. But Cora? She was so different. So real. She had a genuineness about her, and I found it so interesting. Captivating really. I kept trying to force her to fit into my world, but try as I might, she didn't. God, she'd make me so angry."

"And so you hit her?" I seethed.

His eyes flashed. "I never said I was perfect. Besides, looks like it all worked out in the end. For you at least."

"For me?"

"Sure, you get to be the hero. Swoop in and steal my place."

"Steal your place? No one is stealing anything here, Blake. You gave up everything the minute you struck your wife," I said, my voice lowered. "This," I said, "them"—I motioned toward Cora and Lizzie—"they could have still been yours if you had just realized you already had everything you wanted and stopped acting like a pathetic, spoiled little bitch. That woman is amazing. Just the way she is. She doesn't need to be changed or molded into someone else. She's already perfect."

His eyes settled on Cora for a brief second before coming back to me. I saw a flash of pain and then something else. Malice. If there was one thing I'd learned from Cora, it was that, when Blake was hurting, he lashed out.

And that look in his eyes confirmed one thing. Blake had just put on his fighting gloves.

His eyes slowly lingered down toward my left arm to the prosthetic hand peeking out of my suit jacket. "Figures she'd pick someone like you."

I stood up, the sound of my chair scraping against the wood floor grabbing the attention of several people around me. I knew I shouldn't react, but part of me couldn't help it. I'd been a ticking time bomb since this guy showed up, and that daring look in his eyes was like dangling a carrot in front of a starved horse.

I couldn't resist.

"What the hell is that supposed to mean?"

Clearly pleased with himself, he rose to the occasion. "Well, I suppose it means, for starters, you're weak. Crippled." He reached out and flicked my prosthesis for effect. "If I was scared and alone, starving for attention, and ran into you? Well, I just might fall in love with you, too. I'm assuming you have some sort of sad, sappy story to go along with this piece of plastic on your arm? Something that really gets the girls' juices going. How many times have you used it?"

My body was humming with raw, untapped anger as he rambled on, smiling nonetheless. I could see what he was doing as he was doing it.

Egging me on.

But it was as if my body and my brain disconnected, and my body took the helm of the ship.

"How long exactly did it take my overly emotional ex-wife to jump in bed with you? A day? She's a real fire pistol, too, isn't she? And that mouth of hers? Really hoovers the thing right in there."

"Dean?" My brother had taken notice and ditched his bridesmaid to try to step in.

"Go, Taylor," I said. "Just go."

"Taylor? This your brother Lizzie was telling me about? The other fisherman? The one who actually fishes? Hey, what are the chances you could get me to shore tonight, buddy?"

"No," I barked. "No one is taking you anywhere in this weather, Blake. I told you that. Besides," I said, pulling out the set of keys I'd taken away hours ago, "Taylor has the night off. Don't you, brother?"

"Right," he said, his eyes darting between Blake and me before he stepped back to join his bridesmaid.

"Man, you guys on this island are a bunch of pussies when it comes to weather," he said. "But at least you have plenty of it. Pussy, I mean. Maybe I'll just go find some of my own. Your brother looks like he found a good one. I think I spotted a bridesmaid earlier who looked promising—a pretty blonde with a funny name. Minnie or Mickie?"

Millie, Molly's younger sister.

My stomach heaved and my fists clenched.

"You have yourself a good night," he said. "Well, who am I kidding? Of course you'll have a good night. You'll be burying yourself over and over in my ex-wife, and as we both know—"

I hit him.

I hit him so hard, he flew back into the table, shattering glasses and breaking chairs. It was like one of those slow-motion scenes from a movie. Only there was no slow motion, and the blood wasn't fake.

For as drunk as he was, it didn't take him long to pop back up and take a shot at me. Thankfully, there must not have been much roughhousing or boxing classes in finishing school because the guy punched like a toddler. Still, he managed to get a few shots in.

"Son of a bitch!" he roared before someone—Jake, I realized—grabbed him from behind to separate us.

My brother tried to do the same for me, but I shrugged him off.

"I'm fine!" I hollered, taking my first look around. "I'm fine."

There were flower petals everywhere as glass littered the floor. The remaining wedding guests were all huddled together, looking shocked and scared.

I scanned the room, finding the two most important guests.

Cora and Lizzie.

They both stood in a corner, clinging to each other, staring at me with disbelief in their eyes.

Disbelief and disappointment.

"Okay!" Jake announced. "Show's over. Let's get this cleaned up. I'm gonna grab some ice."

I gave him a look of apology, and he just shook his head, waving it off as he headed for the kitchen.

As I walked off in the direction of Cora, I knew her forgiveness wouldn't come nearly as easy. I watched as she whispered in Lizzie's ear, sending her toward the kitchen after Jake.

"Cora," I said, barely able to make eye contact.

"I can't do this," she said.

"You can't do what?"

"This," she said. "Any of this. I can't go through life like this with the two of you at each other's throats in front of Lizzie all the time."

A frustrated breath escaped my lips. "I know. I'm sorry. He egged me on, and I shouldn't have let him."

"Stop," she said. "It doesn't even matter." A tear ran down her cheek. "And I can't believe I have to do this.

But you're making me choose between the two of you. You're making me choose between the man I love and the father of my child."

"Please, no," I begged, pulling her into the hall for privacy. "I'm not making you choose anything. I can do this. I can."

She let out a strangled laugh. "You just proved that you clearly can't, Dean. You just clobbered him at your best friend's wedding. Lizzie has one father. And I need him to be a bright light in her eyes, not the horrible monster that he became to me. So, I'll fight for that, and if that means walking away from this, from what we have, I'll do it. For her, I'll do anything. Even if it means giving up my own happiness."

"Has anyone seen my keys?" Taylor's voice resonated through the house at the same time I heard Jake call out, "Where did he go?"

Cora and I must have sensed it.

Something was up.

We both turned toward the parlor, and I found Jake with a small med kit and ice and a bewildered-looking Taylor.

"Where did who go?" I asked.

"Blake," Jake said. "I set him down at this table before I went to the kitchen, and he's gone."

"And so are my keys," Taylor said, pointing to where I'd set his keys down right before Blake and I went to blows.

The giant set of keys that had access to every boat we owned in the harbor.

"Well, maybe they flew off the table when you hit the guy," Taylor said.

"Maybe he's in the restroom," Cora said.

Everyone started looking around at once. After five minutes, he was a no-show. And so was Taylor's truck.

"Why the fuck would he take my truck? He has a car of his own."

"Does it really matter at this point?" I asked.

"Where do you think he went?" Cora asked, moving on to more pressing issues.

"I don't know, but he was pretty drunk. Wherever he went, we need to find him before he gets hurt. Or worse, before he hurts someone else." I pulled my keys out of my pocket just as Taylor's phone began to ring. "I'll go look for him."

"What?" Taylor said loud enough to make everyone turn. He held up a finger, signaling for me to wait. "When?" he asked the person on the phone before turning to us. "Someone just took one of our boats out of the marina."

"Oh my God, in this weather? He wouldn't," I said. "Does he even know how to operate a boat?"

Cora nodded. "Unfortunately, yes. It's one of his hobbies."

Grabbing the phone from Taylor, I held it up to my ear. "Hi, who is this?"

"Dean, is that you? This is Dwight Bosley. I live just behind the marina, over on the—"

"I know where you live, Dwight," I said, feeling too impatient to wait for the old man to continue.

"Oh, yes, of course. Anyway, I saw Taylor's truck skate into the parking lot just a few minutes ago, which was alarming because it wasn't too long ago that the Mrs. and I left the wedding, and I remembered you taking away his keys."

"Dwight, which boat did he take?" I pressed.

"Smaller one," he answered. "One of the boats meant for the inshore tours—or at least, that's what it looked like from my window. I was so worried it was Taylor. That's why I called him first. But, now, I feel terrible I didn't call Macon first, knowing someone stole it. Do you want me to call him? Macon, that is."

"I'll do it myself," I said, knowing Macon wouldn't do a lick of good right now.

He couldn't steer a boat in a straight line to save his life.

Never could.

Handing back the phone to my brother, who was still three sheets to the wind, and then glancing in the direction of my best friend, still dressed in his wedding attire, holding a med kit and a bag of ice, while his new wife stood by his side, I knew I was the only option.

So, I took a deep breath, and I made a choice.

"I'm going after him," I announced to the room.

And, before anyone could change my mind, I charged out of the house and toward the churning dark water that had already tried to steal my life once, and I begged it not to do so a second time.

SIXTEEN

Cora

Dear Friends and Family,

I could say something cliché like, Long time, no see, but from the long gap between my last post and this one...well, that much is already obvious. And, besides, a stupid phrase like that doesn't really say anything, does it?

It doesn't explain the why. It's just an excuse people use to camouflage the truth.

And I've done enough of that in my life.

So, here it is.

The truth. All of it.

Or at least, most of it.

My life fell apart a while ago, and I headed back into the world to start over. Too embarrassed to tell anyone of my failure, I kept it a secret. But, in the depths of all these secrets and lies I was telling to the outside world, something amazing happened. I began to find balance again.

And love.

So much love.

I've met a man—a beautiful, broken man—who is teaching me how to trust again. How to open my heart once more to the possibility and vastness of love.

The forever kind of love.

It's funny how, in the midst of tragedy, life can offer up something so pure and magnificent. And yet, I still can't seem to find the strength to trust myself.

To take that leap into forever.

I watched Dean storm out of the house with a look of determination so fierce, it felt like the air crackled around him as he moved. By the time the door slammed and I heard the roar of his truck engine, the reality of what was happening sank in.

My eyes flickered to the windows as rain beat against them, falling in thick sheets against the glass, while the wind howled, and the trees bent.

Oh god, what have I done?

"Someone, go after him!" I screamed, searching the crowd until my eyes fell on Taylor.

He shook his head, remorse and regret painting his face. "He knew I couldn't," he said. "I've had too much to drink. I'd be more of a hindrance than help out there right now. But—"

Panic turned to anger as I blinked several times, trying to keep the tears away. Turning away from him, I moved on. "Jake?"

His gaze morphed into something of the same.

"I am not a seaman, Cora," he said. "Never have been."

Letting out a frustrated breath, I found myself nearly

yelling, "Can anyone help him? Or are all of you just going to sit around and wait for him to die out there?"

"Cora," Taylor called out.

I could feel myself beginning to lose it as the room began to close in around me, and I knew, once I allowed it to, I'd never pull myself back together. So, I ran. I ran for the door. I ran out into the storm, water beating down on me, soaking my skin in seconds.

The world was crying.

"Cora!" Taylor yelled from the doorway.

"What do you want?" I screamed, my head lifted to the heavens as the world wept for me.

"You never let me finish. Drive me to the docks," he said. "I'll do what I can from land. But I'll need some help. I'm not exactly operating at my peak here."

Nodding, I met his gaze, one that matched Dean's in so many ways. "I'll go get my purse."

Twenty minutes and a change of clothes later, Taylor, Lizzie, and I had made our way to the docks.

My little girl was scared, so scared that she was huddled up to my side like she had no plans of ever leaving.

It made me secretly wish we could trade roles from time to time, and I could be the outwardly scared one who curled up to her while she stroked my hair and told me everything would be okay.

Because, as I'd dodged tree branches and driven at a turtle's pace just to be able to see through my windshield to get here, I knew it was definitely not. I couldn't imagine what it must be like in the water with the waves tossing and turning you in every which way, making you lose your sense of direction.

Not to mention, the inebriated state Blake was in.

The idiot.

I'd conveniently left that part of the story out when

relaying the information to Lizzie. Making excuses for him, just like old times.

When would I ever learn?

Maybe Dean was right. Maybe Blake didn't deserve a place in our lives.

Sitting in the office of Sutherland Fishing Company, I watched Taylor get set up, switching on the radio. He tried to get a signal from Dean or Blake. There were a few other things he turned on, but from my layman's point of view, nothing really made sense.

"Okay, I'm going to radio the Coast Guard and let them know we've got a couple of missing boats in the inlet, so they can start looking as well—might take a few tries. It's going to be hard for them to get a helicopter out in this weather, but hopefully, Dean will get to him first."

I nodded, giving Lizzie an extra squeeze while he sent out the distress call to the Coast Guard. My usually talkative and inquisitive girl was anything but as we waited on news of Dean and Blake.

"Is there any way you can track them? Don't boats have trackers?" I asked once he was finished on the radio.

"Yes," he answered. "That's what I'm trying to do now." He pointed to a screen. It was pretty much black, except for two green dots. "But nothing is showing up."

Taylor held the radio up to his mouth, switching several dials before pressing a switch just below his lips. "*Endeavor, Endeavor, Endeavor*, this is Sutherland Fishing Company. Please state your location. Over."

We all waited with bated breath for an answer. Several minutes passed, and all we were met with was static.

Never-ending static. I looked toward the window, the rain battering the glass so hard, it shook. Letting out a shaky breath, I tried to remain calm.

"Okay, let me try Blake. You said he's a decent boatman, correct?"

I nodded.

"Well, let's see if he can figure out a radio as well as a boat."

"*Wave Runner, Wave Runner, Wave Runner,* this is Sutherland Fishing Company. Please state your location."

Lizzie squeezed my hand as we once again waited, a lump so big forming in my throat, I could barely breathe.

What if I lost both of them in one night?

The man I loved and Lizzie's father. Gone. Just like that.

Suddenly, the static changed, a hiccup in the frequency, and then suddenly, Dean's voice filled the small office.

"Sutherland Fishing Company, this is *Endeavor*. I've found him. I can see the lights in the distance."

The dam broke, and tears fell from my face. Tears of joy, tears of relief.

He was alive.

He was—

"Mayday, Mayday, Mayday!" he yelled, making my heart fall to the floor as I jumped to my feet. "Taylor, the boat is capsized. Jesus, I don't know for how long. I've got to go in. I've got to go after him. Tell Cora I love her."

And then the static returned as Taylor turned to me with wide eyes of terror.

I'd thought my heart broke a long time ago. The moment Blake had betrayed my trust and his fist collided with my face.

But I was wrong.

Turned out, it wasn't quite done.

That night was the longest of my life.

The waiting.

The constant, never-ending waiting.

I didn't know how long Taylor, Lizzie, and I were in that office at the marina, listening to that radio for some sort of answer. Every glitch and jump in the otherwise mundane sound of the static would send my heart into overdrive as I prayed that it would be followed by Dean's voice.

I didn't know how long we sat there.

It could have been minutes, days…hours.

But, finally, when I'd nearly lost hope, imagining Dean out there, in the angry black water, fighting for his life, thinking about those horrible, angry words I'd said to him, hoping they wouldn't be my last, we got the call.

The Coast Guard had found them. Both of them.

And they were en route to Virginia Beach.

Taylor and I looked at each other, knowing this nightmare wasn't over yet.

"Why are they going to Virginia, Mommy?" a sleepy Lizzie asked as we headed out toward the car.

I swallowed deeply, knowing this was one of those moments as a mother when I had to make a decision. Lie to protect her innocence or trust her with the truth, knowing she deserved to know everything just as I did.

"It means they're doing everything they can to take care of Dean and Daddy, sweetheart. And, like you know, the hospital Mommy used to work for in Virginia Beach is the best place to do that, isn't it?"

She nodded, looking more childlike than I'd ever seen her. Sometimes, with so many big words and thoughts coming out of her head, it was hard for me to remember how young she really was.

"You know we can't drive up there yet," Taylor said the minute we were seated in the car.

My hands gripped the wheel as rain pounded down all around us. If it were just me, I would have said screw it and done everything in my power to get to him.

Bribed a pilot, stolen a boat...

Whatever it took.

But it wasn't just me.

And that kind of selfish thinking was what had gotten us into this mess. Blake had been so hell-bent on getting off this island, getting away from us, that he put his own needs before anyone else.

I couldn't do that.

"I know," I said, feeling defeated but resolute.

"As soon as the weather clears, Cora," he vowed, placing a warm hand on my shoulder.

I nodded, knowing he meant it. We pulled out of the marina and headed back to the inn.

I knew sleep wouldn't come easy to anyone that night.

Not as long as the rain held and the winds whipped around the island, holding us here like prisoners from the one we loved.

"We're coming, Dean," I whispered, tears stinging my eyes. "I promise. We'll be there soon."

"Cora."

My eyes opened slightly, blinking several times as the sunlight from the window hit me square in the face. Molly was sitting on the edge of my bed, holding a cup of tea.

What was she doing here? Didn't she get married—

Suddenly, the events from the night before came roaring back.

The wedding.

A fight.

Blake stealing Taylor's boat.

It'd capsized.

And Dean.

I shot up, causing Molly's tea to spill.

"Sorry!" I said. "But how did I—the weather." I pointed to the window. "I need to go."

Placing the cup on the dresser, she held her hand out in front of her, like she was trying to calm a wild animal. The wild animal—me—wasn't having it.

"I need to get dressed, Molly. I need to catch the ferry to Hatteras and—"

"I already pulled out some clothes for you right over here. Lizzie is eating breakfast as we speak, and since I knew you wouldn't sit down and eat, I packed you something for the road. Or air, I guess."

"Air?"

"Taylor was going to take you by boat, but the water is still pretty choppy. So, one of the pilots in town was gracious enough to offer you a ride. So, you don't have to deal with traffic. And the ferry."

"That is very generous."

I looked around the room, feeling immensely guilty. "I can't believe I slept."

An expression much the same as mine painted her face before she said, "I might have put something in that tea I made you last night. You were death on your feet. I knew you needed some rest before today."

"And you expect me to drink another cup of it now?"

She laughed. "Oh no, that one is perfectly normal. Promise. But I'll give you a minute to get ready. Taylor is already at the airport. He left about five minutes ago, so when you are ready, I'll have Jake drive you over. He's going to head up there with you. He offered to take Dean's mother as well, but after everything Dean went through before, she can't set foot in that hospital again. So I'll stay back and wait with her."

"Thank you, Molly," I said. "I know this isn't exactly

the wedding you imagined. Or the first day of marriage, for that matter."

She shrugged. "It's not the wedding that counts. Besides, it wouldn't be a small-town wedding without some drama," she said with a wink. "And, as for my first day of marriage, well, I definitely wouldn't have wished for Dean to be back in the hospital, but everything else? Jake and Molly Jameson helping friends and family when they need us? That sounds just about perfect." She paused for a moment, her cheeks staining red. "Jake and Molly Jameson. I think that's the first time I've said it out loud."

"And how does it sound?"

"Like a dream come true. Now, go bring home Dean," she said, heading for the door. She stopped short just at the threshold. "And, Cora?"

"Yeah?" I said, grabbing the things she'd pulled out for me.

"Don't forget that home now includes you."

With a warm smile, she vanished into the hallway.

It didn't take me long to get ready, thanks to Molly. I threw on the clothes she'd picked out, ran a comb through my hair, and brushed my teeth, all within the span of ten minutes. We were at the airport in another five and taking off. I'd never seen Ocracoke from the air before. In a different circumstance, I would have taken the time to look for the inn, point out Lizzie's school to her, and soak in the beauty of the island we'd adopted.

But all I could do was stare down at that vast water and wonder what had happened the night before.

"Jake, do you have any updates?" I asked.

He looked to Lizzie, who was staring out the window, as if he were asking for permission to speak candidly in front of her.

I gave it with a single nod.

"Both of them were in pretty bad shape when the Coast Guard pulled them up into the helicopter. Blake more so since he'd been in the water longer and was, uh…intoxicated to begin with. They were worried about the lack of oxygen."

"And now?"

"I don't know," he said. "It's only been a few hours, Cora, and being the middle of the night, information was hard to get. Even for me."

I looked at the clock on my phone. He was right. Even though the sun was bright in the sky, it was still very early in the morning. I'd only been asleep for a handful of hours. Knowing this somehow relieved a bit of the guilt that had been coursing through me since I awoke in my comfy, dry bed, knowing Dean was somewhere suffering.

"Mommy?" Lizzie said, her gaze tearing away from the window as she turned toward me.

"Yeah, sweetheart?"

"I have something to tell you," she said, her eyes betraying her remorse.

"What?" I asked, suddenly worried. I sat up and grabbed her small hand as she looked away.

"You know how I like to go on the computer late at night after you go to sleep?"

I let out a sigh. "Yes."

"Well, a while ago, when we first moved to Ocracoke, I made up an email address—SmartieBeachGirl5," she explained before adding, "I guess I shouldn't have put the five at the end of it since I'm six now. Can I change that?"

"Lizzie?"

"Right, okay. So, I made an email address, and I emailed Dean. I had taken a business card from his office that day he took me to the marina."

I glanced over at Taylor and Jake, who were both

doing a good job of minding their own business as both men looked out the window with feigned interest.

Curiously tilting my head to the side as my attention went back to my daughter, I asked, "Why did you email Dean?"

The side of her mouth scrunched up as she thought about it. "I told him you needed a friend," she said. "And that Daddy had made you frown a lot, and I thought you needed someone to make you smile again."

My heart melted.

"But that wasn't the whole truth," she said. "I wanted someone to make me smile again, too."

"What do you mean?"

That same guilty face washed over her once more.

"It's okay, sweetheart. You can be honest with me."

She tried to look away again, but I turned her head back toward mine.

"It's just that, when you don't smile, I don't smile."

And, just when I'd thought my heart couldn't melt any more, it liquefied all over the floor.

"Oh, come here," I managed to say before the tears started to roll. She curled into my lap as I wrapped my arms around her. "I'm sorry I've been such a terrible mom lately."

"But you haven't," she said, looking up at me with those giant brown eyes. "You keep saying you're a horrible mom, but you're actually the best one ever. It's called self-doubt."

I let out a strangled laugh, catching Taylor doing the same. "Oh," I said. "I didn't know that."

"You need to trust yourself more, Mommy. And give yourself more credit. Or at least, that's what the free self-help guide I downloaded from Amazon says."

"Did this self-help guide also tell you to email a handsome fisherman on my behalf?"

She giggled. "Dean isn't handsome. That's gross. And no, not exactly. But it did say to surround yourself with people who make you happy."

I stroked her hair, loving my daughter more in that moment than I'd thought was possible. "And you thought that person was Dean?"

"He makes you happy, right?"

"Yeah, sweetheart, he does," I answered honestly.

Her smile beamed up at me. "Me, too."

She settled back into me, laying her head on my chest for the remainder of the short flight, while I thought about her words.

"When you don't smile, I don't smile."

That kept replaying in my head.

I'd thought I was making the right choice, choosing Lizzie and therefore Blake over Dean. Lizzie needed her father, and if Dean couldn't handle that, I had to walk away.

I'd thought it was a simple choice.

"When you don't smile, I don't smile."

But I'd be giving up a lifetime of happiness.

A lifetime of love.

"When you don't smile, I don't smile."

Would I also be sacrificing her happiness as well?

The moment we all stepped foot in the hospital, Jake went to work. Dean had always joked around about his best friend having two distinct sides. So far, I'd mostly only been around the doctor side of Jake Jameson. But after I'd spent the last few days with him, witnessing him marry the love of his life and seeing him interact with mine, the stark contrast was palpable.

Sitting in the waiting area was a foreign concept for me.

I'd never been on the opposite end before.

I'd never been the anxious friend or the basket-case family member waiting for news. I'd always been the one on the other side, caring for those loved ones so that there would be a next day.

And a day after.

Finally, after what seemed like an eternity but was probably a matter of minutes, Jake returned with news.

"Dean's fine," he said, causing me to let go of the breath I'd been holding since the night before.

"Are you sure?" I asked, Lizzie squeezing my hand with excitement.

He nodded. "He's a little banged up and bruised from being thrashed around in the water, and he's tired from the lack of oxygen. But he's good."

"And Blake?" I asked.

"He's a little more banged up. A little more bruised," he said.

"But?" I asked, feeling it hanging in the air.

"He's going to be arrested, Cora. If he'd just stolen the boat in normal weather, Taylor could decide not to press charges for stealing his truck and the boat, and the whole thing could slip under the rug."

"But he endangered lives."

"And he did so while drunk. So it's out of Taylor's hands. He doesn't have a choice in the matter unfortunately."

I lifted my chin. "I can't keep making excuses for him."

He gave an understanding nod. "Do you want to see Dean?" he asked.

My heart leaped. "I thought you'd never ask." Looking down at my little girl, I knew I had one stop first. "Take Lizzie with you. I'll meet you there in a few."

My stomach was nothing but butterflies as I took the last few steps down the hallway toward the room Dean was in. I still remembered the first time I'd walked down this same corridor, newly hired, barely out of nursing school, nervous as could be.

By the time Dean had shown up, I'd thought I was an old pro.

But nothing could have prepared me for those soulful green eyes and that mesmerizing smile. I thought it was just his sad story—a poor fisherman who had lost everything to one fateful night at sea. But I was wrong.

His memory had stayed with me through it all. The pain, the suffering, and ultimately, the strength that had risen from it all.

He was always there.

Calling me home.

The door was cracked open, and I could hear the sounds of Taylor and Jake laughing as I stepped inside. They caught my movement and quieted down as I entered. Turning the corner, I saw him.

My beautiful, broken man.

Curled up against him was Lizzie. Like a barnacle on his side.

"Well, I could use some coffee. You, too, Jake?" Taylor said rather loudly.

"Oh, yes," he replied. "Coffee sounds nice. How about you, munchkin? Hot cocoa from the coffee shop?"

Lizzie's eyes widened, and she hopped down off the bed. "See you later, Dean! Be right back, Mommy!"

"Okay, honey. And, Jake?"

"Yeah?" he said, stopping next to me before he left.

"Do you think you can take Lizzie to see her daddy? He's awake."

He looked at me before nodding, and the noise of the three of them dissipated down the hallway. Silence fell around us as I made my way up to the bed, taking a seat in the chair that'd been placed next to him.

Dean's eyes had followed me the whole way there. Finally, he opened his mouth to speak, but I beat him to it.

"The other night, Lizzie was telling me about arch bridges. No doubt, she'd been up late at night, learning about them, when she should have been sleeping. Anyway, she was amazed by them; she couldn't stop rattling off facts about these stupid bridges. And I let her because you know how she gets if she doesn't get a chance to tell someone this knowledge she's learned; it's like she overheats, and then we risk her exploding in the middle of art class or something."

He smiled a ridiculous, handsome smile that did funny things to my already fluttery stomach.

"Turns out, these unbelievable arch bridges date back as far as 1300 BC, and people still use them. So, I asked her how they worked. She explained that they would actually build the bridge or arch from each side, and it would only be strong or fortified when it was connected. When the two sides connected and became one. Do you see where I'm going here?"

His brow lifted. "Not really. But I am kind of out of it. Keep going. Maybe I'll catch on."

"That was an incredibly stupid thing you did last night," I said.

"Incredibly brave, you mean?"

"You could have been killed, Dean. You could have been snuffed out of existence just like that, and you didn't even ask me how I felt about it. You didn't even turn to me before you ran out the door. I mean, did it even occur to you before you leaped into that boat to, I don't know, consult me? I thought we were a team. Or at least, headed that way. Hence, the crazy bridge talk."

"Is that where you were going with that?" He grinned.

"Yeah, because after the arch is formed, it can bear all sorts of stress and stuff. Two sides becoming one. Like a team."

He looked down at me, that same grin plastered on his face.

"Oh, shut up!" I threw my hands up, and he managed to grab on, holding it close to his chest. "It made sense in my head."

"You'd just dumped me, Cora," he reminded me. "I figured, consultations between us were kind of on hold. At least until I could prove to you that I was willing to make an effort when it came to Lizzie's father. I had to fight for us by first fighting for him."

"But by doing so, you nearly killed yourself in the process."

"I'm still here," he said. "Still here. Still dumped."

I bit my lip. "Right. That. Can we forget that part? Maybe strike it from the record?"

"I'd like nothing more," he said. "But first, I need to say something. Or rather, a few things. I was wrong to judge you in this situation with Blake."

I opened my mouth to stop him, but he continued, "I know it's been a rough situation for you, and I've only made it harder during the last week. I realized that last night when you said I was forcing you to choose between me and Lizzie. I never want to make you feel like you have to choose like that again because, of course, it should be Lizzie. Every time. I wouldn't expect anything less.

"Since you came back into my life, I spent so much time being angry over what Blake had done to you; it was hard for me to see him as anything other than what I'd made him out to be in my head. He might not deserve my respect, but I haven't earned the right to cast him out of Lizzie's life."

"You might not, but I have," I said, causing his eyes to widen with surprise.

"What?"

"I'm going to file for full custody of Lizzie," I said. "And Blake is going to, as you said, have to earn his place in Lizzie's life. His return in our lives this week reminded me of a woman I didn't like very much. One who made excuses for a man who didn't deserve them. And one who allowed others to fight her battles for her."

"But what about Lizzie?"

I squeezed his hand in mine. "I still believe Lizzie needs her father. But not like this. Not one who rolls in like a giant thundercloud, bringing nothing but destruction in his wake."

"He made a mistake."

I smiled. "He's made a lot of mistakes," I said. "And it turns out, he made even more while I wasn't around. The reason he could be here all week? He didn't shuffle his work schedule around. He doesn't have one. He was fired from his own family's law firm. His father told him to go dry out somewhere and come back when he wasn't an embarrassment to them anymore."

"Ouch. So, what is he going to do?"

"Well, for starters, he's going to give me full custody —you know, after he gets out of jail. And then he's going to enroll himself in rehab. I don't even care if it's one of those ultra-rich ones on the West Coast where they do yoga all day and drink fancy cucumber water. Whatever gets him sober. Some anger management wouldn't hurt either. And then we'll see."

"And us?" he asked hesitantly.

I smiled, rising from my chair to curl up next to him on the bed, much like Lizzie had done just moments earlier. "Well, I was thinking we could work on getting you out of this hospital. Again."

"And then?"

"And then I was hoping you might take me on a romantic tour of the island."

He kissed my head and ran his hand through my hair. "I thought I already did that."

I looked up at him, smiling. "Yes, but I've heard the view from the water is to die for, Captain Sutherland."

A soft chuckle fell from his lips as he pulled me closer. "I think that could be arranged. And then what?" he asked.

"And then…everything."

"Everything?"

I nodded. "Everything. I want it all. With you."

Dean

EPILOGUE

SIX MONTHS LATER...

"Ready?" Taylor asked as I stared out onto the crystal-blue water, the waves gently lapping at the docks below us.

I took a deep breath, smiling to myself. I could already hear the eager voices of children outside the office door. "Yep."

"Good, 'cause they're hyper today. Better you than me. I'll take a fishing party over that any day."

I chuckled, grabbing several life vests on my way out. "Suit yourself. But just remember, at the end of the day, I get Popsicles. What do you get?"

He gave me a sly grin. "If everything goes right? A hot, single tourist in my bed. Now, go do your job."

I stood up straight, dropping several of the life vests to the ground, and I did my best to mimic a soldier, my left hand moving to the top of my forehead. "Yes, sir!"

He shook his head, chuckling, as he gathered the necessary paperwork for his upcoming excursion. "You salute with your right hand, asshole."

Looking to my right side, currently devoid of any prosthetic, I laughed. "You love having me back. Admit it!" I said, holding my hand out wide, baring my chest, with an equally wide grin.

"I'd love it even more if you weren't such a smart ass about it."

"That's the brother I love," I joked, reaching down to pick up the child-sized life vests before heading out the door.

I was flying high this week. This simple idea that I'd come up with less than a week after coming home from the hospital, still bruised from the beating I'd taken in the water, had finally come to fruition.

And with such success.

I never thought I'd go back into the water, but that night, I'd faced my darkest fear.

I realized in that moment, when I bolted out the door, intent on saving Blake from his own stupidity, that, for Cora, I'd face all my demons a hundred times over.

But out there, on that boat and in the water, I discovered just how stupid I'd been. I'd been so focused on Cora, I hadn't thought about myself. Blake wasn't the only stupid one that night. It was sheer luck that I managed to keep both of us afloat before the Coast Guard found us.

I needed to retrain myself. Not only how to steer a boat, but also how to survive in the water.

I'd been avoiding the water because I felt betrayed. But it'd had me wondering how many handicapped people out there avoided the water and all its many forms because of sheer fear.

"Damn, you look mighty fine today, Mr. Sutherland," I heard Cora call out.

I looked across the street and saw her and Lizzie heading toward me. Lizzie was dressed similarly to me—

bathing suit and not much else. Unfortunately, Cora was going to work and had far more on.

I'd have to remedy that. Later.

"There are my girls!" I hollered as both came closer. "Are you ready to be my big helper again?" I asked Lizzie, causing her to immediately nod her head with enthusiasm.

"I did a bunch of research on sinking ships. What to do, what not to do—those kinds of things. Did you know the first lifeboat launched from the *Titanic* when it was sinking only had twenty-eight people on it, but it was equipped to hold sixty-five? Do your boats have lifeboats? How many?"

Cora gave me an amused, sideways glance as I looked down at the curious little girl who'd stolen my heart.

"We have lifeboats on the big boats and inflatable rafts on the smaller ones. Not to mention state-of-the-art equipment. Promise. Now, come on. Say goodbye to your mom. She's got to go to work, and so do we!"

Cora bent down, and Lizzie gave her a huge hug. The sight of it made me smile and even more so when Lizzie let go, ran over, and affixed herself to my leg.

"Now, you know it's Tuesday, so—"

"So, she goes to the tutor at school at one," I said, finishing Cora's sentence. "I got it."

"Okay, just checking," she said, stepping forward. "Would it be totally unprofessional to kiss you in front of all these kids staring at us right now?"

I looked over, and indeed, my class of spring-breakers —handicapped kids from all over the country who'd come to learn about water safety and fun—were completely absorbed in our conversation.

I met her the rest of the way. "I think it would be rude not to," I said, placing a tender kiss on her lips.

As expected, it was met with a chorus of, "Gross," and surprisingly, a few, "Aw," from the girls.

"I'll see you later," she said.

"When later?" I asked. "Lunch?"

Her face scrunched in disappointment. "We're pretty busy. Spring break and all. But don't worry," she said, pulling out a familiar notebook out of her bag. "I'll be with you in spirit! It's the last one in the pile, by the way. What does that mean?"

I tried to keep my face as neutral as possible. "It means, you're nearly caught up. I guess you'll have to find something else to read during your lunch breaks from now on."

"Hmm," she said, looking at the notebook with a bit of sadness before she shrugged it off. "I guess so. I do have a giant stack of books gathering dust in my bedroom. But there will be more of your notebooks. Eventually I mean."

I smiled as Lizzie squeezed my leg. "Yep."

"Okay, well, I'm off. See you later."

Both of us watched her cross the street once more, hop into her beat-up SUV, and drive away before I dared to move.

Lizzie's jump caused my heart to nearly bolt out of my own skin.

"Operation Notebook? It's a go?"

I looked down at her, a grin forming across my face, one that stretched from ear to ear. "Operation Notebook is a go," I confirmed.

Cora

The clinic was almost empty. With only one patient left in the room with Jake, I took advantage of the few minutes of peace and grabbed my bagged lunch. I headed for the front desk, hoping to catch a few bites before Mrs. Joyner needed to check out.

Taking out the peanut butter sandwich Lizzie had insisted on making me and a bag of chips, I sat back in the comfy old leather chair and pulled out the black-and-white composition notebook I'd borrowed from Dean the other day.

Since beginning the first one many months ago, I hadn't been able to stop. I felt like I was getting to know the man I loved all over again.

His hopes, his fears, and everything in between.

He'd warned me there would be parts about me, and he'd joked they might be embarrassing, but I couldn't disagree more. Realizing someone had seen me as something special and worthy of love during a time of my life when I felt anything but, it was comforting, especially knowing everything I knew now.

That I'd eventually find my way back to him.

And something so amazing would blossom from it.

Sometimes, reading his entries was difficult. Especially the early days when he'd grieved and lashed out in pain and anger. Even the later years were hard, knowing he was surrounded by so much love but felt so alone at the same time.

This notebook was by far my favorite. Every entry was like a single ray of sunshine from the heavens. He spoke of perseverance and even his renewed faith. He wrote of Lizzie and me and how much we meant to him. He even wrote of Blake and how, at night, he prayed for the man he could not forgive. He prayed Blake would find peace with himself, for the sake of Lizzie.

I prayed for that, too.

We hadn't seen Blake since the accident that nearly took both men from my life. But he wrote a lot. Mostly to Lizzie, which was exactly how it should be. He was taking his time in rehab, and yes, it was the kind with the fancy cucumber water and the beautiful beachfront location. I wouldn't expect any less for Blake.

But he was healing.

Like I'd said before, I couldn't forget, and I wasn't sure I'd ever forgive. But, for Lizzie, I prayed. I prayed he would become the man she deserved.

I'd nearly reached the most current entry in Dean's journal when I heard Mrs. Joyner's voice in the hallway.

"I saw Dean on my way here," she said, "with those lovely children he's teaching, all jumping into the bay!" she exclaimed. "I do say, Dean does look handsome without that thing on his arm. So muscular."

She rounded the corner and caught sight of me trying to shove the last bite of my sandwich in my face. "Don't you agree, Cora?" she asked.

"Sorry, what?" I managed to say, peanut butter sticking to the roof of my mouth.

Jake, standing behind her, chuckled.

"The prosthesis," she said. "I think he looks better without it."

I nodded. "I've always thought so. But he's being fitted for another one soon. His original got lost in the boating accident. He said he hastily removed it, knowing it would impair his swimming even more. But the new one he's getting is a vast improvement. Has a few attachments. Lizzie picked it out," I explained with a contented smile on my face. "But in the meantime, he's getting used to being comfortable in his own skin. Finally."

The conversation seemed to be over Mrs. Joyner's head, so I offered to take her payment instead. While I waited for her debit card to run, surprised the old woman even knew what that was, I caught her leaning over, reading Dean's notebook I'd left open.

Figures.

"Oh, that's lovely," she said. "Mr. Joyner used to write me love letters, too. Although never so long, it required an entire notebook."

I curiously tilted my head as I snapped the receipt from the machine, handing it over to her to sign.

"This isn't a love letter, Mrs. Joyner. It's Dean's journal. He's just letting me read it."

"Oh," she said, her bottom lip protruding slightly as she leaned over once more after she signed her slip. She pointed to the last entry before grabbing her purse to leave. "Then, why is he speaking to you?"

I grabbed the notebook with both hands, falling back into the chair.

Recovery Journal: Day 1,342

Today will be my final entry.

You see, I don't need you anymore.

For far too long, I buried myself in my words, in my pain and anger, and I forgot how to live. I was roaming around, searching for nothing yet wanting everything, but giving nothing in return.

I was my own worst nightmare.

But all that is behind me now.

This recovery journal—this long, endless journal—was supposed to be a means to an end. A way for me to heal, but instead, it became a prison, a place for me to dwell in my misery.

Until she came along.
Until you came along.

My heart began to beat rapidly in my chest.

Cora, you've shown me what being brave looks like.

You remind me what trust can feel like again, both inside and out.

Despite three years of telling myself that it was just a silly crush, you in fact stole my heart in that hospital room with your infectious laugh and damn near perfect smile.

When I came back home, everyone thought I was looking for something—a new purpose, a new direction, or perhaps a whole new life.

They were wrong. I was trying to find my way back to you.

The nurse who'd, unbeknownst to her, taken a poor fisherman's heart with her all those years ago.

You wondered why you had chosen Ocracoke.

It was me. Me and that stubborn heart of mine calling you home.

Like a lighthouse beacon.

And now that you're here, I never intend on letting you go.

I no longer need a journal because I have you. You heal my wounds, fade my scars, and ease my pain.

And, if you'll allow me, I have a very impor-
tant question to ask you.
Meet me at the marina at sunset.

My hands were shaking as I read the entry / letter over
once more.

"Jake!" I hollered. "I know you're lurking around in
the hallway. Get in here."

"I never lurk," he said, stepping into the now-empty
lobby.

"Do you know anything about this?" I said, holding
up the notebook toward him.

"Oh, uh…that? Maybe. I was told, if that ever
appeared before me, to tell you to go see Molly. Immediately."

"Molly? Why?"

"Because Dean figured you might not want to be in
scrubs for this specific occasion."

I gulped. "And what occasion might this be?"

He smiled a wicked, evil grin. "Oh, well, you see, that
part was told to me right here, in the office. And you
know what a stickler I am about patient-doctor confidentiality."

I wasn't proud of it, but I might have thrown a stapler
at his head.

❀

Dean

"Think your mom will forgive me for letting you skip
your lesson with the tutor today?" I asked Lizzie as we

headed back to my house after another successful lesson with my spring-break kids.

They'd been instructed to go have a fun day out on the water with their families and report back the next morning, giving me plenty of time to pull off this proposal.

Hopefully.

"After tonight?" She giggled. "I don't think she'll mind at all. Besides, you do take me to the mainland three times a week for all those special classes."

I smiled back at her, pulling into my driveway. "That is a pleasure, believe me. Besides, if it means you can stay in school here, on the island, while still growing that gigantic brain of yours, it's a win for all of us."

"Why?" she asked, big enough now that she could undo her own car seat.

"Because, one day, I'm quite certain that amazing mind of yours is going to do amazing things. Such amazing things that the whole world will benefit."

"You think so?" she asked as we both got out of the car and headed into the house.

"I know so."

I opened the door as Lizzie raced past me in search of snacks.

Nothing much had changed on the inside. A few of Lizzie's toys were scattered on the floor, and there was the sweater Cora had brought over, but for the most part, it remained the same. I'd spent six months trying to convince Cora to move in with me. And, for six months, she'd been denying my request.

I thought she needed to prove to herself that she could make it on her own.

I hoped, for her sake and mine, she'd gotten that notion out of her system, because as far as I could tell, she could do anything if she put her mind to it.

And, starting tonight, I had plans of changing her place of residence. Permanently.

"So, do you have it?" Lizzie asked, her mouth full of cheese.

"Yes, no thanks to you. I thought you were supposed to warn me when she got close to the end of that notebook. You're lucky I was on top of things!"

She kind of shrugged as she stuffed more of a cheese stick into her mouth. *God, how much food could she cram into that tiny mouth?*

"She reads sometimes at night. How was I supposed to know?"

"I thought you were a night owl!" I laughed.

"I am, but obviously, not when she is. I can't be sneaking on the computer when she's looking!"

I shook my head as I headed up the stairs. She followed close behind.

"You know she's aware of your sneaky behavior?" I asked.

"Yes."

"So, why do you guys do it? She goes to sleep, and you wait around until she does. Why not just use the computer while she's awake and save yourself the trouble?"

"Because then, who would talk about it later?"

I blew out a breath as I dug through my closet. "You're going to be a difficult teenager, aren't you? Ah, here it is. Your pappy sent most of it with his blessing. After a search on the internet made my head nearly spin clear off, I let him take charge. So, I really have no idea what's inside. Want to help me out?"

She didn't waste any time and dived right in. "Oh my gosh," she said, pulling out a hat. Or at least, I thought it was a hat. Maybe it was technically a bandanna. "This is excellent."

Stuff started flying in the air. A lot of black stuff.

"Why does this guy wear so much black?"

"Didn't you watch the movie?"

Several other things flew out, including a sword. And a mask.

"Oh Jesus," I cursed. "This was a really stupid idea. I'm going to look like an idiot. Why'd I decide to do this?"

Her head popped up, and she grinned before she stepped forward and wrapped her tiny arms around my waist. "Because you're the best, Dean. That's why."

"Okay," I agreed. "But couldn't I dress up like Thor instead?"

She stepped back and gave me a once-over. She shook her head. "Nope. Definitely not."

"Ouch. Okay, black mask it is."

Cora

I spent all afternoon getting ready.

For what? I wasn't sure.

A question.

A possibility.

A lifetime.

By the time I arrived at the marina, the sun behind me casting long rays of light over the water, I felt like I'd been waiting for this moment for an eternity.

Rather than a handful of months.

Dean had come roaring into my life at a time when I thought I needed no one but myself and the love of my child. He'd been persistent in his friendship, showing me that, while life didn't require a village to survive, it was a hell of a lot better with one.

And thank God I'd found mine.

This quirky little island of the sea.

And the man who loved it.

Walking down to the marina where Sutherland Fishing Company was located, I did a quick check of my hair as it blew in the breeze. Molly had helped me somewhat tame it, creating a French braid along the top that resembled a headband. I didn't know how she had done it, but it was breathtaking.

She was going to be a wonderful mother to the little girl growing in her belly, and I couldn't wait to see her and Jake become parents in a couple short months.

It was Lizzie I caught sight of first, standing outside the office door, looking very pretty in a summer dress I'd bought for her just recently when the temperatures began to rise.

"I should have known you had something to do with this," I said, bending down to place a single finger on her nose.

She giggled, giving me a big hug. "I'm supposed to escort you to the boat," she said.

"Oh, well then, I'd better not keep you from your job."

She held out her arm, looking very official. I took it, and we took off down the dock toward several of the Sutherland vessels. At first, I had no idea which one we were headed for, but the closer we got, the easier it was to pick out.

"Do you see it?" Lizzie asked. "Dean and I did the flowers. We'd collected them from neighbors and some of the shops nearby. They were all really excited when they found out what we were going to use them for."

"I do," I said, tears stinging my eyes. "It's beautiful."

Every rail of the boat was covered in flowers, wrapped in greenery and every spring bloom that blossomed all over the island.

"Don't cry yet, Mommy," Lizzie said.

"Okay." I laughed. "I'll try not to."

As we stepped onto the boat, the flowers only continued, creating a path to the stern.

To Dean.

"Oh my gosh," I said, getting my first look at him.

Dressed in all black, including long black boots, he wore a black bandanna over his head and—*holy hell*—a mask.

"It's too much," he said as I stepped forward.

"I can't believe—"

"It's the bandanna, right? I went too far with the bandanna?" He reached up to touch it.

"Just shut up right now. I'm living out a fantasy, okay?"

A sly grin spread across his face. "Okay."

"You dressed up like the Dread Pirate Roberts for me?" I said, taking his hand. "That's, like, the most romantic thing anyone has ever done for me."

"I know. It's incredibly weird, and I'm not sure I get it. But, for you, if you wanted me to, I'd dress up like a dozen of these guys. Although I draw the line at hobbits. Their feet are really fucking creepy."

She laughed. "What about Marvel? Oh, or DC Comics? There's a Comic-Con in Texas that my dad is trying to get us to go to. We could go as Daredevil and Elektra. I could wear one of those tight black cat suits?"

His eyes traveled the length of my body before he shook his head. "You're distracting me."

I smiled, still focused on all his piratey goodness. "Yeah, well, you're distracting me. Is this rented, or what's the deal? Can we take this home later?"

"Can a guy propose?"

Lizzie laughed loudly.

I pressed my lips together, kissing his cheek. "Sorry. I'll behave."

"That'll be the day." A small smirk tugged at the corner of his mouth. "Lizzie, you want to help me out with this part?"

She nodded wildly, coming up next to him, and together, as if they'd practiced it, they each went down on one knee. He carefully pulled the black mask from his face. My hands went to my mouth as butterflies filled my stomach. I had known this moment was coming. But, now that it was here, I didn't know if I could calmly make it through, watching him look up at me with those determined, soulful eyes.

"Cora Carpenter, you are the other half of my soul. I was nothing but a broken man, but with you and Lizzie in my life, I now know what it feels like to be whole again. That is why I can't go another day without asking you one very important question."

He turned to Lizzie, who was beaming.

"Will you be the Buttercup to his Westley?" she asked her mother.

I laughed, but before I could answer, he continued, "Will you be the Leia to my Han?"

"The River to his Doctor?" Lizzie said.

"The Hermione to my Ron?" He grinned, giving me a wink. "The Ginny to my Harry?"

"The Arwen to his Aragorn?"

"And, finally," he said, motioning to Lizzie, who pulled an already open ring box from behind her back, "the Cora to my Dean? Because, after all, there is no greater love story than the one we make ourselves."

There, inside, was a gorgeous vintage gold band with a simple brilliant stone in the center.

"It's my mother's," he said. "And she gives it to you with her blessing. If you'll have it. Will you marry me, Cora?"

"Yes," I said, tears pouring down my cheeks.

He placed the ring on my finger and lifted me in the air—one-handed, of course.

"I think it's time to set sail, don't you, Captain?" Dean turned to Lizzie, who was busy jumping up and down.

She stopped short and shouted, "Yes, sir!"

"Where are we going?" I asked.

"I do believe you asked for a tour around the island."

I smiled, remembering my request made in the hospital many months ago. "Yes, I seem to remember I asked for something else, too."

"Ah, yes," he said as I walked up behind him, never growing tired of the sight of him manning a boat. "Everything, was it?"

"Mmm, yes, please."

He turned around and gave me a wink. "As you wish."

With the sun setting behind us and the future so bright ahead, I knew this was our forever. Our scars couldn't hold us back anymore.

Not when we had each other.

And a world of possibilities waiting for us.

A Look at Book Three

THE LIES I'VE TOLD

He was supposed to be just another guest. Instead, he became the greatest risk she's ever taken.

Millie never expected to be back on the island long-term, but when her sister goes into early labor, she steps in to manage the family inn. Still reeling from a career scandal and craving a fresh start, she's focused on keeping her head down—until Aiden walks into her life.

He's British, magnetic, and completely off-limits. What should have been a one-night mistake turns into something deeper, something real. Aiden is everything Millie didn't know she needed—kind, funny, and impossible to ignore. But while their connection grows, so do the questions. He's hiding something.

When a sudden accident forces a reckoning, and Aiden walks away rather than open up, Millie is left with a broken heart and a thousand unanswered questions. What is he running from? And can love survive the weight of the secrets he's kept?

AVAILABLE JULY 2025

Acknowledgments

Number fourteen! I am always amazed whenever I get to this part of the book writing process. The part where I thank all the people who make this whole journey even possible—who have made fourteen books possible!

So, here we go!

As always, I must first thank my soulmate, my best friend and the best damn beta reader out there—my husband, Chris. Without him, I wouldn't know what a true hero was, nor how to write one. Thank you, babe.

A big thanks goes out to my kiddos for being extremely patient this time around. After numerous illnesses, I had a tight deadline to get this book finished and they were very understanding when Mom locked herself in her office for days on end.

This book would not be complete without the talent and help of my incredible team which includes Jill Sava, my personal assistant who always keeps me on task and Nina Grinstead, my publicist who makes sure everyone actually hears about the books I write. Jovana Shirley and Ami Waters—I couldn't ask for two better people to work with. Thank you for making me better and keeping all my terrible habits a secret! To my beta and review team— you guys are awesome! Thank you for supporting my words! I couldn't do this without you!

To my readers group—Berg's Bibliophiles! I love you! And I hope you guys are ready for more Ocracoke drama because Millie is coming! And to the rest of my readers, thank you for reading my words and trusting me to give you yet another happily ever after. Here's to fourteen more!

J.L. Berg is the USA Today bestselling author of the Ready Series and has written over a dozen other novels in the past decade. She is a California native but currently calls Virginia home.

When she's not writing, you will likely find her spending time with her family or watching Doctor Who. J.L. Berg is represented by Jill Marsal of Marsal Lyon Literary Agency, LLC

www.jlberg.com
J.L. Berg's Readers Group